SECOND SIGHT

SHARON SALA

SECOND SIGHT

mira

ISBN-13: 978-0-7783-6093-3

Second Sight

Mira
22 Adelaide St. West, 40th Floor
Toronto, Ontario M5H 4E3, Canada
BookClubbish.com

Printed in U.S.A.

Losing trust in someone you love is a hard thing to experience, especially if it puts you at risk or in danger.

The children in this story trusted people they knew, people who said they loved them, and they disappeared.

This is happening daily to children all around the world, and it breaks my heart.

While I can't save those children, I could save the ones in this story and in some small way bring a symbolic kind of justice to the horrendous crime of child trafficking.

Mercy for the lost.

I pray they find their way home.

SECOND
SIGHT

CHAPTER ONE

In two short years, two women were doing to Charlie Dodge what a military career as an army ranger, three tours of duty in Afghanistan and a segue into private investigation couldn't do. Turning his dark hair gray.

Between his beloved Annie's deterioration into early-onset Alzheimer's and Wyrick, the crazy-ass genius who ran his office and his life, they were driving him insane.

Ever since the Dodge Security and Investigation Agency blew up along with the building in which it had been located, Charlie and Wyrick had been working out of his apartment.

Their rapport on a good day was iffy, and they were beginning to get on each other's nerves. Wyrick was touchy as hell, with a tendency to set his teeth on edge, and while he was grateful for her presence in his life, he needed his personal space back.

So when their last case finally came to an end, they went looking for new space, and after days of searching, they settled on a suite of offices in a building between Fort Worth and downtown Dallas.

But that was a month ago. It had taken that long to do the

remodeling they wanted and for the furniture they'd ordered to arrive, and finally it was coming together. Today was moving-in day for Dodge Security and Investigations.

Charlie knew Wyrick was already on-site, but he'd had to wait until the movers arrived to pick up the computers and files from his apartment before he could leave, then once they were gone, it took almost thirty minutes to get to the new office.

But he was feeling good about the day as he drove into the parking garage and up to the sixth floor. He located his personal parking spot and parked his Jeep beside Wyrick's Mercedes, then headed into the adjoining building.

In deference to moving-in day, Wyrick had toned down her choice of clothing to black stretch pants, a pewter-gray-and-silver top, red-and-silver eye shadow, and a careless slash of red across her lips.

Wyrick's safety net with Charlie was whatever it took to keep him slightly pissed off. The last thing she wanted was for him to know she liked him. She had already intimidated the movers this morning by her appearance alone, and then the attitude that came with it kept them anxious over doing something wrong.

She was in the front office directing traffic, pointing out where each piece of furniture needed to go, and already had a red Oriental area rug on the dark hardwood floor in Charlie's office. The massive desk and black leather chair she'd placed over it was a perfect fit for Charlie's size. And the built-in cabinets and bookshelves in both offices provided twice the space they'd had before. It was like going from a diet of grilled cheese to croque monsieur.

Charlie had given Wyrick a budget and she'd done the rest, right down to designing the layout of the renovations, and the interior decor. She knew it looked good—even impressive. But it was the wall of windows in his office overlooking Dallas that she liked best.

She was going over a mental checklist of what was still undone when she became aware of being watched, then turned around.

Charlie was standing in the doorway, all tall and sexy in Levi's and boots and a white knit shirt that set off the natural tan of his skin. He was finally here, and she hated to admit how much she needed him to approve of all this.

Now that he'd been caught staring, Charlie immediately changed the subject by pointing to the outer door of their office, specifically to the black-and-gold lettering on the glass, which read Dodge Security and Investigations.

"Nice," he said, tapping the glass, then paused and tapped it again because it felt different. "What kind of glass is this?"

"Bulletproof," Wyrick said and then pointed up. "What do you think about the crown molding?"

The shock in his voice was obvious. "Bulletproof? Do we think that's necessary?"

She shrugged. "At the moment, I'm the one with people after my ass, but down the road, you might benefit from it, as well."

He blinked. "Sorry. I didn't think."

She pointed up again.

He obliged, then nodded with appreciation. "The crown molding classes up the place. What's the ceiling height?"

"Eighteen feet in both rooms. Come look at your office."

He followed her to the inner office and immediately pictured himself there. *How does she do this? We can't get along for more than ten minutes at a time and yet she reads my vibe like it's written on my forehead.*

He smiled and meant it. "I like it a lot, and those windows are going to be my saving grace when I feel cooped up inside."

Wyrick relaxed. He was pleased. "There's also a private

bathroom in each office. Yours is through that door just beyond the wet bar."

"I have a wet bar?"

"You do now…for your upscale clients," she added.

Charlie eyed the fixtures with satisfaction, then opened the
door to check out the bathroom and stopped.

"There's a bed in here," he said.

"And a closet, and the bathroom is through that door on
the other side of the bed," she said. "For the times when you
might want to work late, or need to change clothes before a
meeting."

He walked into the room in disbelief, checking out the
small walk-in closet and then the bathroom, complete with
a shower actually big enough to accommodate his height.

He thought then of all the details she'd seen to just for his
comfort and turned around to thank her, but she was gone,
and he could hear voices. The movers had arrived with their
files and computers, and from the sharp tone in Wyrick's
voice, someone had already displeased her.

He went back to the outer office, hoping he could sidetrack
mover mutiny. But once he walked in, he realized two sets of
movers were here—one, with the things from his apartment,
and the others, with more new furnishings. And her annoy-
ance was at one of the men for not being careful enough with
the leather sofa they'd carried in.

"That goes against the wall behind you," she said and
pointed.

Three other men came in carrying wingback chairs up-
holstered in red-and-gold brocade. "Those go into the big
office." She led the way, directing the men to put two of the
chairs on the opposite side of Charlie's desk, for client seat-
ing. Two more were placed against a wall, and one went in
the corner of the room, next to the shelving.

Wyrick glanced at Charlie, hoping the design was to his liking, and was happy to see the smile on his face.

"That's really nice," he said.

She nodded, then glanced at the desk.

"The lamp... Where's the lamp?" she muttered and dashed back into the outer office, before coming back with a small gold desk lamp and plugging it into an outlet on the side of the desk.

"Nice touch," Charlie said, and then his cell phone began to ring.

All of a sudden Wyrick felt the room moving out of focus and saw Charlie's wife on the floor, her face covered in blood. Then the image faded. Her heart was pounding, and she was watching Charlie's face. This wasn't going to be good news.

The moment Charlie saw caller ID, his heart skipped a beat. Morning Light Memory Care.

"Hello, this is Charlie."

"Charlie, this is Dr. Dunleavy. Annie had a fall. She cut her head and knees, and one of her elbows is bleeding, too. We sent her to ER because of the head injury. They'll assess her, treat her injuries and they'll let me know if she needs to be hospitalized."

Charlie groaned. "Damn it. Is she bleeding a lot? Is it a bad cut?"

"The cut isn't that deep, but any head injury requires X-rays, and she'll have to be watched for signs of concussion."

"Which hospital?" Charlie asked.

"Baylor University Med Center. We sent one of our staff members to accompany her, with all her information," Ted said.

"I'm on my way," Charlie said and dropped the phone back in his pocket. "Annie fell. Among other injuries, her head is cut and she's bleeding."

Wyrick was in shock. She'd never had a premonition like this before and didn't know what it meant.

"Go take care of Annie. I've got this," she said, and then he was gone.

She was confused about what she'd just experienced, and sad for him, but beyond this office, he was not her business. And so she continued to direct the movers and the delivery people, until finally they were gone.

At that point, she locked herself inside, then began looking around with an appreciative eye. With all of the furniture and decor into place, it was time to get technology up and running. She established the Wi-Fi signal in their new location, then their computers and accompanying printers and scanners in each office. She soon had them booted up and online.

After that, she went to set up the wet bar in Charlie's office, then stocked both bathrooms. She made up the bed in his office with the new sheets and blankets that she'd washed at her apartment, and then got the new bedspread from the closet and spread it out over the bed. It was a rich, dark burgundy that fit the rest of the furnishings, and after tossing a few throw pillows on for effect, she walked out.

She paused in his office, eyeing everything to make sure it would be ready for him, then went back into the front office and unlocked the door.

She'd already placed an ad in the local newspapers with the new address of Dodge Security and Investigations and had checked to make sure they'd run it this morning, which they had. They were officially back in business.

She sat down at her desk and began going through email, but the premonition she'd had about Annie being hurt was such an anomaly that she finally conceded it was likely just one more facet of her abilities waking up—another oddity of her existence.

Charlie was on the I-635 loop, on his way to the medical center where they'd taken Annie. He needed to see her before he could quiet the nightmare of suppositions and what-ifs rolling through his mind.

With the level of her dementia increasing by the month, and her abilities to comprehend decreasing in matching proportions, he didn't know if she would be scared, or if she would even be aware of pain.

Annie...my Annie. Why us? Why you? And how the hell did we get to this place? This isn't how it was supposed to be.

He was in search mode by the time he finally reached the hospital, following the signs through the parking lot that took him to the ER entrance. Once he found a place to park, he got out on the run, then entered the lobby in long, hurried strides, going straight to the front desk.

"Annie Dodge was brought here by ambulance from Morning Light Memory Care. I'm her husband, Charlie Dodge. What room is she in?"

He handed the clerk his photo ID and his private investigator license for identification purposes. She eyed them briefly before returning them, then typed Annie's name into her computer.

"She's in 10A. Through that door," she said, pointing to his right.

Charlie pocketed his ID and wallet, and went through the doors. Within seconds, he could hear people shouting and someone screaming in one of the treatment bays, but it wasn't Annie, and he kept looking at the numbers above the doors until he saw 10A. He heard commotion inside as he approached, and people talking in loud, anxious tones.

He walked in without an invitation.

A doctor and two nurses were attending to Annie, and there was a woman he recognized from Morning Light in the room with them, but standing back out of the way.

The left side of Annie's face was already bruising and

blood-smeared, and one side of her pretty blond hair was blood-soaked.

One nurse was trying to reason with Annie as she held on to her hands, while the other one was assisting a doctor, in the act of putting staples in Annie's head.

"Jesus wept," Charlie said.

It was the only complete Bible verse he could remember at the moment, as he swallowed past the knot in his throat.

The doctor looked up, frowning.

"I'm Charlie Dodge. Annie is my wife."

"I'm Dr. Baker," he said and kept on working.

Annie was agitated and moaning, and trying to reach toward her head, while the nurse attempting to restrain her wasn't having much success.

"May I?" he asked quietly, and then slipped in beside the nurse and laid the back of his hand against Annie's cheek. "Hey, Annie, it's me, Charlie."

She turned toward the sound of his voice. For a fraction of a second it appeared as if she might recognize him, but the flash of cognizance was gone as he reached for her hands.

At that point, the doctor popped another staple into her head, and the frantic look in Annie's eyes startled Charlie.

"She can feel that! You didn't deaden it?"

"The pain of the needles is the same as the staples," Dr. Baker said. "It's just quicker for her in the long run to do it this way, and the cut was too deep to glue it."

Charlie heard it, but he didn't like it.

"Her right wrist is sprained and swelling," the nurse said, cautioning Charlie not to hold her too tight.

"Yes, ma'am, I see," Charlie said and slid his hands a little higher up her arms instead.

At first she fought his restraint just as she had the nurse, but Charlie was stronger, and he kept gently rubbing her hands and arms as he talked to her.

"My sweet Annie… I'm so sorry you fell and I wasn't there to catch you, but I'm here now. Hold on to me. Hold tight. I know you hurt, but the doctor is trying to help. You cut your head, baby, and he's fixing it. You're going to be fine. I love you, baby. I'm so sorry you got hurt."

And slowly the deep sound of his voice began to calm her. Her fingers slowly curled around his hand, and her agitation lessened.

"That's the last one," the doctor finally said.

Charlie breathed a sigh of relief. "How many staples?"

"Six, and we've x-rayed her to check for broken bones but we don't have those results yet," Dr. Baker said.

"Can you tell if she's suffered a concussion?" Charlie asked.

"Not at this point, but from the depth of the cut, I'd say a slight concussion at the least would be likely," Baker said.

Just then, the woman from Morning Light moved up beside Charlie.

"Mr. Dodge, I'm Rachel Delgado. I've seen you in Morning Light, but we haven't officially met. I just want you to know that I'm here with Annie, too, and will be until she's released and taken back."

"Yes, ma'am. Thank you," Charlie said, but his focus was on getting information from the doctor. "Are you going to admit her?"

"I can't say until I see the X-rays. We need to make sure there's no brain bleed," the doctor said.

"Can you give her something for the pain?" Charlie asked.

"I'm sorry. Not yet. I need to wait and see the X-rays first," Dr. Baker said.

But Charlie persisted. "Then can we clean her up a little?"

"Of course," Dr. Baker said and nodded at one of the nurses, who quickly left the room to get the needed supplies.

Now that there were fewer people around Annie's bed, she

seemed less agitated. Charlie watched for changing expressions, but to his sorrow they were almost nonexistent.

"She's just lying there as if nothing happened," Charlie said, then glanced at Rachel. "Did she cry when she fell?"

"She cried out, but there were no tears. People with this disease forget so many things…even how to feel pain, or to be hungry. Showing emotions becomes rare. The most common reaction is usually agitation."

Charlie looked down at Annie in dismay, seeing firsthand what Annie had feared most. The things that had made her unique in this world were already gone, and what was left of her was disappearing rapidly. He wanted to cry for her because she could not cry for herself, but it would have solved nothing for either of them, so he pulled a chair up beside her bed and laid his hand over hers, instead.

Where once her fingers would have intertwined with his, they now lay motionless and limp beneath his touch, her skin cold and clammy, probably from shock.

"She's cold," he said. He unfolded the extra blanket at the foot of her bed and pulled it up over the others, adding weight and warmth, then glanced at her again.

Her gaze was fixed on the television on the opposite wall. It wasn't on, but it didn't seem to matter. She just kept staring at it until her eyelids began to droop.

When the second nurse returned with a basin, soap, some towels and washcloths, Charlie moved out of the way. They began to clean her up, and she seemed to suffer the wiping and the drips without being aware they were happening.

Charlie watched it all without comment. After they'd finished, they put a clean, dry towel beneath her head and left the room, leaving Charlie and Rachel to wait for the doctor.

When Annie finally fell asleep, Rachel moved to the foot of the bed.

"Pobrecita," Rachel said, patting Annie's foot beneath the covers.

Charlie blinked back tears as he looked away. Annie was indeed a "poor baby," but she was his to love, in sickness and in health, and he wasn't the kind of man to forsake a vow.

Just as Charlie was about to go looking for him, Dr. Baker returned.

"Good news!" he said as he breezed in the door. "No signs whatsoever of internal brain bleeds, or for that matter, anywhere else on her body. She has no broken bones. She'll have a black eye for sure. And without knowing where all she hurts, I'd advise keeping her on soft foods for at least a week, in case her jaw is sore."

"Yes, Doctor," Rachel said. "I will tell them. Can she be taken back to Morning Light now?"

"Yes. I'll tell the nurse to order an ambulance, and you'll ride back with her, yes?"

Rachel nodded.

"Then I'll give you all the paperwork." At that point he shifted his focus to Charlie. "Mr. Dodge, you have my sympathies. I don't see a lot of cases of early-onset Alzheimer's, and I can only imagine how hard this must be for you."

Charlie glanced down. If it wasn't for the steady rise and fall of her chest, he would think she was already gone.

"I love her. It's hard to be a witness to this, and it's so damn sad. If I only knew she was unaware and not in pain, it would be easier to bear."

Dr. Baker shook Charlie's hand and walked out, passing a nurse walking in.

"An ambulance is on the way to pick her up," the nurse said. She handed all the paperwork to Rachel and checked Annie's vitals.

"Everything is stable. We'll remove the IV and blood pressure cuff right before we load her up, okay?" She left without waiting for an answer.

Once more, Charlie and Rachel were alone with Annie, and Rachel wanted to give him some private time with her before they took her back.

"Mr. Dodge, I'm going to step out for a few minutes. I won't be long. Ring the buzzer if you need a nurse."

Charlie nodded, glad he was going to have a few moments alone with his wife, and when Rachel left the room, he leaned over the bed and kissed her.

"Hey, sweetheart, it's me, Charlie. The doctor said you're going to be okay. I love you, baby, so much. I miss you. I miss your laugh. I miss making love to you, but I'll never quit you. I'm here for you always."

The ache in his chest was old, but familiar. It was the "losing Annie" ache that came when he let down his guard, but by the time Rachel returned, he had his game face on.

He stayed until the paramedics came into her room and transferred her from her bed to the gurney. She roused briefly, frowning her discontent, and then looked around in confusion as they began wheeling her out of the room.

Charlie walked beside her, still holding her hand, and Rachel followed. Then he stood outside, still watching as they loaded Annie up and Rachel climbed in beside her.

He waited until the ambulance drove away, then went back to his car and started it up to let it cool off before he left.

His heart hurt, his stomach was in knots. The ache in his chest was growing, swelling with every breath he took. Tears welled and rolled silently down his face, but he didn't move. His cell phone rang, but he didn't answer. He wondered what was going on at the new office, but he knew he was in no shape to go back there. Not yet. He also knew Wyrick would be waiting for news. She was the only other person on earth who still cared about Annie's welfare, so he finally sent her a text.

Nothing was broken. No internal bleeding. Six staples in her head. Bruises galore. They're transporting her back to Morning Light. I'll be in later. Text if you need me.

He hit Send, then put the Jeep in gear and drove away.

CHAPTER TWO

Wyrick was unpacking books and putting them on the shelves in Charlie's office when she received the text. The message was terse, but the news not as bad as she'd feared. He wasn't coming back because he was upset and she couldn't blame him. The only thing she could do for Charlie right now was get the final bits of the office set up, so she kept working, getting the hard copy files that had been boxed up in Charlie's apartment into the new file cabinets.

There was an unopened bottle of Irish whiskey in the wet bar, along with a good bourbon, a bottle each of vodka and tequila, some sparkling water, club soda and some mixers. The ice maker was humming along, freezing cubes, and the glassware was sparkling.

It was just after 4:00 p.m. when Charlie came into the office carrying a file folder and a cup from Starbucks.

Wyrick looked up.

"I need you to file this in the folder with my will. You like caramel macchiatos, right?"

Wyrick nodded as she reached for the folder.

He set the cup down on her desk. "Good. It's what I

brought to make up for abandoning you on the day we were moving in. Sorry. Shit happens."

She looked up. His face was expressionless and his sarcasm was verging on bitter.

"Thank you," she said. She set the cup aside to look at the paperwork in the file and then responded with a false sense of calm. "You bought burial plots and made funeral arrangements. I thought you said she was going to be okay. What happened?"

"Let's just say I saw her future today. She's forgotten everything that made her my Annie. She's getting worse so fast it makes my head spin. She's forgetting how to walk. She's not going to remember that she's in pain, and one of these days she's going to forget how to breathe. That's what happened."

Wyrick gripped the folder with both hands as she got up, then moved to the file cabinet and slipped the new info into his personal file, and made herself focus on anything but what he'd just said.

"I sent notes to your laptop regarding new clients. Let me know which ones you want to represent and I'll schedule appointments. Go home. Don't get drunk. You're miserable to be around when you have a hangover…and I'm thinking about moving."

Before Charlie had time to be pissed about her ordering him around, her news startled him.

"What happened?"

She shrugged. "Right after we got back from the Dunleavy case, I took worldwide Universal Theorem down to the bones and left them in ashes for three days without them knowing what the hell had happened. It was something I'd been planning for a while, and when the time was right, I pulled the plug. After the three days had passed, I put them all back online and sent Cyrus Parks a text telling him to leave me the hell alone or I'd destroy them. I'm sick and tired of running, and they won't be bothering me again, so I'm thinking about buying a home."

Charlie blinked.

"Cyrus Parks?"

"He created UT and calls himself my father."

"Calls himself your— Never mind. Not my business. What do you mean, shut them down?"

"Shut down every aspect of technology at all of their locations worldwide, at all of their homes, their banks, their means of communications…their personal phones, all the files containing years of research, etcetera, etcetera."

"Etcetera?"

She shrugged.

"Holy shit, Wyrick."

She arched an eyebrow. "I'm pretty sure they did not consider any part of that holy. The only downside is now they know a bit more about what I'm capable of."

The hair stood up on the back of Charlie's neck. "A bit more? How do you know that stuff?"

Wyrick's eyes narrowed sharply. If it had been any other time, she would have cut him off at the knees for asking, but he needed a distraction from what he'd suffered today, and she was full of shocking information. So she took a deep breath and unloaded.

"Surely you know by now that I'm something of a freak. I am a Universal Theorem experiment that worked, and they've been trying to recreate me since the day I was born, but it hasn't happened. Most likely because they also fucked up and killed the woman who was my biological mother. It was likely a combination of a lot of things, but she is the continuing difference in all of their later experiments…so there's that."

Charlie gasped. "They killed her…as in murdered? Jesus Christ! Why?"

"According to the file I found a few years back, it's because she wanted to keep me. She didn't want to give me back to them."

"Yes...mothers have a way of disagreeing with people who want their children," Charlie said.

"Except, I wasn't ever supposed to be hers. I wasn't supposed to belong to people. Just to UT. I don't identify with normal people. I don't even know what that means. Now thank you for the caramel macchiato, and we're officially open for business."

He stared at her a moment and then frowned.

"I don't know what kind of reaction you expect me to have, but beyond admiration for your brilliance, I don't even need to know why you are who you are. I appreciate you, Wyrick, and I'm glad you work for me. See you tomorrow."

He turned on his heel and walked out.

Wyrick had been holding her breath, wondering how he'd react, but she should have known Charlie Dodge was shock-proof...except for his beloved Annie, who was his Achilles' heel.

She went back to her desk and ordered takeout to be picked up on her way home, logged off her computer, gathered up her bag and her Starbucks drink, and left.

Charlie's apartment was back to normal when he walked in. It appeared his cleaning service had been here today, which was good. They'd sanitized the rooms as always, right down to making a little V-shaped fold on the toilet paper in the bathroom.

He tossed his keys on the table as he went to his bedroom to shower and change. He thought of Annie as he stripped, but not from the time of making love. She'd never been in this apartment, so there was no memory of her in this room, or in this bed. It was the staples in her head and the bruises on her body that were still fresh in his mind. He would call and check on her before bedtime to see how she was doing, but he knew that if something happened, Morning Light would let him know.

He turned on the shower to allow the water to get warm, then grabbed a clean towel and washcloth from the linen closet and shut the bathroom door. After so many years in the military, privacy was a luxury he did not take for granted.

After he was finished, he dried and dressed in a pair of sweatpants and a T-shirt, then went barefoot into the kitchen.

One quick check of the refrigerator, and he was calling in an order of Chinese food. He grabbed a beer and settled down to check the messages Wyrick had sent to his laptop.

He made notes as he read through them but knew, the moment he read the request from a mother with a missing child, that this would be the next case he took.

Wyrick drove through the madness of quitting-time traffic on the Dallas loop, sipping her caramel macchiato and keeping an eye on her rearview mirror to make sure she wasn't being followed. She got off the loop and drove straight to White Jasmine to pick up her dinner, then zipped back on it again. The next time she left the loop, it was to go home.

The aroma of Thai food rode with her as she wound her way through the old elegance of her landlord Merlin's neighborhood, and then just for the hell of it, she gunned the Mercedes as she took the turn into the estate to let him know it was her. She parked at the entrance to her basement apartment and carried her things inside.

The scent of the morning coffee she'd made before daylight was little more than a faint memory as she dumped everything on the kitchen counter, then headed for her bedroom in long, hurried strides, stripping as she went.

The water was still running cold when she stepped into the shower, and she was already soaping when it began to run warm. The need to wash off her public face was always crucial before she could be at rest in her own place, and this time she was hurrying so she could get back to her food.

There was something to be said for never having to worry about shampooing her hair, so she concentrated on removing her makeup, then rinsed the soap off in record time. She turned off the water and grabbed a towel as she got out. Within minutes she was dry and went commando as she dressed, then went back to the kitchen wearing a pair of gym shorts and a tee and began taking boxes out of her to-go bag.

After plating up what she wanted to eat, she grabbed a wine cooler from the refrigerator and carried it into her living room. As soon as she sat down, she turned on the television, then scooped up a forkful of jasmine rice.

"Heavenly," she said, settling in to eat.

It didn't take long for her mind to shift from the evening news to Charlie and work, and wonder if he was looking at the notes she'd sent.

In the weird way of how she'd seen Annie's fall before anyone told Charlie, she'd known as soon as she saw Tara Bien's name that she would be Charlie's next case. In fact, she'd been so certain he would pick it that she'd penciled Tara in on his desk calendar.

Charlie would confirm it tomorrow, and Wyrick could call her then. According to Tara Bien's message, her daughter was missing, she was desperate, she wasn't far from their address, and she would take any time they could give her.

Wyrick thought of that mother again as she was going to bed and could almost empathize. Granted, Wyrick had never been a mother, and after the chemo, it was never going to happen, but she'd been a child who'd lost a mother. The fear had to be similar.

Tara had sent a picture of the missing daughter with the

email, and when Wyrick had focused on her face, she knew the girl was still alive. And as long as she stayed alive, they would find her.

It was just after 9:30 p.m. when Charlie called Morning Light to check on Annie. He was in the kitchen waiting for his popcorn to finish popping when he made the call, and then it rang several times before someone answered.

"Morning Light. This is Wanda."

"Wanda, this is Charlie Dodge. I'm calling to check on Annie. How did she do today after they brought her back from ER?"

"Evening, Charlie. Annie is okay. We just finished bed check and she's asleep. She was a little agitated this afternoon, but the doctor had ordered pain meds, and when we gave her some it seemed to ease her and she settled down."

"Was she able to eat? The doctor mentioned her jaw might be sore after her fall."

"She refused food, but when we offered her a chocolate protein supplement, she drank all of it through a straw, so we know her jaw hurts. We're watching her, but at this point, it appears she didn't suffer anything from the fall that might cause complications."

The microwave dinged behind him. He took the bag of popcorn out and set it on the counter.

"If anything changes, you'll call me, right?"

"Absolutely, Charlie."

He didn't really want to hang up, because she was there and he was here, and talking to people tonight who took care of her made him feel close to Annie, too, but the questions had come to an end and he had no choice.

"Thank you for the update, Wanda. Have a nice night."

"Thank you, Charlie. Rest well. We love your Annie, too. We'll make sure she's okay."

Charlie disconnected, then emptied the popcorn into a bowl and carried it back into the living room to eat. He took the John Wick movie he'd been watching off Pause, and popped a handful of popcorn in his mouth, watching with interest as Keanu Reeves tossed a bad guy up against a wall.

"I could do that," he muttered, got back up for a Coke, and then finished off the movie and his snack at the same time.

It wasn't until he finally gave up each day to the night and to exhaustion that he had to acknowledge the emptiness of his life. If it wasn't for Wyrick's intermittent days of being contrary, it would suck.

Since yesterday was moving-in day and today was the official opening day at the new office, Wyrick decided to go for a subdued version of her usual self, choosing form-fitting stretch pants in a black pinstripe and topping them with a man's white dress shirt. The diamond cuff links at her wrists might be considered a little over the top, but she liked them, and she'd left the collar of her shirt unbuttoned, just shy of revealing any part of her dragon tattoo.

Her eye shadow was black, fading into bright red. The lipstick on her upper lip was She-Devil Red. The lipstick on her lower lip was called Midnight. The name spoke for itself.

She thought about the day ahead as she reached the parking garage and drove up to the sixth level to their designated parking spots. She parked her Mercedes and got out, slinging her computer bag over her shoulder. Picking up the box of sweet rolls she'd bought for the office, she headed inside the building, then down the hall to their new office, with the key in her hand.

She walked in, flipping on lights as she went, then carried the box of pastries to the coffee bar she'd had installed in a mini butler's pantry between their offices.

After starting the coffee, she turned on the lights in Charlie's office, logged on to his computer and put out notepaper and pens on his desk. She aimed the remote at the window shades and raised them all the way up before returning to her desk. The office phone was already ringing as she sat down.

"Dodge Security and Investigations."

"It's me," Charlie said. "I'm on my way in, but I want to get the ball rolling on that child abduction case. Call Tara Bien. Get her in today if possible."

"I've already penciled her in for ten o'clock, pending your confirmation, of course."

"Well, you have it. Call her."

"Fine. Oh, by the way, good morning, and the word for today is *please*." Then she hung up in his ear.

His eyes narrowed when he heard the click. She'd hung up on him. What the hell kind of an employee hangs up on the boss?

Then he shrugged. His kind did, that was for sure. And he had to admit he might have been a bit abrupt, but what the hell?

Wyrick knew it would irk Charlie when she hung up. It was why she did it. Now he would be on edge all day, trying not to piss her off, which was good. Yesterday had gutted him. She'd known that when she saw the papers he'd given her to file. Funeral arrangements were serious business, and now she'd given him something else to think about.

She looked up Tara Bien's phone number, made the call and waited for her to pick up.

Tara Bien was a corporate attorney, and a good one. The day her daughter, Jordan, disappeared, she'd left her at home with Della Whitman, the woman who cleaned her house. Jordan wasn't feeling well, and Tara had to be in court that morning, so she couldn't stay with her. But Tara was also planning to be home before Della finished cleaning. What she hadn't counted on was the judge giving the opposing counsel a brief recess, which wound up making the case run a couple of hours longer.

She was still in court when Della finished cleaning, which left twelve-year-old Jordan alone. In itself, that was not a big deal. She was old enough to stay home alone, but Tara hated it when she had to leave her there, knowing she was sick. And because of the delays, Tara was still in court when her ex-husband, Jud Bien, showed up at their door.

Jordan was a tall, skinny twelve-year-old with black hair, blue eyes and a face that would one day be beautiful. She hadn't felt well all night and was still sick when she woke, so after a short consultation with her mom, she stayed in bed and slept through most of Della's cleaning.

Jordan began feeling better as the morning passed, and by the time Della left, she'd gone downstairs to the kitchen for something light to eat. She was having a cup of microwave noodle soup when the doorbell rang. But she'd been cautioned too many times about never answering the door when she was home alone, so she just kept eating.

The doorbell rang again, then again, until Jordan got up and sneaked into the living room and peered out of a window to see who it was, then she squealed with delight and ran to open the door, her heart pounding.

"Daddy!"

Jud opened his arms and caught Jordan as she leaped, delighted and smiling at the welcome.

"Lord, child, but you have grown. You look like a young lady now. You're not my little girl anymore," he said and then put her back down on her feet.

"How did you know I was here?" Jordan said.

Jud ignored the question. "I brought presents," he said and went back to the porch to pick up the sack he'd dropped, then came back inside.

"Mama should be here any minute," Jordan said. "She'll be surprised. We didn't know where you were in Dallas. Why didn't you ever call me, Daddy? I missed you so much."

"I've been studying," Jud said.

Jordan frowned. "In a school?"

"Kind of like a school," Jud said. "Let's sit in the living room so you can see what I brought you."

Pleased by the idea that her absentee father had brought gifts, Jordan was easily distracted and opened them with delight, and then gasped at the array of makeup.

"This is more stuff than Mama has," Jordan said.

Jud reached out and stroked her hair from the crown of her head down to the middle of her back.

"I like that you've let your hair grow," he said.

Jordan grinned. "Boys like long hair."

Jud frowned. "You have a boyfriend? As in dating?"

Jordan rolled her eyes. "No, I don't date. But I do like boys," she said and then giggled.

Jud relaxed. "Oh. Good. I was about to object."

Jordan didn't like the tone of his voice. He didn't really have a right to disapprove of her life, or what Mama was letting her do—not after moving away without a word to either of them—but she stayed quiet.

Jud felt the emotional shift and realized he'd forfeited his right to object, by his absence. He needed to made amends.

"Hey, honey, would you like to come spend the night with me at the Hilton Anatole? It's where I'm staying for now. We'll do pizza and a movie...or shopping at the mall. Whichever sounds the most fun. And there's always room service for late-night snacks. I have a lot to make up for, you know."

"I'll need to check with Mama," Jordan said.

Jud nodded vigorously. "Oh, definitely. In fact, considering everything, I think I should be the one to talk to her and let her know. You go pack."

Jordan got up. "Yes, okay. I won't take long," she said and took her presents with her as she ran upstairs.

Jud watched his daughter leave, her long legs flying and her dark hair swinging as she ran. He smiled. The Seraphim was going to be pleased with his daughter.

Jordan had pajamas and underwear in her overnight bag, and was adding an outfit for school tomorrow, plus an extra one in case they went somewhere special to eat. She knew her daddy was calling for permission, but she felt obligated to contact her mother, too. He had abandoned them without a word, and she didn't want Mama to feel hurt in any way that she was leaving with him, even if it was just for the night. So she sat down on the side of the bed and sent her mama a text.

Mama, you won't believe it...but Daddy came back. He brought me presents, and I'm going to spend the night with him at the Anatole. We're doing pizza and a movie, and he said he'd take me shopping at the mall if I wanted. I feel better. I'll be fine. I'll have Daddy drop me off at school in the morning, and I'll see you tomorrow after school like always. Please don't be mad. I am so glad to see him.

Then she hit Send and tossed her phone and charger on the bed. At that point, Jud knocked on the door and walked in.

Startled that he'd just walked in without waiting for her to answer, she frowned.

"Dad! Really? What if I'd been changing clothes or something?"

Jud frowned again. He was out of practice with this older version of his daughter.

"Sorry. I keep forgetting how much you've grown up. I'll carry your bag down to the car while you get dressed. Do you have everything in it you want?"

"The phone and charger go in," she said, pointing to them near her bag. "It won't take me long to get dressed."

She grabbed underwear and the jeans and T-shirt she planned to wear, and went into the bathroom to change. Then did something very out of the ordinary and locked the door between them.

Jud's eyes narrowed as he heard the lock click. He shoved her phone and charger beneath the pillows on her bed and took her bag out to the car. He paused a moment at the doorway to look up and saw the cameras. He'd almost forgotten about them; he took off down the hall to the room where the security equipment was kept.

He'd been the one to install it all, so he knew what to do to disable it. Within moments, he'd erased all the footage featuring him, then disabled the entire system. He wiped it down so as not to leave fingerprints, and was on his way back to the foyer when Jordan appeared on the landing above him in skinny jeans and a pale pink T-shirt.

"I still can't believe you're here," she said and took the stairs down on the run.

"You are a beautiful young woman," Jud said, as he slipped her hand beneath his arm.

Hearing her dad talk like that made her feel weird. He wasn't acting like he used to, and she shook her head in denial.

"Dad, give me a break. I'm not even a teenager," she said.

Then as they went out, she locked the door and dropped her key into her bag.

Tara was giving her summation when the text from Jordan came, but she didn't know it because her phone was on Mute and in her briefcase. It wasn't until after the judge made his ruling and the court had adjourned that she began to check her messages.

When she saw the text from Jordan, her first reaction was shock, followed by anger. How dare Jud do this without talking to her first? They hadn't seen or heard from him in over two years, and she had even begun to wonder if he was still alive. *Now he shows up like nothing ever happened and sweeps her away for good times?* Oh, no way! Not when he was more than two years behind on child support.

Tara was pissed, but not at Jordan. Jordan had been such a daddy's girl, and his absence had nearly destroyed her. She could only imagine how overjoyed Jordan must have been to see him. What bothered her most was how Jud knew Jordan was at home on a school day, and why he had waited until he knew Tara would be at work?

She grabbed her things and walked to her car, and the moment she got inside, she called Jordan. The phone rang, then went to voice mail. Frowning, she sent Jordan a text to call her immediately, then headed home. She was angry and upset at the whole situation, but fear had yet to set in. That came later, after she was home and calling every few minutes without getting an answer.

The strange part was, every time she called, she thought she could hear the Bon Jovi ringtone Jordan had set up to indicate the calls were from her mama. But every time she tried to run down the sound, it would quit ringing and go to voice mail before Tara could find it.

So she began calling the number over and over, going all through the ground floor before starting upstairs. It wasn't until she was on the second floor that she realized the phone was ringing in Jordan's room. She ran inside and then called again, and within moments, found the phone and the charger cord stuffed beneath a pillow on the unmade bed.

That caused the first wave of panic.

This made no sense. Jordan didn't accidentally forget it was there. It was always in her hand. She would not have left the house with her father without it, which meant the text was sent before she left the house.

And it was obviously hidden. But why hide it? Why would Jud hide Jordan's phone from her before he took her away?

Then came the second wave of panic.

So she couldn't tell her mama what was happening, or where they went.

"The security cameras!" Tara cried and ran downstairs, only to find everything off. When she started it back up again and discovered it had been erased back to the point of Della leaving the house, the third wave of panic struck.

"Oh my God, Jud Bien. What the hell are you doing?"

Now she was trembling, and the fear within her was choking. She stumbled to the nearest chair and pulled up her Contacts list, then called the only number she had for Jud, which went straight to voice mail.

"This is bad. So bad. I can feel it," Tara said. She knew calling the police was never going to help, because she and Jud shared legal custody, and she'd never changed that after he disappeared.

Jud *was* Jordan's father, which meant it wasn't stranger abduction. Right now, she didn't have even one bit of information as to where they went beyond the Anatole, or that anything was wrong except her mother's instinct. She knew in her gut that something bad was happening, and she needed as much information as she could get.

She called the Anatole, asking for Jud Bien, they told her that there was no one registered there by that name. Now she knew something was wrong!

She ran to her office and began digging through the drawers in the desk until she found Jud's old address book. She started calling the men Jud used to hang out with, hoping he'd stayed in touch with at least one of them. She needed to get a handle on what he'd been doing so she'd have a starting point as to where he might have gone.

Her hopes continued to fade with each call she made—

she'd called three men on the list with no luck. The next one down was Gordon Butler. Jud had always called him Gordy, and she remembered him well.

The phone rang several times without an answer, and she was expecting it to go to voice mail when she suddenly heard Gordy's voice.

"Hello, hello! This is Gordy!"

Just like old times, Tara thought, and then responded.

"Hello, Gordy, this is Tara Bien, Jud Bien's ex-wife. Do you have a few minutes to speak with me?"

"I sure do, gorgeous! How the hell have you been?"

Tara sighed. It didn't sound like Gordy had done much changing or growing up.

"Not so good right now, Gordy, and it's why I'm calling. By any chance would you know what Jud has been doing since he left Dallas?"

There was a brief moment of silence, like Gordy was try- ing to decide whether to give up a brother or not.

"Uh, I might. The last time I saw him was two years ago when we went on a trip together, but we kind of parted com- pany after that, and I haven't seen him since."

"Please, Gordy. This is important. Jud came by my house today while I was gone. Our daughter, Jordan, stayed home from school because she wasn't feeling well, and somehow he knew she was there and he took her...without calling me... without letting me know a thing. We haven't seen him in over two years and now he just whisked her away. I was in court, so I didn't get Jordan's text until later, but she went somewhere with Jud to spend the night, and he's not answering his phone."

"Uh... I thought y'all had joint custody of the kid," Gordy said.

"We do," Tara said.

"So what's the big deal? He came to visit. He'll bring her back in the morning."

"The big deal is... I think Jordan is in some kind of trouble. I tried to call and text her numerous times to no response. Then I got home and found her phone and charger hidden beneath her pillow. She would never leave her phone behind, let alone hide it, so what do you know that I don't?"

Gordy took a quick breath. "Look, Tara. All I know is two years ago we both left Dallas to go to a psychic conference held at this big estate in the mountains above Eureka Springs, Arkansas. You know how Jud is about what he called his gifts, but he didn't want to go alone."

Tara's heart skipped a beat. Of course! *That* was how Jud knew where Jordan was! That psychic part of him was something she'd always known about, but he'd never done much with it.

"So what happened at that conference?" she asked.

"He took to it like he had walked into a family reunion or something. He was more at ease and excited than I'd ever seen him. He kept saying this was what he was supposed to be doing. I felt like it wasn't much of a conference. It wasn't about workshops or speakers. They were just testing all of the attendees in several ways to see what they were best at. Jud scored off the wall on everything, and the dude running the conference got really excited and offered Jud the opportunity to come study with him and his group."

Tara's heart was beginning to pound. "What kind of group? What did they do?"

"I don't know," Gordy said.

"What's the name of the group? What was the man's name? Do you know where it was located?"

Gordy sighed. "I don't remember the dude who recruited Jud, but I do remember the name of the group. It was Fourth Dimension, and no location was ever mentioned in my presence. That's all I know, and he could be doing something else by now. That was two years ago, right?"

"Yes, two years ago," Tara repeated, writing furiously to take down everything Gordy had been telling her. "Thank you. Thank you so much, Gordy."

"You're welcome, Tara. I hope your kid calls in real soon, and this all turns out to be nothing."

"So do I," Tara said and hung up.

Only she didn't have to be a psychic to know that wasn't going to happen, because she knew something about Jordan that no one else but Jud knew. When it came to psychic abilities, Jordan was her father's daughter.

Tara needed help. She needed a good private investigator to track Jud Bien and find out where he took Jordan, and she knew who that would be. She turned to her computer and googled Charlie Dodge, and Dodge Security and Investigations. He was the best there was in Dallas, but when she called, it went straight to voice mail, and this mess was too complicated to just leave a message. So she sent an email to him, instead.

CHAPTER THREE

The first stop Jud made was at a nearby gas station to fill up. All of Jordan's luggage was in the back of the SUV and she wanted her phone, but she couldn't get out on her side because he'd pulled up too close to the pumps. So she sat, waiting for her dad to come back and get it for her.

She watched him go inside to pay before he gassed up and wondered why he hadn't just used a credit card, but when he came out he was carrying two bottles of pop, one of which was a Dr. Pepper, her favorite. She smiled that he'd remembered.

Jud opened his door, handed Jordan the bottle of pop with the cap already loosened for her, along with a package of Peanut M&Ms, another favorite, and then went to fuel up. Jordan dug into the candy and pop without thinking about her phone again until they were driving away.

"Oh darn it, I was going to have you get my phone out of my bag," she said.

"We don't have far to go. You can get it then." He filched a couple of M&Ms from the bag, popped them in his mouth, then took a drink of his Coke. He put it into the cup holder, then pointed at Jordan's Dr. Pepper. "Drink up while it's still cold," he said, wanting the knockout drops he'd put in it to work so he could get her out of the city.

Jordan giggled, took another big drink and then palmed some more M&Ms. The sun was on her side of the car and even with the tinted windows, it was hot on her skin. The effervescence of the pop and the slight burn of it going down her throat was refreshing. She took one last big drink and then set the bottle in the console, put the leftover candy in her pocket, leaned back and closed her eyes.

She never knew when they headed north out of Dallas, or when they crossed the border into Oklahoma. The sun continued to move toward the western horizon as they took an eastbound highway in Oklahoma an hour later.

It was dark when she finally roused, confused as to where she was and who she was with. Then she saw her father's profile in the lights from the dash and, in that moment, saw a stranger. He turned his head and looked at her. She heard his thoughts, she saw his purpose and knew he'd lied to her, and that she'd been drugged.

"Where are we, Daddy?" she asked, her voice shaking.

"I'm taking you somewhere special," Jud said. "To a place where you will help make great changes in the world."

Jordan panicked. "I don't want to make great changes!" she cried. "I want to go home. Take me home now!"

"I can't do that," Jud said. "You're too important to me."

"I'm important to Mom, too!" she cried. "I have a life of my own to live, and this isn't part of it," she said and started to cry.

Jud reached for her, and when he touched her, she yanked her hand back in sudden rage.

"Don't touch me! Don't you ever touch me again!" she screamed. "I should never have trusted you when you showed up. I was right all along," Jordan shouted, wiping away angry tears.

Jud frowned. "What do you mean?"

"You aren't worth the tears I shed before, and I will die before you'll make me cry again."

The words were like a gut punch. "You don't understand, baby. You're like me. We belong together. There is so much that we can do with our powers."

"Don't talk to me, Jud. I'm not like you. I'll never be like you. You're a runaway coward. Life got too boring… too hard…and so you ran away from us. I don't know what you think I'm going to do for you, but I won't. I will never play your games."

Jud was trying not to panic. Bringing trouble into Fourth Dimension was frowned upon. It wasn't unusual for the Sprite novitiates to cry and miss home, but no one had ever come in defiant. He reached across the console and grasped the soft flesh on her arm, remembering the years when she was little and they'd curled around his neck.

"They aren't games, daughter."

But the moment Jordan felt his touch, she saw her future, and the horror within her rose up into her throat.

"I'm going to throw up," she said. "Either pull over, or prepare to ride the rest of the way to Kentucky with vomit."

Shocked that she knew where they were going, Jud hit the brakes and wheeled off onto the shoulder of the road, then got out running, opened the passenger door just as she leaned out and threw up…over and over and over, until she was so shaky she couldn't breathe.

Jud pulled a handkerchief from his pocket and tried to hand it to her. She spit on his hand and closed the door in his face.

Jud stood there in the dark with her vomit at his feet and then wiped her spit off his hand. He threw the handkerchief in the ditch.

He got back in the car, put the keys back into the ignition and hit the child lock on the door. She couldn't get out now if she wanted to.

"Do you want a bottle of water?" he asked.

"Fuck you, Jud."

Jud slapped her across the mouth before he thought, and then groaned.

"I'm so, so sorry, baby. I was just startled to hear such an ugly word coming out of your mouth."

Jordan turned to face him then, while the blood trickled down from the lip he'd busted.

"You're bothered by a curse word, but you're going to pimp me out to some old man just like you. Some old man who *will* fuck me. So what's it to you, *Daddy*?"

Jud started the car and peeled out, slinging gravel behind him as they left. His gut was burning. His heart was pounding so hard that he thought he might be having a heart attack. The shame he felt was transient, but it was there, because he could not deny one word of her accusations.

He was bringing her to Fourth Dimension for breeding. But it wasn't as if they were going to be marrying children. They weren't allowed to pick their mate until after they'd reached puberty. He had his bride already picked out, but until he brought back a donation for someone else, he couldn't claim her. Jordan would have time to learn about them before it was her time to be chosen. She would come to understand the importance of her place there. She was only twelve and he knew she had yet to bleed. She'd grow into the idea. It was the path of women to bear children and make the house a home.

While Jud was convincing himself what he'd done was okay, Jordan had blocked all of her thoughts from Jud and was thinking of her mother and how panicked she must be. She knew now that her phone was not in her bags, or they would have heard her mother's desperate calls trying to find her. Thank God she'd sent that text. At least Mama would know who took her.

Jordan saw the shadowy reflection of her own face in the window as she looked out into the night. She didn't look like herself anymore. Maybe because she'd thrown up the last vestige of her innocence on the side of a highway, and it had been too dark to see the place where she'd died.

She didn't know it yet, but in a strange way, her favorite movie was going to be what saved her. Ever since she'd seen the movie *Wonder Woman*, she had been completely taken with the idea that a young, beautiful woman could also be powerful and fight bad people, and in Jordan's mind, she was entering a world filled with bad people, and her father was her betrayer. She wasn't an innocent in this deception. She would fight them every step of the way.

Jud was popping uppers to stay awake for the drive, and the knowledge of what awaited Jordan was enough for her to never close her eyes again.

They were in Kentucky by daylight, but once again, Jud needed to stop and refuel, and this time he didn't trust her not to run. If she got away and told what was going on at Fourth Dimension, they'd all wind up in prison.

"I'm going to stop for gas," Jud said. He slid his hand in his pocket and grasped the syringe filled with Nitramal. It was something they'd developed at Fourth Dimension for quiet transport, and he needed control of his recalcitrant daughter.

"Good. I need to pee," Jordan said. "And I need water, but I won't drink a drop of what comes from your hands, just know that."

Jud frowned. "Stop defying me. I am your father."

"No, you're not, Jud. You're the stranger danger Mama talked about."

"Then you leave me no choice," Jud said. He flipped the

cap off the syringe, jabbed it into her neck and shoved the syringe all the way down.

"No!" Jordan screamed, frantically grabbing at her neck, but it was too late. She could already feel the drug moving through her bloodstream, through her body...into her brain... and then everything went black.

Jud yanked out the syringe and the cap and dumped them in the trash at the pumps, then ran inside to prepay.

He bought a case of bottled water and some chips in a can, and carried them back to the car. He put the water beneath her feet and the chips on the dash, then filled up the car and left.

It was a four-hour drive into the Appalachians to reach the compound, and Jordan was asleep for two of them. When she finally woke up, they were deep in the woods and he pulled over to let her pee.

"You are now in more danger from the animals in these mountains than you are from me. Pee, then get back into the car and there will be no more injections."

Jordan got out without looking at him and closed the door between them to do her business. She staggered as she got back in, and Jud thought she was going to faint, then guessed she was dehydrated.

"That case of bottled water has not been opened. You can see that. Nothing has been injected into them. None of them are leaking. Drink some water or you'll arrive unconscious and won't know what's happening. Is that what you want?"

Jordan was trapped and she knew it. She reached down between her legs to get a bottle of water as he began driving away, and then struggled to tear through the plastic wrapping before she finally got one free. She was weak and she knew it. That was dangerous. If she was going to survive this ordeal until Mama found her, she had to stay strong.

She drank half the bottle before she took a breath, and then opened the can of chips and ate them one at a time, chewing slowly and washing each bite down with another drink of water. She ate half the can of chips and emptied two bottles of water before she stopped.

"Feel better?" Jud asked.

"I feel like the turkey that's being force-fed before Thanksgiving. That's how I feel," Jordan said.

Jud sighed. "Look. You're not going to be gang-raped. You're not going to be sold at auction. You're going to live with girls just like you who are waiting for their turn to get married. They've all been chosen. They're just not ready."

Jordan didn't respond. She didn't want him to know how much she'd seen of what that place was about when he'd touched her before. She didn't want any of them to know. She'd been blocking her skills for years so that she wouldn't do or say the wrong thing at school, or out in public, so this was just more of the same. The only difference was that all of the men were more or less like Jud. The plus was that the girls they'd brought in weren't like her, so the men would not be expecting her to have powers to use against them, and she didn't think her father was going to tell them, for fear she'd cause trouble for him. If she was a failure, he wouldn't get to marry the girl he'd chosen.

Her eyes narrowed as she glanced at his profile and saw the frown on his forehead.

How do you like me now, Jud Bien?

He gasped, then stared at her in disbelief before returning his attention to the road.

"How long have you been aware of your skills?" he asked.

"All my life."

"Why didn't I know this?" he asked.

She smiled. "I don't know. Why didn't you? I knew about yours."

He said nothing more to her. If he could, he would have

turned around and taken her back right then, but then she'd tell, and he had no one else to donate.

The ride was silent for the next couple of hours, except for the crunch of Jordan chewing as she ate the rest of the potato chips and drank another bottle of water.

They passed through a little town called Shawnee Gap, but when they left the highway at the edge of that town and started up a mountain on a blacktop road, Jordan glanced in the outside mirror, watching the last vestiges of civilization disappearing behind them.

The road went up, sometimes curving, sometimes a straightaway, but always gaining altitude. And the forest was getting so dense it was difficult to see beyond the shoulders of the road.

"We're almost there," Jud said.

Jordan didn't comment.

He reached across the console again, wanting to reestablish some kind of relationship before they arrived, but when he started to touch her, she jerked back.

"In your dreams, you bastard," she said.

Jud frowned. "You do not embarrass me in front of my people. Do you hear me?"

"Or what?" Jordan said. "I'm not afraid of you. Not of any of you. You disgust me, Jud. Your little cult is nothing but a bunch of child molesters. Even if I haven't experienced it yet, I know how sex works. You've got to get it up before you can get it in, and I will laugh at them, whether they're limp or hard. I will call them ugly. I will make fun of how they look. They may beat me. And they may rape me. But I won't cry, and I will not submit."

Jud couldn't believe he was hearing these words coming out of his little girl's mouth. He'd gone after a child, but he'd been gone too long. His stomach was in knots as he braked to turn onto a narrow, one-lane road off to the left. After winding through brush so thick it scraped the sides of his car as they passed, they arrived at the gates to a massive, walled-in compound. He glanced at Jordan. She was motionless... staring at what was before her, and he wondered what she thought. The two-story house she could see through the gates was quite ornate, but the rest of what she could see was little more than long metal buildings erected on bare ground. Considering the wealth of green growth around the place, it looked strange for there to be nothing green inside.

"We're here," Jud said unnecessarily and then leaned out the window to key in a code at the entrance.

An alarm sounded as the gates began to open.

Jordan's heart skipped a beat. As defiant as she'd been, she was scared, but they'd never know it. Her own walls were up and there wasn't a code for getting into her mind. She was in control of that.

Men came out of buildings from all over the compound as Jud circled the drive that led to the front of the estate, but Jordan was looking for the girls. Then she saw faces at the window of a long single-story building at the far end of the compound. There they were. That was where she would be kept.

The front door at the big house opened, and a man of great girth and height walked out wearing a long white robe. His hair was gray with a few remaining streaks of mousy brown. The length of it was well below his shoulders, but his face was clean-shaven and shining like it had been greased.

Jud got out of the car, went around to the passenger side and opened the door. When he started to take his daughter's arm, he remembered her warning and stopped.

"You have to get out now. I'll get your bag."

Jordan grabbed two unopened bottles of water and then got out, tossed her long dark hair with a flip of her head, and

stared into their faces without taking a step beyond the hood
of the car.

The others saw her defiance, but it wasn't the first time a
Sprite had resisted, and they thought nothing of it.

Aaron Walters was the man in white, but in Fourth Dimension, he was the Seraphim, and addressed as that, or Master.

He felt omnipotent, and purposefully sent psychic waves
of energy toward the girl as a means of calming her while he
waited for Archangel Jud to approach and present his donation.

Jud got Jordan's bag. "Follow me," he whispered.

"No," Jordan said.

Jud set the bag beside her and approached the Seraphim
alone.

"Master… I present my daughter, Jordan Bien, as the
needed donation to claim my bride."

"She does not show obedience," Aaron said.

"I have not seen her in some years. It is her mother's fault.
She has taught her to hate me."

Aaron's eyes narrowed, but he said nothing as he gestured
toward two of the men to bring her closer.

Jordan saw them coming and tightened her grip around
the full bottles of water. When the first one reached for her,
she swung her fist and hit him on the side of the face, the
weight of the bottle still in her hand. He staggered backward
and grabbed his face.

When the other man leaped at her, she sidestepped him
and did the same with her other fist, hitting him square in
the nose. The man screamed out in pain as blood spurted. He
bent over, clutching his face.

"Nobody touches me!" Jordan said and walked forward,
past the men, past her father, and straight up to the bottom of
the steps upon which the Seraphim was standing, still holding
both bottles of water. "I am here against my will. I will die
before I'll submit to any of you, so kill me now, or let me be."

Jud moaned. He couldn't bear to see her murdered before his eyes.

But the Seraphim held up a hand, and the men stepped back.

"So, Jordan Bien, you have spirit."

Jordan said nothing.

And that was when Aaron realized he couldn't read what she was thinking. His eyes narrowed. He'd never had this happen before. Was she like them? Was she blocking? If so, then she was more valuable than the others, but of what use would she be if she defied them? He'd have to meditate to get answers. They obviously could not put her with the other girls, or they might wind up with a rebellion on their hands.

"Take her to the old dormitory. She does not share quarters with the other Sprites. She is a bad influence," he said.

Three men came forward.

"Someone get my bag," Jordan said, as if ordering a bell-hop in a fancy hotel.

They surrounded her and marched her toward an older building a short distance away, and once she was inside, the man carrying her bag threw it onto the nearest bed.

"The bathroom is in there. Food will be brought to you here. You will not be allowed to eat with the others," he said.

Jordan lifted her chin in defiance. "I will need a pillow and bed linens to make up my bed. I will also need soap, towels and washcloths for my bath."

He blinked, and then they left without answering.

Jordan heard the door lock, but she didn't cry. They'd be back. They didn't know what to make of her yet, but as long as she kept them unsure of what to do with her, she was somewhat safe. But it was the biggest bluff she'd ever run. Her heart was racing. She'd never been this afraid in her life. Yes, her level of defiance startled them. She didn't know how long this would last, but she'd raise hell for as long as they would tolerate it. They couldn't turn her loose or take her back. And if no man wanted to mess with her, she didn't trust Jud to save her life. She had to be aware at all times of a chance to escape. She didn't know where she was, but she knew Shawnee Gap was at the end of the only road they'd come up on, and she knew what the people here were all thinking. Except for her mother knowing who took her, it was the only edge she had.

"Please, God, help Mama find me," she said, willing herself not to cry.

CHAPTER FOUR

Tara kept calling the number she had for Jud's phone, but he never answered. She was scared, angry and confused. She didn't sleep all night, and she knew when she got up the next morning that she couldn't function at her job when she was in this state. Since the shared custody in their divorce was still valid, she knew the police wouldn't help. She needed to talk to her partners directly. Maybe one of them would have an idea of what she needed to do next.

She put on another pot of coffee and then showered and dressed. Sick to her stomach from a night of nothing but coffee, she made a piece of toast, then filled her to-go cup and headed to the offices downtown, eating as she drove.

She raced into the lobby, so far removed from the perfectly dressed and coiffed lawyer she presented to the public that the receptionist almost challenged her, then recognized her at the last minute.

"Tara? What's wrong?"

"Is Mr. Richter in?" Tara asked.

"He just arrived. He and Eric are talking about a case."

"I need help. I'll talk to both of them," Tara said.

"I'll tell him you're on the way," she said as Tara barreled through the door separating the lobby from the bank of offices.

Toby Richter was the eldest son of Harmon Richter, who'd founded the law firm thirty years ago, and being the eldest, he was now the head of the firm, even though his two younger brothers were also partners here. He was licking the sugar off his fingers from the cruller he'd just eaten when the receptionist buzzed in.

"What is it, Milly? I told you I didn't want to be disturbed."

"I know, sir, and I'm sorry, but Tara Bien is on her way to your office. Something is wrong, and she said she needs your help."

Eric Prince heard enough of Milly's message to be concerned. He had the office next to Tara, and admired her work ethic and the sharp wit she exhibited in the courtroom. So when the knock came at the door, he turned to look.

Tara burst into the office wearing blue jeans, tennis shoes and a rumpled cotton shirt. Her hair was a mess and wadded up into a bun on top of her head, and her eyes were so red and swollen she looked like she'd been crying for hours.

Toby took one glance at the haunted look on her face, the dark circles beneath her eyes, and jumped to his feet.

"Tara! What's wrong?"

"My daughter was abducted by my ex while I was in court yesterday. We share custody, but I haven't seen him in two years. He just showed up out of the blue and talked Jordan into spending the night at his hotel. If she hadn't sent me a text telling me what was happening, I still wouldn't know where she was. There's nothing on my security cameras to even indicate he was there, and he's not registered in any hotel anywhere in the surrounding area."

"Wait! What? So did you call him?"

Tara sank down into a chair and started to cry.

"All night. He never answered."

"Your daughter isn't answering, either?" Toby said.

"I found her phone hidden beneath a pillow on her bed. She texted me from it, and all I can guess is that he hid it from her when they left so she couldn't contact me. I already know the police won't help because of the shared custody settlement in our divorce papers. And there's something I've learned that's even more frightening. I found out from one of Jud's old friends that the last time he saw him was at a gathering for psychics." Tara sighed at the look on their faces. "It's just something he can do. He was never into it much, but finding this out and then having Jordan go missing is horrifying on a whole other level for me, because Jordan has inherited some of her father's abilities."

"Have you checked out the people behind the gathering he went to?" Eric asked.

"All I know is that the group was called Fourth Dimension."

"That might be bordering on cult behavior," Toby said.

"I know, and I don't know what to do," Tara said and then covered her face.

"Tara, I'm so sorry," Eric said.

"Do you have any idea where he's been living?" Toby asked.

"No," Tara wailed. "He dropped off the face of the earth, and now this."

"My first instinct is to get a really good private investigator on this. Someone like Charlie Dodge."

Tara grabbed a handful of tissues from the box on Toby's desk and began wiping her eyes.

"Yes, I've already sent him an email, but I haven't heard back. I don't even know if he'll take the case."

Eric leaned forward. "My brother-in-law is a special agent

with the FBI. He's headquartered at the office here in Dallas.
I can talk to him…see if he has any suggestions."

"I'll take any and all help," Tara said. "I'm just so scared. I
feel like the bottom fell out of my world, and that's the other
reason why I'm here. I am in no way able to deal with clients
right now. I don't have another court case pending, and am
requesting leave. I'm so sorry to put—"

"We'll handle it," Toby said. "Just go home. If Dodge
doesn't take the case, find someone like him. Get an investigator on this before the trail gets too cold."

Tara stood. "Thank you. Thank you for the help and the
advice, and Eric, let me know if your brother-in-law has any
advice for me, too."

"We're having dinner with him and his wife tonight. I will
do that," Eric said.

Tara left the offices with more hope than she'd come in
with. At least now she had a direction. She got back in her
car, then sat long enough to check and see if she'd gotten a response from her email to Charlie Dodge, but there was nothing. Now she had a call to make to Bronte Middle School.
She had to let the principal know what had happened, too.
Because the last bell had just rung for class, and Jordan was
going to be late for school.

Tara's plight was on Eric Prince's mind all day. He talked
to his wife, Mona, about it while they were getting ready to
go out to dinner.

"I told Tara I'd ask Hank if he had any advice for her,"
he said.

Mona nodded. "Good idea. Hank works on a lot of kidnapping and serial killer cases. He should have some suggestions that might help her."

"That's what I thought" Eric said.

A couple of hours later, Hank Raines and his wife, Barb,

were sharing appetizers with Eric and Mona, when Eric brought up the subject, explaining the details as he went.

Hank listened, more than sympathetic to the situation. He and Barb had kids, and he couldn't imagine anything worse than having one of them go missing.

"The private investigator angle is good, and your boss was on target suggesting Charlie Dodge. He's one of the best I've ever heard of. I'd like to meet him sometime. Tell her to try to find out where her ex went when he disappeared. That might be the best starting point."

"She may already have one good starting point," Eric said. "She claims her husband is psychic, and one of his friends told her that he might be mixed up with a group called Fourth Dimension."

Hank sat up a little straighter. "Fourth Dimension?"

Eric nodded. "Have you heard of it?" he asked.

"I've heard of it," Hank said. "But I don't know anything about it. I'll dig around a bit and see what I can find out for you, okay?"

"Thanks," Eric said. "And my apologies to the ladies for bringing such a disturbing element into our evening out."

The women quickly assured him it was fine, but it wasn't lost on either man that their wives were glad to move on to something more pleasant and lighthearted.

The evening ended on a good note, and Hank was nodding in all the right places as Barb chatted about the food, but he was already thinking about Fourth Dimension, and would be checking in with the deputy director when he got to work tomorrow.

Tara had prayed more in the last twenty-four hours than she had in her entire life. It was the morning of the second day of Jordan's disappearance and her phone was still silent. No returning phone call from Jud. No check-in from Jordan.

She hadn't heard back from Dodge, either, and was debating with herself about calling the agency. It was just after 8:00 a.m., and she was pouring herself a cup of coffee when her phone rang. When she saw caller ID, her heart skipped a beat. Finally!

"Hello, this Tara."

"Tara, this is Wyrick from Dodge Security and Investigations, calling on behalf of Mr. Dodge. He has agreed to take your case. We have a ten o'clock opening this morning. You said in your email that you could come at a moment's notice. Is this too soon?"

Tara was shaking. "No, no, it's not. Oh my God, thank you. I'll be there."

"I'll text you the address of our new offices. Bring pictures of your ex-husband and a recent one of your daughter. Also, please bring the phone you said she left behind. Does she have a laptop?" Wyrick asked.

"Yes, she does. Do you want me to bring it, too?" Tara asked.

"Yes, please. We'll see you soon."

Tara was overwhelmed with relief. Someone was finally going to help her. She left her coffee on the counter and ran upstairs to get dressed, then began gathering up everything she'd been asked to bring.

After checking her phone to make sure she had the directions, she loaded everything up in her car, entered the address into OnStar and drove away. It felt good to have forward momentum now, but she was so scared for her daughter's welfare that every moment she spent in traffic felt like a delay in getting her daughter home. She knew Charlie Dodge by reputation only, although she'd been in court when he'd testified at hearings before, and right now he was her only hope.

A short while later, she arrived at the office building, parking with ten minutes to spare. She gathered up her things and ran into the building, then rode the elevator up to the sixth floor. It was five minutes to ten when she entered the offices of Dodge Security and Investigations.

When the woman sitting behind the desk looked up at her and then stood, Tara knew this must be Wyrick, the formidable assistant.

"Mrs. Bien?" Wyrick asked as she circled the desk.

"Yes. Please call me Tara."

Wyrick nodded. "Please have a seat. Mr. Dodge is on a phone call, but it shouldn't be much longer. May I get you a coffee?"

Tara thought about the coffee she'd left sitting on the counter.

"Yes, thank you, and black, please."

Wyrick stepped into the butler's pantry, got a coffee and a napkin, then set it on the small table beside Tara's chair. She paused, eyeing the woman's obvious exhaustion and pale skin, and felt instant empathy, but she said nothing as she went back to her desk.

A couple of minutes later, she glanced at the PBX on her desk. Charlie had ended his call, so she buzzed him.

"Yes?"

"Tara Bien is here," she said.

"Show her in," Charlie said.

Wyrick stood. "Mr. Dodge will see you now. Do you need a refill on your coffee?"

"No, but thank you," Tara said, following Wyrick through a short hall and then into the office.

Charlie was immediately on his feet, and when he gave Wyrick a look, she knew what he meant.

"I know. Hold all your calls," she said.

"Just put them on voice mail for a bit. I want you to sit in on this interview," Charlie said.

Wyrick nodded and came back a few moments later with an ink pen, a notepad and a recorder.

Charlie seated Tara before he sat back down.

Wyrick was at a table at the end of his desk.

"Now, Mrs. Bien, I understand your daughter left with your ex-husband under mysterious circumstances, and you haven't seen or heard from them since."

"Please call me Tara, and yes, she's been gone for two days now, and with no word from either of them."

"Did you call the police?" Charlie asked.

She shook her head. "No. I'm a lawyer. I already know their answer. After our divorce, Jud and I shared joint custody and that was never changed, so they won't consider her as having been abducted."

"Then what makes this visit so different from any other one?" Charlie asked.

"Because there haven't been any visits since Jud disappeared over two years ago. We haven't seen or heard from him, then he just appears at a time when he knew I would be in court and on a day when Jordan stayed home sick from school. I wouldn't have even known he was the one responsible for her absence, except Jordan sent me a text right before she left."

"Maybe your daughter has been in touch with him and you just didn't know it," Charlie suggested.

"No. She was devastated when he disappeared. They were very close, and for him to just dump her like that broke her heart," Tara said. "Oh, when I got home and then found her phone had been left behind, it worried me. Then I discovered my security system had been disabled, so I started it back up again, only to find out it had stopped at the point Della, my housekeeper, left the house and nothing had recorded after that. Jud set up that system, so he knew what to do to erase any signs of his presence. If it hadn't been for Jordan sending me that text, I would think this was a stranger abduction."

Charlie was beginning to get a sense of how detailed this man had been in his abduction. So far, he hadn't missed a thing.

"How old is Jordan?" Charlie asked.

"She just recently turned twelve, but she's tall for her age."

Charlie nodded. "If she hadn't been in contact with him, then how did he know she'd be home and not in school?"

Tara glanced at him, hesitant to use this as an excuse, but she knew in Jud's case, he was the real deal.

"Jud is psychic. He always knew stuff. I guessed that's how he knew she was alone."

At that point, Wyrick looked up at Tara but said nothing.

"You said in your email to us that you found her phone in her room. May we see it?" Charlie asked.

Tara handed over everything, including the photos, the phone and the charger, and Jordan's laptop.

"May we keep them for now?" Charlie asked.

Tara nodded.

Charlie handed them to Wyrick, who took them without comment.

"What else can you tell us?" Charlie asked.

Tara went into detail about calling Jud's old friends, and then shared what Gordy Butler had told her.

That was when Wyrick interrupted the interview, and the moment she did, Charlie realized she was onto something.

"Excuse me," Wyrick said. "But did you say the invitation Jud received two years ago had to do with Fourth Dimension?"

Tara nodded.

"So Gordy Butler didn't remember the name of the man holding the conference, but did he say where it was held?" Wyrick asked.

"Yes, at a large private estate somewhere in the hills around Eureka Springs, Arkansas."

When Wyrick got up and walked out of the office without a comment, Tara was startled.

"No worries," Charlie said. "She's already doing what she does best, which is research."

"Thank God," Tara said and then started crying. "I'm just so scared. Jud was never a bad person. This is so unlike him, I keep thinking of cults, and how they can get people to do outrageous things. I'm afraid for Jordan."

Charlie pushed a box of tissues toward her.

"Thank you," Tara said, wiping her eyes. "I never asked because it doesn't matter, but I'll pay whatever you charge. What's your retainer?"

"Wyrick will give you the rates and a receipt. We'll stay in touch with you by phone or text. When you get one from us, return them as soon as possible because we may be needing the answer to an important question in a timely fashion."

"Yes, of course," Tara said.

"Is there anything else you can tell us?"

"Not that I can think of," Tara said. "Oh, wait. About Jud being psychic. It may mean nothing, but Jordan inherited the gift. She doesn't really know how to use it, and to my knowledge doesn't practice it in any way…but she is her father's daughter."

"How do you mean?" Charlie asked. "Does she see the future, or know things about people? How does it manifest with her?"

"The things I know for sure are that she knows when someone is going to die, because she says their faces melt down to a skull. And the person does die within a month of her seeing that. She also has a photographic memory and has dreams of cataclysmic events before they happen."

"Anything else?" Charlie asked.

Tara shrugged. "Not that she's shared with me, but there's no telling. Her powers may have changed as she's aged."

"Okay, Tara. We have some good information to begin

with. Go home. Eat some food. Try to get some sleep. You are no longer in this alone, understand?" Charlie said.

Tara wiped her eyes again. "Understood, and please, find my baby. She's all the family I have in this world."

"I don't ever quit on a job I take," Charlie said.

Tara nodded. "I know. It's why I chose you."

Charlie walked her out into the front office.

"Tara is paying the retainer today," he said.

Wyrick stopped what she was doing and got out a receipt book as Charlie went back into his office.

He waited until he heard Tara Bien leave before he went back to talk to Wyrick.

"Is Fourth Dimension a cult?"

Wyrick shrugged. "Some people think so."

"What do you know about it?" Charlie asked.

"No one knows where it's located, so there's that. But the buzz about the place is that the only people who belong are psychics. No one knows what they're doing, or if they're doing anything illegal. But when they join, they do leave behind every facet of the lives they lived before, including family."

"Tara said Jordan is also psychic," Charlie said.

Wyrick frowned. "That might explain why her father came to get her."

"How so?" Charlie asked.

"If he's become deeply indoctrinated into the group, he might believe it would be best for his daughter to be with people like them. Adults who are psychic aren't fooled by other people's motives, but children who are psychic can be brainwashed to a level of loyalty that is often dangerous."

"Then we need to find her fast," Charlie said. "If you can find the names of any people who quit the group, reach out to them and see if they will talk to me. We might get some details as to what Fourth Dimension is about and where it's located."

Wyrick turned back to the computer and Charlie grabbed a sweet roll from the coffee bar on his way back to his office.

In another part of the city, Special Agent Hank Raines arrived for work. As soon as he reached his desk, he made a call to his boss's cell phone, rather than his office phone.

Deputy Director David Arnett glanced at caller ID and then answered.

"This is Arnett."

"Sir, do we have any interests in a group of psychics going by the name Fourth Dimension?"

"We do," Arnett said. "Why do you ask?"

"It's a bit of a story," Hank said.

"Then come to my office and fill me in," Arnett said.

After Tara Bien left the office, Wyrick spent the next couple of hours online, digging through information about psychic workshops, trying to find out who had held the one two years ago near Eureka Springs, Arkansas.

It was noon when Charlie came out of his office.

"I'm going to check on Annie. If anything breaks, just text me," he said.

Wyrick nodded but didn't look up.

Charlie frowned. "Don't forget to eat," he muttered and left, letting the door bang just a bit behind him.

Wyrick sighed, paused long enough to put in an order at a sandwich shop for delivery and then kept working. The delivery guy with her food showed up about forty-five minutes later.

"Delivery for Wyrick," he said and then took an unintentional step back when Wyrick spun around in her chair and glared. "Uh…"

"Well…set it down," she said, eyeing the box he set on

the edge of her desk, and yet he just kept staring. "Staring is rude. Take your ass out of my office."

In four long strides he was out of the office, moving so fast he didn't bother shutting the door behind him.

"Idiot," Wyrick muttered and got up to shut the door before going into her washroom to clean up.

She came out a few minutes later, got a cold bottle of Pepsi from the mini fridge below the coffee bar and took it to her desk. She ate as she worked, running a search for organizations called Fourth Dimension. By early afternoon, she knew a man named Aaron Walters had held the psychic workshop in Arkansas.

She also found a connection between Walters and Fourth Dimension, and two more names connected to it. Peter Wendell Long, who had been a member of the cult, was now residing in a federal correctional institution in Phoenix, Arizona.

The other name belonged to Farrah Leigh Walters, Aaron Walters's ex-wife.

Peter Long was in prison for kidnapping his eleven-year-old niece, Justine. But unlike Jud Bien, who got away with Jordan, the police had caught up with Peter Long at the border between Arizona and New Mexico. His niece had been returned unharmed to her mother, and Long was in prison, serving time for kidnapping.

And now that Wyrick had two solids, she picked up the phone and sent Charlie a text.

I have names.

Charlie was in the solarium with Annie, playing music for her from the playlist on his phone. He'd taken her a stuffed animal—a long-haired white cat with shiny black eyes and a fluffy tail. She was holding it in her lap, her eyes closed, as the music swirled around them.

When Charlie got the text from Wyrick, he quickly read it, then replied.

On my way.

Duty called.

He ended the music, then leaned over and kissed Annie on the forehead, careful not to get close to the staples.

"I have to go now, baby. I love you and I'll see you soon."

Although she didn't respond, she hadn't let go of the stuffed toy, either, which was an anomaly. But with Alzheimer's, there were no constants.

He left the room, pausing once in the doorway to look back. One of the workers was already checking on her, but she hadn't moved. When he got to the lobby to sign out, Pinky, the receptionist, was at the desk.

"I'm sorry about Annie's fall," she said.

"Yeah," he said and signed out.

He and Pinky had gotten off on the wrong foot early on at Morning Light, and now they sort of danced around cordiality without conversation. He left in a rush, on his way back to the office.

CHAPTER FIVE

Wyrick was waiting for him when he walked in with a look of satisfaction on her face. The same intent expression she wore when she had new information.

"What do you have?" Charlie asked.

"Aaron Walters is the name of the man who hosted the psychic workshop, but no info beyond that on him. I have the name and contact information for his ex-wife, Farrah Walters. And the name and location of a Fourth Dimension member who got caught trying to get away with his niece, and is serving time in a federal prison in Phoenix."

"Good work," Charlie said. "Where does Walters's ex-wife live?"

"Boca Raton, Florida, now, but both she and Aaron grew up in Louisville, Kentucky."

Charlie frowned. "We have a number for her?"

Wyrick nodded and handed him a paper with all the info she'd gathered. He looked down at it.

"I'm going to call her now. In the meantime, get me a number to the warden at the prison where Peter Long is being held. Hopefully, he'll let us interview him."

"The number is already on your paper, along with the warden's name, Thomas Wilhite."

Charlie glanced at it, again. "Oh, right. So I want you to sit in on the phone call to the ex-wife."

Wyrick grabbed her iPad, along with a pen and a notepad, and followed him into his office.

Charlie plopped down behind his desk, laid the paper in front of him and reached for the phone. A few seconds later, the call he'd just made to Farrah Walters was ringing...and then it went to voice mail. Charlie left a message.

"Mrs. Walters, this is Charlie Dodge. I'm a private investigator from Dallas, Texas. I am calling on behalf of a client, hoping you can help me. My client's twelve-year-old daughter was taken by her father against her will, and we have reason to believe they are on their way to an organization called Fourth Dimension, which is run by your ex-husband, Aaron Walters. She's been missing for two days now and her mother is frantic. Please call me back as soon as possible."

Then he hung up. "Now we wait," Charlie said. "Either she's so pissed at him she'll ignore the call, or she'll be kind enough to cooperate. Is there anything sweet in here to eat besides the sweet rolls from this morning?"

"Bottom draw of your desk, left side," Wyrick said.

Charlie opened it, his eyes widening at the assortment of chips and candy bars.

"Wow! This may become a little too convenient," he said. "Want something?"

Wyrick eyed the sharp cut of his jaw and wide shoulders, and the way the sunlight coming through the windows highlighted the gray at his temples.

"Anything chocolate," she said and went to the wet bar at the end of the room to ice a couple of glasses.

"Coke, Pepsi or Mountain Dew?" she asked.

"Which one has the most caffeine?"

"Mountain Dew," she said.

"That one," he said as he chose a Payday candy bar for himself and pulled a Hershey's bar with almonds out for her.

They poured the pop over the ice in their respective glasses and then tore into the candy, eating and drinking in comfortable silence.

It wasn't until Charlie happened to glance up and saw Wyrick sucking chocolate off the end of her thumb that his gut knotted. He took another drink and looked away. Thankfully for the both of them, the phone finally rang.

"Want me to answer?" Wyrick asked.

He shook his head and picked up the receiver. "Dodge Security and Investigations. Charlie Dodge speaking."

"Mr. Dodge, this is Farrah Walters. I'm going to be upfront with you now and tell you I haven't seen or talked to Aaron in over five years, but if I can help you in any way, I will, and please call me Farrah."

"Call me Charlie, and I'm going to put this call on speaker phone so my assistant, Wyrick, can take notes as we speak."

"That's fine," Farrah said.

"Thank you for agreeing to do this," Charlie said. "I guess the first thing we need to know is how much do you know about Fourth Dimension?"

"I never heard of it until you mentioned it in your call. What is it?"

"Supposedly, some kind of psychic organization," Charlie said.

"Oh, good lord! Aaron claimed to be psychic, and I guess he had some kind of powers. He had clients in his office in our home all the time, doing readings for them and helping them find lost objects...that kind of thing."

"Did he do that for a living?"

"Yes, and made about fifty thousand a year in what he called donations."

"Did you know he began holding psychic workshops a few years back?" Charlie asked.

"No."

"Would you have any idea where he might have chosen to locate his Fourth Dimension group?"

"Not really. We're both from Kentucky, and he missed living there, but I'd grown up in a small town and I wanted to live in the big city."

Wyrick slid a piece of paper across the desk to Charlie. He glanced down.

Ask if they have children, and if so, where are they now?

Charlie gave her a thumbs-up.

"Farrah, did you two have any children while you were married?"

"No, I couldn't have children. He had two from a previous marriage, but one passed away when she was ten, and his son, who was always a kind of rolling stone, disappeared six years ago. He'd been living in Arizona at the time and is still listed as a missing person with the Phoenix Police Department as far as I'm aware. I'm really sorry I can't be of more help, but that's truly all I know."

"Thank you, Farrah. If you do think of anything else, please call."

"Yes, I will, and I wish you luck."

She disconnected. Charlie sighed in frustration and popped the last bite of his candy bar into his mouth.

"The number I gave you for the warden's office is his direct line," Wyrick said.

Charlie nodded, chewing and swallowing, and then made the next call.

The call rang four times before it was answered.

"This is Warden Wilhite."

"Mr. Wilhite, my name is Charlie Dodge. I'm a private investigator from Dallas, Texas, and—"

"The same Charlie Dodge who found missing billionaire Carter Dunleavy?"

"Yes, sir, and I'm working on another case that you might be able to help me with."

"And how might that be?" Wilhite asked.

"I understand you have an inmate named Peter Wendell Long in your facility. He was convicted for kidnapping his niece."

"Just a moment. Let me pull up his name," Wilhite said.

Charlie could hear keys clicking, and then a brief pause, and guessed the warden was reading the charges against Long.

"Yes, we have an inmate here by that name," Wilhite said.

"Would it be possible for my assistant and me to question him? We know Long kidnapped his niece and was taking her to a cult-like organization called Fourth Dimension when he was caught. That's the same scenario for my current case, except this time a man took his own daughter—and got away with her. He shared joint custody with his ex-wife, so the mother can't claim kidnapping, which is why I was called in. We don't know where Fourth Dimension is located, and are hoping Peter Long would help us."

"Yes, I will grant you an interview with Long, but there's no guarantee that he'll cooperate."

"Understood," Charlie said.

"When do you want to do this?" Wilhite asked.

"As soon as possible," Charlie said, then watched as Wyrick slid another note to him. *The chopper is ready and standing by.* Charlie gave her a thumbs-up.

"Would tomorrow morning be too soon? Say around 11:00 a.m.?" Charlie asked.

"That will work," Wilhite said. "Do you know how to get to the prison from the airport?"

"Just give me an address and I'll find it," Charlie said, and then gave the warden his email address.

"I'll email you all the particulars," the warden said.

"Will we be allowed to bring recording equipment into the interview?" Charlie asked.

"Yes, but they'll search it first. As soon as you arrive, I'll be notified. It would be an honor to meet you and shake your hand," Wilhite said.

"Thank you, sir," Charlie said, adding, "See you tomorrow" before he hung up.

"Be at the hangar at 7:30 a.m. It's less than a two-hour flight, but it's always good to leave time for delays," Wyrick said.

Charlie nodded and then glanced at the clock. It was less than an hour before quitting time.

"Switch the office calls to voice mail. I'll lock up. You've done a good job today."

Wyrick was surprised and she let it show before she thought, and then she tried to blow off the compliment.

"It's a kid in danger. That always changes the level of trouble," she said. "Don't forget to log off your PC. I'll empty the coffeepot before I go," she said and left his office.

Charlie eyed the computer on his desk and frowned.

"I would have remembered to do that," he muttered but did as he was told.

Wyrick dumped the coffee grounds, rinsed out the carafe and made sure all of the appliances were turned off, then logged out of her own computers, grabbed her things and left the office.

Charlie wasn't far behind.

Hank Raines's visit to the deputy director's office had raised new interest in a cult already on their radar. He was already initiating contact with the Kentucky division of the Bureau, who would be coordinating contact to take them to the location.

Telling his partner, Luis Chávez, they were leaving in two

days for Lexington, Kentucky, had been easier than he'd expected. Normally, Luis liked to stay close to his family in Dallas, but his mother-in-law had been visiting from Phoenix for over a week, and he was ready to get out of the house.

Jordan had already explored the old dormitory, looking for anything she could turn into a weapon. The power and water were still on, which must have made it acceptable quarters for them to put her there.

Windows opened from the inside, but there were bars on the outsides of every one. The back room was devoid of furniture, and water still dripped from rusty showerheads in the gym-style showers. The bedsprings on which the mattresses rested all squeaked, and there were obvious signs of rats having nested within the stuffing.

She found an old flashlight in one of the bed stands but the batteries were dead. Still, it felt good to have something solid in her hand. After poking around in the storage closets, she found a piece of two-by-four about five feet long, so she took it with her back into the main room. The place was cold and creepy and she wanted Mama and home like she'd never wanted anything before.

When the sun began going down, she turned on the lights in every room to remind them she was there, still needing the necessities. She was headed toward the bed where they'd tossed her bag, when she caught movement from the corner of her eye, then shrieked in panic.

A six-foot-long rattlesnake was slithering across the floor, and when she screamed, it coiled up and began to shake its rattles in warning. Her heart was pounding so fast it was hard to breathe, but she couldn't let it get away. She couldn't spend the night in here knowing there was a live rattlesnake anywhere on the premises. Holding the two-by-four like a baseball bat, she began inching her way closer.

The snake's tongue was flickering like the flame of a tiny candle as the rattles grew louder. It was coiling tighter now, readying to strike when Jordan swung the board down onto the coils with all of her strength.

The snake began writhing in a way that Jordan knew it was injured, so she swung again and again until it was broken and bleeding in multiple places, and the head was nearly severed from the body. She had been sobbing with every blow.

Once she finally realized it was dead, she shoved it all the way to the front door and left it as a greeting for the next people to walk in. She turned around to scan the room, making sure there wasn't a second snake anywhere in sight, but all she saw was the pool of blood and the blood streaks where she'd pushed it to the door.

She didn't want to be in here, and the thought of accidentally walking in that blood in the night gave her the creeps. She was looking around for something to wipe up the blood when she heard rustling in the shadows behind her. Fearing it was another snake, she spun around and caught a glimpse of three huge, fat rats scurrying away.

"Nooooo!" she screamed and began chasing after them, then swinging the board at the windows and the walls, shattering glass from one end of the dormitory to the other until there wasn't a solid piece of glass left in any window.

She could hear shouting outside, so she knew they'd heard her, but she wasn't through. There were rats at the door now, eating on the snake, and she ran toward them screaming in rage. She stomped one as it ran past, then finished it off with her two-by-four, before killing another one.

She was standing in the middle of the room with the two-by-four held across her body like a soldier holding his weapon, splattered in blood, her chest heaving and her hair as wild as the look in her eyes, when the door flew inward.

The first man to come through the doorway stumbled

when he saw the snake, and the one behind him ran into him and knocked him flat onto the bloody carcasses of two rats and one snake.

He began shrieking and screaming, trying to get up, and his screams brought even more men coming. They saw the snake, the dead rats and the girl standing in middle of the floor, waiting for her next victim, and they froze, suddenly realizing what they'd done by putting her here.

But it was Jud who pushed past them and walked toward her, horrified by what he'd allowed to happen, and holding out his hand.

"It's okay, baby. It's okay. You aren't going to stay here. I won't have it," he said softly.

Jordan shook her head once from side to side, as if trying to clear away the horror of what she'd endured, and then backed up, still holding the wood.

Her voice was flat, completely devoid of emotion, which made the scene that much more horrifying.

"Stay away from me. All of you."

A two-way radio suddenly crackled.

Jordan heard the man answer, then begin to explain what the noise had been about.

"Yes, Master. Right away, Master," the man said, then signed off and pointed. "Archangel Troy, get her bag. The Seraphim has ordered for her to be taken to the dormitory with the other girls."

Two of the men started toward Jordan, and when they did, she swung the board back over her shoulder like she was at bat waiting for the next pitch, and hunched slightly to center her stance.

"Don't come near me!" she screamed.

Jud wanted to weep. The blood splatters on her hands and arms were telling, but it was the streaks on her cheek and clothes that told the full story of how frantic she'd been.

"Don't!" Jud told the others. "I'll take her."

Jordan was cornered and she knew it. She didn't want another knockout injection in her neck, and when Jud started toward her, she dropped the board and held up her hands like she was being arrested.

"Damn it, Jordan! Don't do that," Jud said.

"Is that other dormitory a lockdown facility?"

He sighed.

"That's what I thought. Then I'm a prisoner, and you're all still perverts waiting for your old pimp to pick the next girl for you to fuck. I hate you. I hate all of you."

And with that, she walked out of the building with her hands still up in the air, stepping over the dead rats and the bloody snake as they escorted her to the other girls in angry silence.

The girls had also heard the glass breaking and all the screaming, and they'd watched through the windows as the Archangels went running. They knew why she'd been isolated, because they'd witnessed her fighting the men and defying orders. So when they saw her being marched toward them with her hands in the air, they stared at each other in disbelief.

"She's all bloody. What happened to her? Did they already beat her? Is she going to fight us, too?" one girl asked.

Miranda Powers, who called herself Randi, was secretly in awe of the new girl's defiance.

"Of course not," Randi said. "She's just scared, like we were when we first came."

The girls agreed with the explanation, but they were still huddled together with uncertainty when the men brought Jordan inside.

"Don't talk to her," they ordered.

The girls ducked their heads and looked away.

"You will sleep here," Jud said and left her bag on a bed that was already made up. "The girls will show you where everything is. They'll all go to dinner soon, so get cleaned up. You can't go looking like that."

"You're not my father anymore. You can't tell me what to do," Jordan said and turned her back on him.

Jud's heart was hurting, but he left with the other men without arguing with her.

Jordan turned around as soon as the men left. The girls were all staring at her. She guessed they were afraid of her because she'd fought back. But instead of talking to them, she just lay down on her bed, rolled over to face the wall and curled up into a ball.

"Aren't you going to clean up?" one girl asked.

Jordan closed her eyes, listening to their whispers and the occasional giggle. The door opened again later, and she heard them all marching out, then heard a lock turn.

Her belly was grumbling from want of food, but she'd rather go hungry than obey. However, now that she was alone, she got up and scoped out the building. The only entrance was the one she'd come through, and it was locked. These windows didn't have bars, but the heavy wire screens over the windows were permanent and served the same purpose.

One thing she noticed was the lack of mirrors. There was a bookshelf full of books about psychic phenomena and mediums, as well as books on astrology and child-rearing. Ridiculous reading for kids.

The ancient refrigerator in the corner had nothing in it but bottled water. There was a small sitting area with a sofa and a few easy chairs, and a long craft table with a dozen straight-backed chairs lined up around it. The projects were simplistic and in various stages of completion, along with a stack of men's clothing that they were obviously mending...or learning to mend. Things they would need as married women. The absurdity of it all equaled the horror of their situation.

She went back to her bed, unfolded the blanket at the foot, then wrapped it around her like a cocoon. Unwilling to undress or remove her shoes in case she got a chance to run, she lay down and curled up, facing the wall.

She knew when the girls came back, but they thought she was asleep. Oddly enough, now that she was no longer alone in the building, she felt safer and fell asleep listening to their chatter.

It was 4:00 a.m. when Charlie's phone began to ring. He woke abruptly, always afraid it would be Morning Light calling about Annie, and then saw it was Wyrick.

"What's wrong?"

"There's a huge thunderstorm heading this way. We either cancel the appointment or try to leave ahead of it. If you can be at the hangar in an hour, I can get us out of here. It's your call," Wyrick said.

"I'll see you at the hangar," Charlie said, rolling out of bed. This was going to be the day he went to work without a shower or a shave.

He dressed in record time, grabbed his things and raced out the door. The traffic shouldn't be bad at this time of the morning, although there was always traffic in Dallas. By the time he hit the loop, he had a little over forty minutes to get to the hangar on the outskirts of the city.

Wyrick was already dressed and heading for her Mercedes when she called Charlie. She knew what he'd choose and she wasn't going to call her flight mechanic at this time of the morning. She could get the chopper out of the hangar on her own, and she'd already called her flight mechanic to get it ready after Tara Bien's visit. If their timing didn't get messed up, they'd be in the air and on the way to Phoenix before the storm reached Dallas.

For once, she drove without checking headlights behind her. Focused on the urgency at hand, she darted in and out of lanes and accelerated in the open spots until she finally reached her exit. She took it without slowing down, and was checking for headlights coming and going at the cross street before she reached the stop sign. Since it was clear both ways, she blew through it and took a right. Ten minutes later she came over a hill, saw the security lights at the landing field and gunned the engine. She sped through the gate and headed toward her hangar, then came to a sliding stop. Within moments she was out of the Mercedes and running toward the doors. She keyed in the code on the security panel, then waited impatiently for them to open.

As soon as she was in, she began flipping on lights and then made a run for the aircraft caddie she'd pimped out to tow her chopper. Once she had it out of the hangar, she drove her Mercedes inside, grabbed her things out of the passenger seat, then locked her car and set the alarm.

She used a flashlight to do her exterior check of the chopper and was almost finished when she felt the wind change. She looked up just as the distant rumble of thunder sounded, and glanced toward the south. She saw a flash of lightning, and then it was dark again.

"Come on, Charlie Dodge. We don't have much time," she muttered and then finished what she was doing.

When she noticed her little ice chest behind the pilot seat, she guessed Benny had gone above and beyond when he'd fueled up the chopper for her yesterday. She jumped in and started it up, going through the preflight check and hoping Charlie would show up soon.

The rotors were spinning when she saw headlights come

over the hill. At that point, she breathed a sigh of relief. He'd made it.

She jumped out, waving him into the hangar to park, and when he got out running, she pointed toward the chopper.

"Get in and buckle up!" she shouted.

Charlie didn't miss a step and kept running while Wyrick keyed in the code to shut the hangar doors.

Charlie jumped into the seat and slid his door shut before he bothered to look up, then watched Wyrick sprinting toward the chopper. She was in blue jeans, a plain white T-shirt and a denim jacket. He'd never seen her without makeup, and his first thought was how beautiful she was. The moment that went through his mind, he froze. *Oh hell no, you don't go there, Charlie Dodge.* Then he looked away as Wyrick jumped in and buckled her seat belt. Within seconds she had her headset on and was revving up the rotors.

The storm was close now, because she could see trash blowing across the runway. She looked back just as a bolt of lightning shot across the sky. She glanced at Charlie once to make sure he was ready, then lifted off and made a half circle over the landing field before heading west, less then fifteen minutes ahead of the rapidly approaching storm front.

Charlie adjusted his headset and turned up the volume so he could hear her speaking.

"That was close," he said. "Thanks for this. It was a good save."

"Didn't you watch the weather last night?" she asked.

"I didn't think to, but you obviously did," Charlie said.

"Obviously," Wyrick replied.

Conversation was sparse after that.

Charlie dozed.

Wyrick chewed gum and wished for coffee. Without her usual outrageous clothing and makeup, she felt naked, so there was that to add to the stress of being this close to Charlie without her armor.

About an hour into the flight Wyrick remembered the ice chest, then swallowed her gum and poked Charlie's arm to wake him.

He woke abruptly, making sure that land was still before them rather than coming up at them.

"What?"

"I need caffeine," she said. "There's an ice chest behind my seat, likely with pop and candy. Hand me a Snickers candy bar and a Pepsi."

"And...what do you say?" Charlie drawled.

Wyrick's eyes narrowed warningly. "Please, dammit, hand me a pop and a bar of candy."

Charlie laughed out loud and reached behind her seat, rummaged around inside the contents that were kept cold with ice, and pulled out two cans of pop. He opened the top on hers and handed it to her, then put his can between his legs as he reached for the candy.

Wyrick took a quick sip of the Pepsi, relishing the carbonation tingle as it went down the back of her throat, then took a few more sips until she felt the caffeine beginning to kick in.

After that she tore the wrapper off her Snickers with her teeth and ate while trying to ignore Charlie's presence.

The caffeine and sugar were enough of a pick-me-up to last until they landed in Phoenix.

CHAPTER SIX

The sun had already risen behind them when Wyrick began talking to the tower at Phoenix Sky Harbor International, requesting landing instructions. It was barely 7:00 a.m., which meant they were going to have some serious time to kill before their 11:00 a.m. appointment.

A short time later they were directed to a smaller runway and came down on a landing site near a hangar. They emerged from the chopper, and then Wyrick reached back inside, got a bag from the back and slipped the strap over her shoulder.

Charlie promptly transferred the bag from her shoulder to his, then narrowed his eyes, daring her to argue.

She shrugged.

"You're welcome," he said and followed her all the way to the car rental.

After standing in line for a bit, they picked up the key and then the SUV—a white late-model Jeep Sahara.

"Nice," Charlie said, and Wyrick tossed him the key.

As soon as she was seated, he handed her the bag and then got in and started it up.

"Breakfast calls. Your choice of places," he said.

"IHOP," Wyrick said. She googled the nearest location and off they went.

She navigated, Charlie drove, and despite a long breakfast line, they were seated and waiting to order within an hour of their landing. She knew she would be less of a curiosity without her flashy clothes and makeup, and she was right. People saw her and thought "cancer victim." And she knew the less flashy she looked, the less trouble her appearance would draw in the prison, too.

On one level it bothered her to be labeled that way, because she was no one's victim, but this wasn't the day to challenge society's opinion of judging people by how they looked, and Charlie was doing enough frowning at people's stares for both of them. It was yet another reason he rocked her world, but the last damn thing she'd ever let him know.

The waitress came, poured coffee and took their orders. Charlie knew before Wyrick opened her mouth that she would order Belgian waffles with whipped cream and fruit, and she did. And then the moment he thought it, he was startled he knew that. It had to be from the time they'd spent together on the Dunleavy case. The longer he knew her, the more secrets of Jade Wyrick were revealed, including her penchant for Belgian waffles. Her taste for waffles was a safe thing to know. His growing interest in the rest of her wasn't. She was his trusted employee. He wasn't sure if the word *friend* would apply, but that was as far as interest could go. It bothered him that was even in his thoughts, and he added sugar to his coffee without thinking.

Wyrick saw it and looked up.

"Since when did you start putting sugar in your coffee?" she asked.

Startled he'd done that, he put down the spoon he'd been stirring with, and frowned.

"Since today. I'm getting off it any day now," he said and drank it like medicine.

"Wake up, girl," someone said softly and shook Jordan's shoulder.

Jordan sat up with a jerk, then saw one of the other girls standing beside her bed, holding a towel and washcloth.

"You have to bathe before you can eat," she said and handed them to her. "The showers are down the hall and to the left. Soap and shampoo are on the shelves. Don't waste."

Jordan swung her legs off the bed, then stood, eyeing the girl.

"What's your name?" she asked.

"Miranda Powers, but everyone calls me Randi. You're Jordan Bien, right?"

Jordan frowned. "How do you know that?"

"We all witnessed Archangel Jud dedicate you to Fourth Dimension before he left to bring you in."

Jordan was taken aback by her complacency and wondered if they had been instructed to spy on her.

"Where's my bag?" she asked.

"In that closet," Randi said, but she kept shifting from one foot to the other, unwilling to leave. Finally, curiosity got the best of her. "How did you get that blood on you?"

"Killing snakes and rats," Jordan said.

Randi gasped and then gave the room in which they were standing an anxious scan, just to make sure nothing like that crawled out of a corner here.

Jordan got her bag and went back toward the showers. There were a dozen showerheads spaced out along the length of one wall, where four young girls stood with heads down, soaping and washing themselves. Some of them were so young they didn't even have any body hair, while others were further along in maturity.

Jordan set her things on an open bench and stripped where she stood, then strode to the nearest shower and turned on the water. From the corner of her eye, she saw the other girls glance at her, then duck their heads and keep washing.

She stepped beneath the spray and got her hair wet before reaching for a bottle of shampoo. She squirted a little into the palm of her hand, then slapped it on top of her head and started scrubbing until her scalp was tingling. Then she rinsed out the suds and reached for a bar of soap.

A few minutes later, she turned off the water and dried off. When she saw where the other girls had hung their wet towels, she put hers there, too, then dressed in the only other change of casual clothes she had with her. She also had one dressy outfit she'd packed thinking Jud was going to take her some place special, but this definitely wasn't that.

Once she was dressed, she combed out the tangles in her wet hair and carried her things back to the closet and put them inside. All of the girls were standing in line again, waiting.

"Does this happen for every meal?" Jordan asked.

Randi nodded and tucked a loose red curl behind her ear.

"Does nobody here give a shit that this is happening?" Jordan asked, but no one answered. So she doubled up her fists and raised her voice. "Well, just so you know, I will fight this with every breath in my body. I will never willingly go to bed with some old man. That's child molestation. That's rape. I don't care what they call it. It's against the law."

One girl with long blond hair and the bluest eyes Jordan had ever seen turned around and stared.

"They'll beat you for arguing," she said softly.

"What's your name?" Jordan asked.

"Barbie," she said softly.

"Here's the deal, Barbie. I can't control what they do, but I am in control of my reactions, and I will fight back," Jordan said.

"It won't work. You'll see," another girl said.

There was a sudden rattle at the door. Jordan watched the girls go quiet as they bowed their heads and looked down at the floor.

"Don't look into their faces," Randi whispered.

And just like that, Jordan lifted her head.

Charlie swiped his last bite of pancake through the syrup left in his plate and popped it in his mouth, then chased it with the last bite of bacon, while Wyrick finished her coffee.

"Umm, good stuff," Charlie said, then glanced at the time. "We have a little over an hour and a half before the appointment."

"I sent the warden a text and told him we were in town early because of the weather. He told us to come whenever."

"Oh, good call," Charlie said, then picked up their ticket. "I'm going to make a pit stop here before we get to the prison."

Wyrick nodded, and when Charlie went into the men's room, she went into the women's.

There was a woman at the washstand, and another coming out of a stall. They both glanced at her, then went about their business. Wyrick already knew she invited derision with her normal public persona, but she didn't give a damn. She didn't do it for shock value. She did it in defiance of what she'd endured, and it was on other people as to how they received her.

When she went back out to join Charlie, her chin was up, her stride long and certain. They walked out together, and as they were driving away, Wyrick was already navigating to the new address.

CHAPTER SEVEN

Wyrick pulled a notepad out of her bag as Charlie maneuvered through Phoenix traffic.

"Since this Peter Wendell Long we're going to interview was a member of Fourth Dimension, have you taken his psychic abilities into consideration for when you question him?" she asked.

Charlie frowned. "No, I have not, probably because I'm a skeptic of the whole process."

"That's what I figured," Wyrick said. "If he's going to be hostile in helping us, and is truly psychic on some level, I want you to ask him these questions. He doesn't have to answer them, but he needs to hear them."

"What the hell good will that do?" Charlie asked.

"For one thing, it will keep me happy," Wyrick snapped, then tore the page from her notepad, folded it up and stuck it in Charlie's shirt pocket.

"Fine," Charlie muttered.

He'd either find out later, or he wouldn't, but he wasn't going down that road with her. A few minutes later they arrived at the prison. Charlie pulled into a parking place in front of the main building and killed the engine.

"Homey little place, isn't it?" Wyrick said, eyeing the high fencing and the coils and coils of razor wire strung across the top of it. The arid desert landscape had its own cachet, but she wasn't a fan of so much brown. In the distance, a dust devil stirred up by the wind was skipping along the surface of the ground, and when they got out, the air smelled of sage and tasted of dust.

"Prepare to be searched," Charlie said as they stepped onto the sidewalk and headed for the entrance.

Wyrick already knew that would happen, and she also knew that her normal spandex attire would not have been allowed, which was why she was in jeans, a T-shirt and a lightweight jacket for protection against the sun.

Except for the comment Charlie made about the layer of dust on everything, they walked in silence until they were inside. They signed in, naming who they had come to visit, and then they were searched before being escorted into the visitation room. It was a large communal area, with family visitations being held in little groups about the room. Armed guards stood watch, ready to intervene at the first hint of problems or noise.

The officer who was escorting them paused in the doorway.

"Could we sit at that table?" Charlie asked, pointing to an empty table with a good amount of distance to the next group of visitors.

"Sit wherever. They'll bring the prisoner to you. You know the rules. Please observe them," he said and walked away.

Charlie glanced at Wyrick, but she was pale and mute. He lowered his voice.

"Are you okay?"

She glared at him and then looked away. But when he was otherwise occupied, she wiped her sweaty hands on the legs of her jeans and took a deep breath. She'd always been a little sensitive about the energy of places, but this had to be the worst place she'd ever experienced. It felt dark and evil, and she kept glancing at the walls, making sure they weren't closing in on them, because that was what it felt like. It didn't feel like a place that would ever turn loose what had been captured and imprisoned here, but she settled down and blanked her thoughts.

They'd been waiting a little over fifteen minutes when the prisoner they were waiting for finally entered the common room, accompanied by a guard.

"That's him. That's Peter Wendell Long," Wyrick said. "Don't forget the list of questions in your pocket."

Charlie sighed.

"Please," Wyrick added.

And that was when he realized there was more to her request than just trying to control things.

"Yes, I will. Stop worrying," he said and then shifted focus as Long approached.

Long was staring at them in confusion, and when the guard sat him down in the chair across the table from them, he leaned forward, staring at them intently.

Wyrick already knew he was trying to get a read on them, and that he had picked up on Charlie being some kind of cop.

"Are you Peter Wendell Long?" Charlie asked.

"You know I am or you wouldn't be here," Pete said. "So who the hell are you?"

"My name is Charlie Dodge, and this is Wyrick, my assistant. I'm a private investigator out of Dallas, Texas, working on a missing child case, and I believe you might have some information that could help us."

Pete Long eyed Wyrick's bald head out of curiosity, but when the comment Dodge made finally sank in, he was immediately on guard.

"I am not some serial kidnapper, and you're wasting your time," he snapped.

"You kidnapped your niece," Charlie said and knew he'd hit an old nerve when Long's face reddened.

"It wasn't like everyone thought, but I'm here, so justice is being served. I'm not talking about what happened again. I'm not explaining it, and I'm not talking to you," he said.

Charlie pulled the list from his pocket and unfolded it.

"The girl we're looking for is with her father. We already know that, so no one is accusing you of that crime, okay?"

The tension in Pete Long's shoulders eased. "Then what the hell are you doing here?"

Charlie glanced down at the list, then back up at Long. "We think her father is a member of Fourth Dimension. We think he took his daughter for the same reason you took your niece."

Now that the pressure was off, Pete leaned back in the folding chair, remembering the plans and dreams he'd had there, which had never come to fruition.

"What does that have to do with me?" he asked.

"We don't know where Fourth Dimension is located. We don't even know what state it's in. We were hoping you could help."

Pete was silent a few moments and then shook his head. "I don't out my brothers."

"Can you at least tell us what the place looks like? Is it in a city, or a rural area? Is it flat land? Mountains? What's the name of the closest town?" Charlie asked and watched Pete Long's eyes narrow as he stared at them in continued silence.

Wyrick could feel the power it gave Long to refuse their requests, but she was careful to stay off his radar.

Charlie sighed. There was one last question on the list.

"Look, man…this is a kid…she's got to be scared to death. She's missing home. She's missing her mother. At least tell us why she was taken? Why did you take your niece? What's the purpose of taking little girls? If it's human trafficking, then why take someone near and dear to you? Why not a stranger?"

The question hit a nerve. Pete's hands curled into fists.

"You go to hell. It has nothing to do with human trafficking. It's not a bad place. It's a pure place, and I'm done here." He stood up, and the moment he did, his guard was at the table. "Take me back to my cell," he said.

The guard looked at Charlie.

"We're through," Charlie said.

The guard handcuffed Long and walked him out.

"That was a bust," Charlie muttered, then he and Wyrick got up and walked out.

Wyrick got just as many stares going out as she had coming in, but she didn't care what they thought. Coming here was the break they needed. They stopped to sign out and then left the building.

Walking out into the dry, dusty land was, for Wyrick, like walking out of a dungeon. But what she knew now about Fourth Dimension made her skin crawl. They got into the rental car and then sat for a few moments, waiting for the car to cool off while Charlie checked his phone for messages.

Out of the blue, Wyrick started talking.

"Fourth Dimension is a cult of men who claim to have psychic powers," she said.

"But we sort of guessed that after our meeting with Tara Bien, right?" Charlie said.

"But we didn't know why Jud Bien kidnapped her," Wyrick said.

"Tara Bien guessed it was because Jordan was also gifted like that in some ways," Charlie said. "What we needed to know was where to find them."

"The cult is in a heavily wooded area in the mountains of Kentucky. The closest town is a place called Shawnee Gap. And the reason they're taking young girls there is to donate them to a slush pile from which their wives will be chosen. Once a member makes his donation, he's then free to choose his wife from any of the others."

Charlie gasped. "What the fuck are you saying?"

"If the little girls are all blood kin to the members, then there's the supposition that the DNA that made the member psychic could be carried through into the girls in their families. They're using them as breeders to grow their own cult of psychics. Jud Bien's payment to choose his own mate was to donate someone. He donated his daughter."

Charlie's face went pale. "Just when I think I've heard or witnessed every depravity man can do to another, something like this happens, and I am horrified anew." He wiped a hand over his face, then looked at her in disbelief. "How the hell do you know that?"

Wyrick shrugged. "I saw his thoughts like a movie."

"Have you always been able to do this?" Charlie asked.

"I don't know. But when I thought about it, I knew it would work. However, it's all beside the point."

"So when we find Jordan, we have to rescue all of the girls there, not just her," Charlie said.

Wyrick nodded.

Charlie glanced at his watch. "We need to get back to Dallas and pack for the trip. Has the storm moved out yet?"

"I'll check," Wyrick said, pulling her laptop from the bag at her feet as Charlie backed up and drove away.

He could hear the click of the keys as she typed, and knew Wyrick would have an answer soon.

"So are we going home today or not?" Charlie asked.

"We're going home. The storm is already moving into the far northeast part of the state."

"Good. Now look up Shawnee Gap. Are we flying or driving?"

Jordan had eaten the breakfast of oatmeal and toast that they served to everyone. The girls were silent, so she stayed silent, too. She saw her father sitting at a long table with other men and knew he was trying to catch her eye, but she ignored him. There was another table where couples sat. She supposed those were the "married" ones. What horrified her most were four young girls with fat little babies in their laps. They didn't look much older than the girls who were still in the dormitory. But they'd obviously been married close to two years, because it took nine months to grow a baby, and the two babies looked to be anywhere from nine months to a year old. She knew it hurt to have a baby. And she knew it hurt to have sex. At least at first. That was what her friends said. Her mother had told her all about getting her period and about reproduction, but unless a miracle happened, her first sexual experience would be rape.

When the meal ended, the man in the white robes entered the common area.

"It's the Seraphim," Randi whispered.

Jordan frowned. She didn't know what that title meant, but she wasn't going to ask. She knew he was in charge, and that was enough. Then, to her horror, he waved to two of the men and pointed at her. When the men started toward her, Jordan stood up.

"You're not supposed to do that," Randi hissed.

"They're the ones breaking the law. Not me," Jordan said.

The men obviously weren't willing to lay hands on her again, but when they reached the table where she was standing, one of them spoke.

"The Seraphim wishes to speak with you. Come with us."

Jordan circled the table and then walked with the men to the front of the room, and when the men stopped behind her, she turned and glared.

"Don't stand behind me," she said.

The Seraphim waved his hand, and the two men moved away as he turned his full attention to Jordan.

Jordan had all of her defenses up, including her psychic ones, and stared back at the man without flinching.

Finally, the Seraphim spoke.

"You broke all of the windows," he said in a loud, booming voice.

"You put me in a building with poisonous snakes and rats," Jordan said, and the loud, accusing voice with which she answered him rang out all the way to the back of the room.

"Woman! Do not shout at me," he roared.

"There are no women here!" Jordan cried. "There are only children…and old men. You are the abomination my preacher spoke of in church. I do not honor you. I do not obey you."

The Seraphim was pissed. He glared at Jud Bien from across the room, and when Jud started to get up, the man waved him away.

"You will be put to work mending clothes today," he said. "Your food will be brought to you. You will not join us again until you have learned your manners."

When Jordan rolled her eyes and then laughed, the shock of her insubordination was evident on his face.

"Now I'm a child who must learn manners, when moments ago you called me a woman? Make up your mind, old man."

In that moment, Aaron Walters didn't feel like the Seraphim. If he hadn't been in front of all his people, he would have put his hands around her neck and squeezed until it snapped.

"Get her back to the dormitory. She will not be allowed into this common room again until she has learned to respect her elders."

Jordan saw the rage in his eyes, but she stood her ground. At that point, all of the girls stood.

"You! Get in line with the others," one man told her, and after she did, they were marched back to their residence.

As soon as they were inside, the man stepped out of the

group and approached Jordan until he was so close she could
smell the coffee he'd had for breakfast on his breath.

"I am Archangel Thomas. I am in charge of the Sprite
residence. You heard the Seraphim. The girls will show you
where the mending is. They will show you what to do. Your
food will be brought to you at noon, and then your supper
will be brought to you in the evening. Your progress with
the mending will be judged at that time. It is in your best interests to obey," he said.

Jordan eyed the tall, skinny man with as much hate as she
had the snake just before she'd killed it.

"Get away from me," she said softly.

Archangel Thomas blinked. He started to chastise her, then
realized the gaze of every girl in the room was on him, so he
turned to them instead.

"You heard me. Show her what needs to be done, then
shun her. She has brought discord into this place of peace."

"You perverts are the ones who brought me here," Jordan
said, then turned her back on him and walked away.

The men left, shutting the door and locking it behind them
as they left.

CHAPTER EIGHT

The girls stood in silence, each looking for someone else to volunteer to show the new girl anything. They were partly in awe of her and partly afraid of her. She'd upset the status quo of a situation they'd felt hopeless to fight, but now that the seeds of discord had been sown, it remained to be seen if any of them would take root.

Randi stepped forward. "I'll show her," she said and hurried to catch up.

Jordan was standing in front of two large baskets full of clean clothing and one straight-backed folding chair.

"Is this it?" Jordan asked.

"Yes," Randi said. "Thread, needles, extra buttons and some small embroidery scissors are in the top drawer of that little dresser. We don't get regular-size scissors," she added.

"Probably afraid someone would stab them," Jordan muttered and opened the drawer. She saw the needles stuck in a small pincushion and the rest of the sewing notions in a jumble around it.

Randi continued her instructions. "You have to inspect each item of clothing carefully to find out what's wrong with it, so look for torn seams or hems or missing buttons. If you don't have any thread that matches, use the next best color."

Jordan nodded, then carried the chair to the nearest window for better light, dragged the baskets over beside it, piled all of the mending into one basket and set the empty basket aside for the items that had already been repaired. She then pulled the drawer out of the dresser with all the sewing notions and carried it over to her makeshift workstation.

Randi panicked. "What are you doing? We're not supposed to—"

"I moved where I can see better," Jordan said. She threaded a needle with white thread, poked it back into the pincushion and picked up a shirt.

"How do you know to do all this?" Randi asked.

"My mother is a lawyer. She lives a very busy life. She taught me lots of ways to help myself when she wasn't around to do it for me," Jordan said. She began checking the shirt and found it was missing a button.

She dug around for a replacement button and quickly sewed it in place. As soon as the other girls quit watching what she was doing, she proceeded to sew every buttonhole shut, as well, and then tossed it into the empty basket and kept working.

She didn't know what the repercussions were going to be for what she was doing, but at this point she didn't care.

When she came to a long white robe with an entire hem that had come undone, she guessed it belonged to the fat man and used bright red thread to fix it. And so the morning went, with Jordan quietly and persistently sabotaging every item in the basket.

When noon came, Archangel Thomas arrived with two others, one of whom set a tray of food on the table for her.

"I don't trust you not to poison me or drug me, so I'm telling you now I won't eat this. You may as well take it back," Jordan said.

Archangel Thomas was startled, and it showed. "We would never harm a Sprite," he said. "It's not our way."

"You're all child molesters. My own father stabbed me in the neck with a needle and drugged me to get here. Your *ways* are an abomination," Jordan said.

Thomas was taken aback as much by the emotionless tone in her voice as he was by her accusations.

"Our purpose is for good," he said, lowering his voice to one of gentle persuasion. "The members of Fourth Dimension are all gifted. Our intention is to build a community of people all born with different levels of powers and gifts. We aren't killers. We don't traffic in humans."

"Did you ask any of these girls if this is what they wanted to be when they grew up?" she asked, pointing at the girls.

Their silence bothered Thomas. "Take the Sprites to eat their meal," he ordered, and they were escorted out by the two other men.

Jordan expected him to leave with them, but he didn't, and when she found herself alone with him, she backed away and doubled up her fists.

"What are you doing? You have no need to fear," Thomas said.

"The better question is…why are you still here and what are you going to do to me?"

Thomas's face flushed. "I am not going to hurt you. I just want to help you understand."

"Oh, I understand plenty," Jordan cried. "You are all liars. You are all crazy. You're kidnappers. You are rapists. My mother is a lawyer, and she will never stop looking for me. If you kill me and burn my body to ashes, she will come for you, instead. And she won't stop until every one of you is sit-

ting on death row. And that's what *you* need to understand.
Get away from me. Get out. Get out! GET OUT!"

Thomas was still trying to come to terms with what she'd
said when she started shouting, and when her last words came
out in a scream, he bolted out of the dormitory just ahead
of the tray of food she threw as he was locking the door behind him. It hit with a crash and a clatter. He could smell the
spilled stew from where he was standing. He hurried back to
the main house as fast as his legs would carry him. He needed
to report this to the Seraphim.

After the run-in he'd had with the new Sprite this morning, Aaron Walters had gone straight to meditation. He knew
his powers were less when he let anger interfere, and as the
Seraphim, he needed to be clearheaded at all times. After a
couple of hours in solitude, he got up to get ready for lunch.
He was putting on his robes when there was a sudden knock
at his study.

"Enter," he called out, expecting his houseman, Archangel
Robert, to be reminding him it was time to go to eat.

Robert opened the door. "Master, I am sorry to disturb
you, but Archangel Thomas has a matter regarding the new
Sprite that he wishes to discuss."

Aaron frowned. "Send him in," he said, and then took a
deep breath to center himself as Thomas came in, his head
down, his hands folded in a gesture of penitence and prayer.

"You may speak," Aaron said.

Thomas looked up. "The new Sprite has refused to eat
anything brought to her in fear that it has been poisoned or
drugged. She said her father drugged her to get her here, and
she doesn't trust any of us. She threw the food at me as I was
leaving, and it hit the door as I was locking it behind me. She
said her mother was a lawyer and would never stop looking
for her, and that if we killed her and burned her to ashes, then

her mother would come after all of us, instead, and would not stop until we were all on death row."

Then he stopped and took a deep, shaky breath.

The shock that ran through Aaron was real. In all this time, no one had ever put together what happened to their daughters. He knew because they were all on the national website for missing children. He needed to talk to Archangel Jud before he did anything else.

"Thank you, Archangel Thomas. You may go to lunch now, and don't worry. Those are all just words of fear. She will settle, as all the others have."

"Yes, Master," Thomas said.

Aaron rang for his houseman. "Robert, summon Archangel Jud for me. I will speak with him now."

"Yes, Master," Robert said and got on the intercom, which sounded in every building except for the one where the Sprites were housed. "Archangel Jud, the Seraphim has summoned you. Report immediately."

Jud had just walked into the dining hall when the call went out, and the moment he heard his name, he groaned.

What the hell has she done now?

He turned without comment and headed straight for the Master's private quarters. When he knocked at the front door, Archangel Robert let him in.

"Follow me," he said briefly and led him through the stately mansion to the study, only to find the door open, and the Seraphim waiting.

"Thank you, Archangel Robert. You may go to lunch. I will join you shortly… Oh, and please close the door on your way out."

"Yes, Master," Robert said.

Jud's heart skipped a beat when the door went shut between them, but he stood as all others did who entered the

Master's quarters, with his head down and his hands in a gesture of prayer.

"Archangel Jud, please sit," Aaron said.

Jud sat and then grabbed hold of his knees as the Seraphim took a seat on the other side of the desk.

"Your daughter has made a grave accusation. I need to verify the veracity of it to make sure it's only fear talking, or if the real possibility exists. She claims her mother is a lawyer. Is this true?"

Jud nodded. "Yes, Master, that is true."

"She also claims that her mother will never stop looking for her, which is what all of the Sprites assume, and that is fair. They are all on the National Registry for Missing Persons now. What I need to know is if there is any reason her mother would suspect you."

"Absolutely not," Jud said. "We have not been in touch for more than two years. I had not seen my daughter in all that time, either."

But Aaron was picking up on something that shot through Jud's mind when he asked that question, and pursued the line of questioning.

"Your daughter said you drugged her to get her here. Tell me how you got your daughter out of her home."

Jud blanched. "That's not how it started at all. I knew she was alone at home. I knocked and she let me in, elated to see me."

"Did they have a home security system? Were you seen on camera?"

"I knew about that, so after a brief conversation, I invited her to spend the night with me in my hotel room and told her we would go do some fun things together before I took her back the next day. She was excited and said she needed to let her mother know. I told her it would be better if it came from me, and she agreed and ran upstairs to pack. I used to live there and knew where everything was. I easily disabled the security camera and erased the footage where I first appeared, then went upstairs to get her."

Aaron frowned but kept listening. "And what did you find when you went into her room?"

"She was angry with me for walking in without knocking, but she got over it. She had everything packed, except her phone and the charger. She'd been sick all night, and her phone was on the bed. She asked me to put it and the charger in her bag, and then she went to get dressed. Instead, I hid it beneath a pillow and we left."

"You are certain she did not call her mother on her own?" Aaron asked.

Jud tensed. "I did not witness it, but if she had and intended to take it with her, why then was it not in her bag?"

What Jud didn't know, because he'd left before Jordan was old enough for a phone of her own, was that kids never put their phones away, that they were always in their hands or at the ready in a pocket.

And Aaron had raised his children before giving phones to kids was even a thing, so he didn't see the hole in Jud's explanation.

"Yes, yes. I see the logic in that," Aaron said. "All right, then, and you're certain she had no other opportunity to call her when she realized she wasn't going to your hotel room?"

"Yes, Master, but I had to drug her to keep her from running, when I stopped to refuel."

Again, Aaron saw the logic in the drugging at that point in the journey.

"Thank you for your honesty and for clearing up my concern," Aaron said.

Jud bowed his head. "Yes, Master. Always."

"Just so you know, she is refusing to eat and threw her tray of food at the door as Archangel Thomas was leaving. She now believes she will be poisoned or drugged, which is unfortunate, because she will have to eat and drink sometime."

"She would not eat a bite of the food I offered her on the trip here until I bought unopened snacks and a case of unopened bottles of water. Only then did she eat and drink."

"And that was after you drugged her, I assume?" Aaron asked.

Jud sighed. "Yes, Master."

"So *you* have created our little monster."

"Master, she was already enraged and threatening everything before I drugged her. She did not expect it, nor did she see it coming."

Aaron's viewpoint of the Sprite initiate shifted again.

"Was she always a troublesome child?"

"Not while I was there," Jud said.

"And maybe your absence from her life is resented," Aaron said.

"Yes, Master. I am sure it was."

"Then part of your duties now will entail spending time with her at the dormitory while she is on lockdown. Find some food that is unopened and take it to her...water, as well. You will eat your meals with her in this way until she is ready to accept her place here."

Jud groaned inwardly. *That could very well be when hell freezes over.*

"Let's hope not," Aaron said and smiled.

Jud blinked. Aaron had just read his thought. He'd forgotten one of the Master's gifts was clairvoyance.

"I'm sorry, Master. Please forgive me for doubting," Jud said.

Aaron waved him away. "Go get the food. Archangel

Thomas will let you into the dormitory, and you will be locked in with her until the Sprites return."

"Yes, Master," Jud said and left in a hurry. Jordan wasn't going to like this any better than he did, but an order was an order.

CHAPTER NINE

"It's past noon. Are you up to stopping long enough to get something to eat before we head back to the airport?"

"Mexican?" Wyrick asked.

"Works for me," Charlie said. "Pick one and give me driving directions."

Wyrick opened her laptop again, her fingers flying over the keys, looking for restaurants with good ratings.

"Okay, I have the directions pulled up. Turn right at the next stoplight and we'll go from there."

"Where are we going?" Charlie asked.

"Cocina Madrigal. It has a five-star rating on their website and rave reviews."

Charlie turned right at the stoplight, and together they found their way to the restaurant without an issue. But when they pulled up and parked, Charlie frowned at the nondescript appearance of the sandy-brown building.

"Doesn't look like much from the parking lot," he said.

"I don't look like much from the outside, either, but we both know it's what's on the inside that counts," Wyrick snapped.

Charlie glared. "I don't know how my opinion of the outside of a building suddenly became about you, but do me a favor, get your ass out of the car and stop griping."

Wyrick put her laptop in the floorboard, then tossed her bag on top of it and got out, marching toward the building without waiting for him before going inside on her own.

"Damn, aggravating female," Charlie muttered and lengthened his stride, entering only a couple of steps behind her, and just as the hostess walked up.

"How many?" she asked and then eyed Wyrick curiously.

"Two, and seat us against the wall so we can see the enemies coming," Wyrick said.

Charlie arched an eyebrow. Obviously the hostess had stared at Wyrick's bald head a little too long, and when the hostess looked up at him, he glowered.

She grabbed two menus. "This way," she said and led them all the way to the back of the room. She seated them against the wall, near the kitchen.

Charlie turned around and swept the room with what he hoped would pass for a steely gaze, and then nodded.

"It'll work," he said.

Wyrick was enchanted that he'd actually gone along with the impulse she'd had, and now she was stuck with having to be grateful. She sat without looking at him and picked up a menu, then laid it back down.

"I read the menu on the way here. I already know what I want," she said.

Charlie picked up a menu, then paused. "Do you know what I want, too?"

"Beef tenderloin steak tacos," she said.

"Whoa! They have that?" Charlie asked.

"I am not answering that question," she muttered.

Charlie stifled a grin. He'd finally gotten under her skin.

Moments later, a waitress appeared with glasses of water.

"Are you ready to order, or do you need a few minutes?"

"I'll have the mushroom enchiladas," Wyrick said.

"And I'm having the beef tenderloin steak tacos," Charlie said and then took a drink of the water she'd brought to the table.

"Are we having an appetizer today?" the waitress asked.

"Charlotte and I are having guacamole and chips," Wyrick said.

Charlie choked on the water he was swallowing.

"Yes, ma'am," the waitress said and hurried away to turn in the order.

"What the hell is wrong with you?" Charlie asked.

"That prison was smothering," she said. It was all the explanation she was going to make.

"Ah...yes, it was," Charlie said.

Now it was all making sense. She needed the silliness to offset the darkness. He'd felt it. And with her abilities, he could only imagine how deeply it had impacted her.

A few moments later the chips and guacamole arrived, and the tension between them lessened with food in their bellies.

"Can we fly to Shawnee Gap?" Charlie asked as they ate.

"No. The population is less than two hundred and fifty residents, and it's right in the midst of the Appalachians. From the maps I looked at, there's not much of a road, either. I'm saying we drive it. We'll have to check out the entire area to see what the security is like. As much as I hate to say this, the only overnight housing we'll have will be camping. Do you have tents?"

"Yes, but for safety's sake, I'm going to suggest both of us in one. At the least, there will be bears."

"Ah, shit," Wyrick said.

"Look, we can sleep in separate tents if it will make you feel—"

Wyrick pointed a chip at him! "That was for the bear comment. Not you. I'm not afraid of you, Charlie Dodge."

"Well, that's a relief," Charlie muttered. "If it will make you feel any better, I am somewhat afraid of you."

Wyrick smirked, but inside she was laughing out loud.

By the time their main courses arrived, the tension between them had been set aside.

Wyrick rolled her eyes in ecstasy as she took her first bite of the mushroom enchiladas, then chewed and swallowed.

"This is the best stuff I've ever tasted in my life," she said and chased the bite with a scoop of beans and rice peppered with homemade pico de gallo.

Charlie's first bite of the steak taco was tender and spicy, and the warm tortilla made it the perfect mouthful. He downed the first one without saying a word and didn't even look up until he stopped to take a drink.

"Sorry you aren't enjoying your food," Wyrick said.

He picked up his second taco. "Mind your own business," he said and took a big bite.

She laughed, and the sound rolled through him like the ripples of an earthquake, cracking the mental wall he kept between them. *No, you don't, Dodge. No. You. Don't.*

They were almost finished when their waitress came back.

"Have you saved room for dessert?" she asked.

Charlie already knew Wyrick's penchant for sweets and was waiting to see what she ordered.

"I saw a photo online of something that looked like pudding, with a caramel swirl on top. What is that?" Wyrick asked.

"Ah…the dulce de leche flan. It's served with cinnamon sugar churros. A great choice," the waitress said.

"A flan is like pudding, right?" Charlie asked.

The waitress nodded.

"Do you have pie?" Charlie asked.

She smiled. "A very decadent Mexican chocolate pie served with whipped cream, nuts and a drizzle of dulce de leche on top."

"That's caramel," Wyrick said.

"I know that," Charlie said.

"Just trying to be helpful," she said.

Charlie ignored her. "I'll have the pie," he told the waitress. "Oh…and I'd like a cup of coffee with that."

The waitress nodded and glanced at Wyrick, who just pointed at her empty glass and smiled.

"Oh, sorry. I'll bring you a refill," the waitress said.

"Back to the trip," Charlie said. "What else do we need to prepare for?"

Wryick thought. "By any chance do you own a drone?"

"No, why?" Charlie asked.

"Never mind. I have something. I'll bring it. I thought it might be helpful in locating the property from the air, since I saw heavy forest all around it."

Charlie eyed her curiously. "You own a drone?"

"I own a company that makes them," she said. "Do you have an extra sleeping bag? I'd happily buy one, but the sooner we get on the road to Kentucky, the faster we'll get Jordan Bien home."

"I'll deal with the camping equipment. My Jeep has plenty of room for all of it, and I have an assortment of MREs, so that will limit the need to build a fire, which could alert them to our presence."

Wyrick frowned. "What are MREs?"

"It stands for Meals Ready to Eat. It's what soldiers eat when they're doing fieldwork or on patrol."

"Ick," Wyrick said.

Charlie grinned.

And then their desserts arrived. They eyed their own desserts and then each other's, before getting down to business.

Wyrick had an iced tea and Charlie had his coffee. As soon as they finished, Charlie paid up, and then they were back in the car and headed for the airport.

CHAPTER TEN

The flight home was turbulent and took longer than the trip going to Phoenix, because they had to fly around another storm. Three hours later, they finally arrived at the hangar.

"There's no sense driving at night now after the day we've had, and I need time to get all the gear together," Charlie said. "Why don't you meet me at my apartment around 8:00 a.m. and we'll leave from there. Pack a couple of changes of clothes, and shoes and socks for rough terrain, and if you have a rain slicker, pack that, as well. Do you have a backpack large enough for all that?"

"Yes," Wyrick said. "Reception is going to be bad in the mountains, but I'll handle the technology and you deal with the camping aspect."

"Agreed," Charlie said and got out of the chopper just as Benny came out of the hangar to help Wyrick. "Go home and get some rest. It may be the last night of good sleep we have for a while."

Wyrick watched Charlie pause to speak to Benny, trying not to think about how Charlie looked naked, which had been a total accident that happened during the Dunleavy case. She sighed and turned away, and when she heard his Jeep start up and leave the hangar, she refused to give in to the urge to look back and wave.

Jordan was back at her sewing station when she heard someone unlocking the door. It wasn't time for the girls to come back; she guessed it was about her throwing food at the door. She was scared, but she wasn't going to let on. She dug through the stash of spare buttons to find one to replace on the shirt in her lap.

She heard the sounds of men talking about cleaning up the food, and then footsteps coming through the dormitory to the back room where she was sitting.

Seeing Jud walking in with another tray of food surprised her, as did the calm expression on his face.

"Can you please take a break? I brought food that hasn't been opened, and I will eat with you to prove none of it has been drugged. Deal?"

Jordan was hungry but unwilling to be amenable. She set the sewing aside and got up.

"We can sit at one of the craft tables," Jud said and put the tray down. "There are bottles of water still in the refrigerator, so grab us a couple."

Jordan did as he asked, then sat down on the opposite side of the table and placed the bottles between them.

"Thanks," Jud said and then slid a paper plate, a plastic fork and a can of Vienna sausages toward her. Then he put a whole sleeve of saltine crackers and a box of Little Debbie oatmeal cookies, both unopened, in front of her.

Jordan noticed he had the same thing, and realized he really was going to eat with her. She didn't know how she felt about it,

"Want me to open the can for you?" he asked.

Jordan popped hers and peeled back the lid without an-

swering him. She dumped the little sausages out onto the
paper plate, and reached for the crackers and a bottle of water.

Jud shrugged, accepting her silence as a positive, and they
began to eat. He tried conversation a couple of times, but after
continuing silence from her, he quit talking.

The men cleaned up the food she'd thrown, then the door
and the floor before leaving, locking them in as they went.
About an hour later the girls returned, and when they did,
Jud took their food trash with him, leaving her to return to
her sewing.

The girls were curious about Jordan's father coming to eat
with her, even somewhat envious that he'd actually spent
time with her. They had no personal contact with the family members who'd brought them here.

Randi, being the brave one of the group, went back to
where Jordan was sewing, and sat down on the floor beside
her.

"So why did your dad get to come eat with you?" she asked.

Jordan shrugged. "They probably made him, after I refused to eat what they brought, and threw it at that Thomas
guy when he left."

The other girls had followed Randi into the sewing room
and gasped en masse when they heard her say she threw her
food.

"Why didn't you eat it? You ate breakfast this morning,"
Randi said.

"I saw everybody being served from the same pans, so I
guessed they weren't drugged. I had no way of knowing they
hadn't drugged the food they put on my tray."

Randi's mouth opened, but she was so shocked she didn't
speak. It was the little blond-haired Barbie with the blue eyes
who responded.

"Why would you think that?" she asked.

"Because Jud drugged me twice to get me here, that's why."

"Oh," Barbie said, then moved a little closer and sat down on the floor beside Randi. "Why don't you call him Daddy?"

Jordan looked up from her sewing, her eyes blazing.

"I don't have a father. He walked out on me two years ago, and the man who showed up the other day kidnapped me and fed me drugs. When I wouldn't eat anything else he gave me, he stabbed me in the neck with a syringe and drugged me again. I hate him. I hate all of these men. They're evil."

The other girls stared at each other and then wandered off to the craft tables to find something to do. But Randi and Barbie stayed, and it was Randi who began looking through the basket of finished mending and discovered what Jordan had done.

"Jordan! You sewed the buttonholes shut!"

"I know," Jordan said.

Randi groaned. "They're gonna be mad."

"Yes, well, I'm mad at them," Jordan said.

The two girls looked at each other, then nodded. That made sense. They weren't brave enough to rebel, but they had mad respect for the new girl's fearless stunts.

And so the afternoon progressed. Most of the girls took a nap out of boredom, but Jordan kept her head down and worked until the other basket was empty and the mending was finished.

The ends of her fingers were sore and a couple were bleeding from needle pokes. She had a headache from squinting and thought of her reading glasses back home. But the minute she thought of home and her mother, her eyes welled.

Mama, I miss you so much. I'm so scared. Please find me.

Without a clock to know what time it was, she went to her bed, rolled over onto her side to face the wall and closed her eyes. She could hear the air-conditioning units humming outside the nearby window and fell asleep to the sound.

She woke up as Archangel Thomas came to bring the girls

to supper, and when she rolled over and sat up, she saw Jud coming in with another tray of food.

She sighed. Was the shit going to hit the fan before or after they ate? Then she saw the Seraphim walk in with his usual entourage. Her belly rolled, but she stood up, ready to face the consequences, and noticed the other girls watching her with measured levels of sympathy as they were being marched out.

"Bring the mending!" Aaron ordered. He pointed at Jordan and said, "You. Come here to me."

She lifted her chin and walked toward him without hesitation as one of the men went to get the basket.

He carried it back to his Master and set it before him.

The pile of clothing displeased Aaron.

"You didn't fold it!" he said.

"You didn't tell me to," Jordan said.

Aaron leaned over and picked up a shirt, checking the buttons to make sure they had been sewn on properly. He went to button it without thinking, but when he realized the buttonhole had been sewn shut, he began checking more of it, flinging it aside.

"You little bitch!" he screamed and began going through the basket piece by piece, finding that every piece in there had been sabotaged one way or another. He was beside himself with rage.

But when he came to his white robe and saw the red hem she'd sown into it, he dropped it, drew back his hand and began slapping her, from one side of her cheek to the other, until he hit her so hard it knocked her off her feet. She fell backward and didn't get up.

Jud cried out before he thought. "No! Stop! Stop!"

But when the Master turned on him with his fists doubled up, Jud realized how close he was to getting hit, as well.

"Get out!" Aaron ordered.

Jud was trembling inside, but this was his daughter unconscious on the floor. Instead of obeying, he knelt down beside her to check for a pulse.

"Get up and get out!" Aaron screamed.

"This is not our way!" Jud said. "You talk about a better world, and kindness and peace controlled by people who can see into the future. You caused harm to my daughter! I trusted you, or I would never have brought her here."

The other Archangels were in shock. One of their own had challenged the Master. But they had also been stunned by what the Master had done, and began thinking of their family members with unease.

Jordan's face was bloody and already swelling and bruising as Jud picked her up from the floor and carried her to her bed.

"You will pay for this insubordination," Aaron screamed as Jud ran to get some wet washcloths and then rushed back to Jordan's bedside.

Jud paused, staring at the man he'd worshipped. "I already have, and at the expense of my child," he said, then began wiping away the blood from his baby's face.

Aaron turned to the Archangels with him, ready to demand they take Jud into custody. But he saw their expressions and changed his mind. He'd just lost face with them. Granted, it was just a few of his followers, but word would spread. He needed to do something fast to regain control.

"Archangel Rubin, go get the medic. Have him come see to the Sprite's injury."

Rubin bolted out of the building.

Aaron took a deep breath. "It is unfortunate that this happened, and I will commune with Spirit as to the correct path to take with her. What none of you know...but what I do realize is that this Sprite has powers far beyond most of you, and I believe that is what causes her constant disobedience. She has not yet learned control." Aaron took a deep breath and then apologized to Jud. "Archangel Jud, I am sorry for striking your child. It won't happen again. Archangel Franklin, bring the mending with you. It is best not left in her care again."

Franklin was a tall, skinny man in his early thirties, and horrified by what he'd just seen, yet it was habit that made him obey.

As they were walking out the door, the medic came running into the building with the first aid bag, with Rubin right behind him.

Aaron paused at the doorway. "Tend to her and report her condition back to me. Archangel Rubin, lock up when you leave, and bring Jud with you."

Then he walked out, knowing they would all obey.

It was the cold, wet cloth on her face that brought Jordan back to consciousness, and then she heard Jud's voice, begging her for forgiveness, promising her this wouldn't happen again. She kept wondering what he was talking about until the pain surfaced, and then she remembered.

She'd suffered the consequences of her rebellion, and they were painful. She opened her eyes and saw that Jud's were filled with tears. Noticing the bloody washcloth in his hands, she pushed him away.

Another man was coming toward her that she'd never seen. She didn't know what he was about to do to her, but she wasn't going to be lying down and helpless when she found out. She struggled to sit up and swung her legs off the bed.

"Wait, Jordan," Jud said. "He's a medic. Let him look at you. He won't hurt you, I promise."

"I don't trust your promises," Jordan said, but when she tried to stand up, the room started spinning around her.

Jud caught her before she fell, and eased her back down on the bed as the medic suddenly loomed above her. Jordan's heart skipped a beat. She was trapped.

"My name is Archangel David. They told me you fell backward and hit the floor. All I want to do right now is check you out and listen to your heartbeat. Okay?"

She nodded as he helped her sit up again. She held her breath when he reached toward her. She felt his fingers in her hair, and when they came away bloody, she assumed that was why it hurt. He checked her pulse, listened to her heartbeat and then asked her to track his finger as he moved it back and forth across her line of vision.

All the time this was happening, her lips were continuing to swell. She could feel them growing tighter and tighter, until they were so swollen it was hard to talk.

Finally, David straightened up. "I need to feel your nose and your jaw to see if anything is broken. I'm sorry that it will hurt, but I'll be as gentle as I can, okay?"

Tears had welled in her eyes, but she had yet to cry. She groaned when he began feeling along the edge of her jaw, but when his fingers touched her nose, she gasped. Quick tears from the shock of the pain spilled like water over a dam, rolling down her cheeks in fluid succession.

"I'm so sorry," he said. "One last thing...open your mouth as far as you can so I can check to see where your lips are cut."

Jud reached for her hand, but she snatched it away.

"Don't," she mumbled and then parted her lips.

She was unprepared for the wave of nausea that rolled through her when David gently raised her upper lip, but as he was feeling along the lower one, the room began to spin and then everything went dark.

"Oh my God! What happened?" Jud cried as he caught her from lurching forward, and eased her back down onto the pillow.

"She passed out from the pain," David said. "Her nose isn't broken, that I can tell. Her jaw isn't dislocated, and her lips will heal without stitches. Without medical equipment, I can't say she didn't suffer some kind of concussion, but I can say that her pupils are normal and focusing properly. Let's get her comfortable here," he added, and together, they stretched her back out on the bed and covered her up. "I have some pain pills I can leave for her to take when she wakes up again. That's all I can do," he added.

"And I'm not leaving her unconscious and alone," Jud said. "So I'm here until they bring the other girls back."

Archangel Rubin frowned. "The Master said to bring you back with us."

"You'll have to fight me to do it," Jud said and saw the resignation in their eyes as they turned and walked away.

As soon as they were gone, Jud went to get another wet washcloth. He wrung it out, folded it and laid it across her forehead.

Within a few moments, Jordan began to come around again. She opened her eyes to find Jud watching her; he was crying.

"I'm so sorry," he whispered. "None of this was supposed to happen."

Jordan wanted him out of her sight and motioned for him to leave.

"I can't. I'm locked in here with you until they bring the girls back from supper."

"Hate you," she mumbled and then winced from the pain of talking.

He took the washcloth from her forehead, poured some water on it from the bottle on her supper tray and handed it to her.

"Put it on your lips. Maybe it will help the pain."

She knocked it out of his hand, then staggered to her feet and disappeared into the bathroom.

Jud shuddered as he wiped the tears off his face.

"God forgive me," he muttered, then got up and walked to one of the windows.

Looking through the steel screens over the windows, he realized it was the first time he was seeing the compound from their viewpoint. It reminded him of a picture he'd seen once of a concentration camp. Whatever blinders he'd been wearing about Fourth Dimension and their grand plans were gone. He'd been so wrapped up in finding a tribe of people with the same skills he'd been born with that he'd lost touch with reality, and the damage he'd done was irreparable. The scary part was not knowing how to save her without getting them both killed.

Jordan came back carrying a bottle of water she'd gotten from the refrigerator. She sat down on the side of her bed without looking at him, but when she tried to take a drink the water dribbled from both sides of her mouth and down onto her shirt. She looked down at all the blood, but it wasn't nearly as scary as the blood she'd found between her legs.

"Go pick out your baby bride, Jud. I started my period."

Wyrick began shedding clothes as she entered her apartment. She wanted every aspect of that prison vibe washed from her body, and went straight to the shower.

Afterward, she packed a bag with some clothes, then another with her computers, before digging around for something to eat. She put a frozen pizza in the oven, and while she was waiting for it to bake, she went back to a coat closet in the hall and rummaged through it until she found the box she was looking for.

She opened it to make sure everything was still in there, then lifted out what appeared to be a small model plane made of clear plastic. There was a box inside it where the little engine was housed, and the remote that controlled it was still in the box. She took out the solar cells she used to power it and tested them. They were still good to go.

Then she sat down to check on a search she'd been running on Fourth Dimension while she was gone. There were more than a dozen mentions of it from several psychic sites, so she poured some Pepsi into an ice-filled glass and began to read through them while she waited.

The scent of melting mozzarella and spicy pepperoni filled the small apartment, aggravating Wyrick's hunger pangs. She was beginning to fidget when the timer finally went off. She wasted no time getting it out of the oven, cutting it up and sliding a couple of slices onto her plate. She topped off her Pepsi again, grabbed a handful of paper towels and went back to her laptop. She ate as she scrolled through more comments, wiping her fingers between bites so she wouldn't get the grease all over the keys.

What she did learn was that Fourth Dimension had taken on a cult following, and there were legions of so-called psychics wanting to find a way into the group, but there was no info to aid in their case.

She finished off her second pizza slice and was looking through her stash of chocolate for a Hershey's bar when her laptop signaled new information on her search engine with a robotic voice saying, "Ding-dong, Avon calling."

She shoved aside a package of M&Ms and a Snickers bar before she found the bar she wanted, and began unwrapping it as she headed back to the laptop. She popped a couple of squares in her mouth and then checked the search engine for the new hit.

Chocolate was melting on her tongue as she read, and she was going back for another piece of candy when it dawned on her what she was reading.

"Oh shit," Wyrick said and hacked into a couple of websites that, on a normal day, would have landed her in a federal prison along with the likes of Peter Long.

By the time the candy bar was gone, she had all she needed to know. She put the leftover pizza in the fridge, loaded her dirty dishes in the dishwasher and started it, then ran to her bedroom and got dressed. After sending Charlie a text, she began repacking her little plane and the solar cells, and carried everything to the car. He responded just as she was getting in behind the wheel.

Charlie made two trips down to the basement of his apartment building to get his camping equipment from the storage locker, then checked it all out thoroughly to make sure nothing was missing, before getting it back up the elevator and into his Jeep. He made one last trip down for a box of MREs and loaded them up, as well, before setting the security alarm on his Jeep and going back to his apartment. He had clothes to pack and the first aid kit to replenish, but his belly was complaining about a lack of food.

He ordered a smoked brisket sandwich and some fries, and then went to pack. By the time the food came he was through packing and had the first aid kit ready to go.

He poured sweet tea from a jug into a glass full of ice and sat down with his food. He paused long enough as he was eating to send a text to Morning Light, letting them know he was going to be out of state on a case, but would be available by phone.

He was finishing off his tea when he got a text from Wyrick.

Are you packed?

He responded. Yes. Why?

I'm on my way over. We need to leave now. I'll explain later.

Charlie frowned. He'd never doubted her before, and this was no time to begin.

You flew us home. I'll drive the first shift.

He got a thumbs-up emoji, then disconnected, dumped his trash and went to change clothes, while Wyrick was pushing the speed limits to get to his apartment building.

She kept thinking of what she'd learned and how it might pertain to Jordan Bien. She kept thinking of David Koresh, the leader of the cult in Waco, Texas, and of Jim Jones and Jonestown in Guyana. Both men had been willing to sacrifice their followers rather than go to jail.

As an adult, getting involved in a cult was on them, but when children were involved, they were innocent pawns to the adults who controlled their lives. Aaron Walters and his Fourth Dimension followers were all adults, but it was the children they'd abducted who were unable to help themselves.

It was nearing 7:00 p.m. when Wyrick reached Charlie's apartment building and turned into the entrance to the parking garage, then drove up to the fourteenth level. She parked beside his Jeep and sent him a text.

I'm here.

A couple of minutes later, he responded.

On my way.

Wyrick stayed inside her Mercedes until she saw him coming out of the building, then got out and began grabbing her things.

Charlie glanced at her choice of clothing as he unlocked the Jeep. The blue skinny-leg jeans accentuated her long legs, and the black T-shirt and blue jean jacket would have been commonplace on anyone else. But for her, it was flying under the radar. As soon as they stowed her things, they got in the Jeep and began buckling up.

"What the hell's going on?" he asked, as he backed out of the parking spot.

"There's an FBI presence near the compound," she said.

Charlie flinched. "I'm not going to ask how you know this. What's the panic? Are they planning a raid?"

"I don't know. But there are agents from Dallas who will be boarding a plane tomorrow morning and heading to Kentucky, as well."

"I don't like the sound of that. Did you get any intel about why?"

"Not yet, but something's happening. From what I could determine, Fourth Dimension has been on their radar for a while as a possible site for human trafficking. There are a lot of children there, but they have no concrete proof beyond a few satellite images of some little girls being moved en masse from one building to another, and some images of what they view as older girls holding babies. Just no adult women."

Charlie frowned. "Well, we know what's happening there, but does the FBI? According to what the warden said at the prison, Long didn't talk to anyone about the cult, ever. I wonder what set them off?"

Wyrick shrugged. "Maybe someone tipped them off. Maybe Tara Bien's story got out within the justice system. It's not like she was hiding her daughter's disappearance. She'd notified Jordan's school, and if everyone in the law office where she works knows about it, too, then people talk."

"Call her," Charlie said. "Find out who else she's talked to about this." He then accelerated out of the parking garage and headed for the freeway. "Just don't let on that she might have triggered something that could get her daughter killed."

CHAPTER ELEVEN

Wyrick pulled up Tara's phone number and called, then put it on speaker phone so Charlie could hear. She waited impatiently as it rang over and over, and just when she thought it was going to voice mail, Tara answered. She sounded panicked and breathless.

"Hello?"

"Tara, this is Wyrick from Dodge Security and Investigations. I have a couple of questions to ask."

"Sorry it took so long for me to get to the phone. I was in the shower."

"We need to know how many people in your circle are aware of what happened to your daughter, and who they are."

"Oh my God. Is there bad news?"

Wyrick asked again. "No, but who all have you told?"

"Jordan's school, of course. I told you that in the interview. I also spoke directly to my boss and one of my coworkers about it, but I'd guess everyone at the law office would know now, because they've all stepped up to fill in for me in court."

"Are they talking about it to other people, or did you tell them in confidence?" Wyrick asked.

Tara gasped. "I didn't ask them not to tell. I didn't think. Was that wrong?"

"No, no, nothing like that. We're just following up on some information we have on the FBI, and were curious if you'd contacted them for help, as well."

"Oh! I didn't do that directly, but my coworker Eric Prince has a brother-in-law who's in the FBI at the Dallas office. He said he was going to talk to him about it and see if he could offer me any other advice. I haven't heard back from him."

"Okay, no problem. By any chance, did you mention Fourth Dimension when you were talking to them?" Wyrick asked.

"Yes, and it was embarrassing. I never told anyone at work that Jud claimed to be a psychic. They both looked at me weird."

"I know all about weird looks," Wyrick said. "I don't have the file in front of me right now, so tell me again the name of the law firm for which you work."

"Richter and Sons," Tara said. "Should I ask Eric about his brother-in-law?"

"No, that's fine, and thank you," Wyrick said.

Tara groaned. "Can you tell me anything? Do you have leads? Do you have any idea where she's being held?"

Wyrick glanced at Charlie, who promptly shook his head.

"Not really. It's all still supposition, but we're following up a lead as we speak. We'll be in touch," Wyrick said.

"Yes, okay," Tara said, and then her voice broke. "I'm so scared for her. Please, please find her for me."

"We're doing everything we can," Wyrick said and disconnected, then glanced at Charlie.

"I'm guessing the Feds have always had an eye on Fourth Dimension," Charlie said. "Cults don't fly under the radar for long with them, and Tara's request for help might have triggered something they needed to know."

Wyrick frowned. "My first thought was the FBI raid at

Waco, and David Koresh's willingness to kill everyone, including himself."

"How many hours to where we're headed?" Charlie asked.

"With no delays, a little over fourteen hours, give or take. We'll switch drivers around midnight," Wyrick said.

"I can drive it straight through," Charlie said.

"And then be too tired to function when we get there? I don't think so," Wyrick said. "If I can fly thousands of feet up in the sky at night and still find cities on the ground below, I can follow road signs right in front of me."

"Point made," Charlie said and headed for the nearest exit to eastbound Interstate 40.

Tara Bien was in a bathrobe and on the phone, waiting for Eric Prince to answer her call. Just when she thought the call was going to go to voice mail, he finally answered.

"Hello, Eric speaking."

"Eric, this is Tara Bien. Sorry to call you at home, but I need to ask you something."

"Oh, hi, Tara. Sure, no problem. Do you have any news?"

"Not yet, but I wanted to check back in with you about your brother-in-law. Did he have any specific advice to share?"

"Oh, I'm sorry. I should have called you back after our dinner that evening. I told Hank everything you told us, from the shared parental custody, to that cult... Fourth Dimension. His name is Hank Raines, by the way, and when I mentioned that cult, he got very interested. I assumed that place was already on their radar, but all he said was, if they knew anything specific, he'd let me know, and I never heard back."

"That's what I needed to know. Thank you," Tara said.

"You're welcome. We're keeping you in our prayers. Hope you get your girl home, soon," Eric said.

"Me, too," Tara said, and the minute she disconnected, she pulled up Charlie's number on her phone and called him back.

★ ★ ★

Charlie was on the freeway heading out of Dallas when his phone rang. It was in the docking station, but when he saw who it was from, he put it on speaker.

"This is Charlie."

"Charlie, this is Tara, again. I called Eric and asked if he talked to his brother-in-law about Fourth Dimension. He said he did, and by the way, the agent's name is Hank Raines. Eric said when he mentioned Fourth Dimension, Hank became very interested. Is that what you needed to know? Does this help?"

"Yes, it does," Charlie said. "If we need to know anything more, we'll call."

"Do you know anything more about Fourth Dimension?" Tara asked.

Charlie hesitated. "Not for sure, but we are actively checking out locations now."

"Okay," Tara said.

"And if you get any kind of news or updates from the Feds, be sure and let us know," Charlie said.

"I will," Tara said and burst into tears as soon as she disconnected.

Charlie glanced at Wyrick.

"Well, there's the leak and you have a name. See what you can find out, okay?"

Wyrick pulled her laptop from the case between her feet and went to work.

It hadn't taken Wyrick long to find out that Special Agent Hank Raines and his partner, Special Agent Luis Chavez, were the agents going from the Dallas office.

"Well, Hank Raines and his partner are flying into Lexington tomorrow morning. It can't be a coincidence—they can't be going there for another reason," she said, putting away the laptop. She then leaned back in her seat and closed her eyes.

Charlie drove into the night with Wyrick asleep in the seat beside him, and that, in itself, spoke volumes about the trust she had in him.

Charlie knew nothing about that, but he did know she didn't look nearly as fearsome asleep as she did when she was awake.

Hours passed on the ribbon of concrete that was Interstate 40, with one state after another looking much the same in the dark.

Charlie finished the coffee he'd brought from home, along with a lukewarm can of soda that he drank for the caffeine. It was nearing midnight when he pulled into a truck stop somewhere near Nashville, Tennessee, to refuel. As he began to slow down, Wyrick woke, raised her seat back into a sitting position and began to look around.

"Where are we?" she asked, eyeing the size of the truck stop where they were stopping.

"Close to Nashville. We need to fuel up."

She scrubbed her face with her hands and looked around for her bag, removed a credit card from her wallet and slipped it in her pocket.

"If they have a deli, I'm getting something to eat," Wyrick said.

"I'm gonna make a pit stop after I refuel. I'll meet you at the deli. Food's on me when we work, remember?"

Wyrick didn't argue, but she wasn't paying any attention, either.

As soon as Charlie pulled up to one of the gas pumps and got out to refuel, she headed into the building and went straight to the bathroom, ignoring the curious stares of the customers milling about. A trio of women were at the sinks, washing their hands when she walked in. One of them glanced up at the wall of mirrors and saw Wyrick, then gasped.

"Hey, dude! This is the ladies' room," she cried.

Wyrick frowned. "I'm not a dude. I'm just bald. Chill out," she muttered, went into a stall and locked the door.

The silence that followed was obvious, and the conversation the trio had been having was suddenly silent. Wyrick heard the door open and the sounds of footsteps exiting, but she was thinking about food, and they were strangers who didn't matter in her world. As soon as she washed up, she went back out into the main area and followed the scent of fried food toward the deli.

She looked out into the parking lot and saw Charlie's Jeep, but since he wasn't there, she guessed he was already inside, and headed down an aisle stocked with chips and candy. By the time she got back, Charlie was at the deli counter.

He raised an eyebrow when he saw her armful of snacks.

"Add this stuff, too," he told the clerk.

Wyrick frowned. "I was going to—"

"Did you get enough for me, too?" Charlie asked.

She nodded.

"Then put it down and stop arguing," he said.

Wyrick dumped her snacks and walked around him to get to the deli case. She already knew from past experience that eating Mexican food from a truck stop would not be a wise move since they would likely be camping out in the woods.

"What do you want?" Charlie asked.

"Two hot dogs with mustard and relish. I'll need to get a—"

Charlie pointed to the oversize cup next to her snacks. "That's yours. It's a Pepsi."

"Thanks," Wyrick said.

A few minutes later they were back in the Jeep, only this time, Wyrick was in the driver's seat and Charlie was riding

shotgun with a lap full of food and the passenger seat pushed
as far back as it would go. She drove back onto the interstate
and began looking for the road she needed to switch from
Interstate 40 onto Highway 736 North.

Once Charlie realized she was on top of the route change,
he settled down to eat, fully aware she was neatly eating hot
dogs, drinking Pepsi and driving his Jeep at seventy miles per
hour without a wobble in her steering or a drop of mustard
anywhere on her clothes. He chalked it up to just another
facet of her unique abilities, and as soon as he'd finished eating
and stashed his trash in the food sack, he checked his phone.
Without anything urgent to deal with, he reclined the seat
back and stretched out.

"You okay?" he asked.

"Yes," Wyrick said.

He sighed and then closed his eyes. He was thinking about
Annie when he fell asleep, leaving Wyrick in charge.

When the girls returned from their evening meal to find
Jordan bloody and beaten, and her father at her bedside, they
were dumbstruck. Then Archangel Thomas took her father
away, and the moment the door locked behind the men, the
girls ran to Jordan's side. Some of them were crying at what
had happened to her, some were silent and still in shock, but
Randi was in awe. Jordan had been brutalized and was still
defiant. She could see it in her eyes.

"Is the pain bad?" Barbie whispered.

Jordan sighed, then nodded.

"Did they doctor you?" Randi asked.

Jordan touched her lips to indicate it hurt to talk, then
shrugged and pointed at a little bottle of pills on the table by
her bed.

"For pain?" Randi asked.

Jordan nodded.

"Do you need one?" she asked.

"Not taking," Jordan said. "Started period. Anything here?"

The girls moaned en masse, while a pretty girl with long brown hair and brown eyes began to cry.

"What?" Jordan asked, pointing at her.

"Archangel Jud chose Katie for his bride. Now he gets to claim her," Randi said.

Jordan looked at Katie in horror, trying to picture her as a stepmother.

"Can you walk?" Randi asked.

Jordan nodded.

"Come with me. I'll show you where that stuff is kept," she said.

Jordan stood up, swayed a little on her feet and then slowly followed, every step feeling like she was moving closer and closer to a destiny she couldn't escape.

Once she had the tampons, it took a while to deal with this all on her own. She'd always expected her mother would be there when this need arose, and now she was figuring it out by herself. The thought of Mama made her heart ache.

She still only had two changes of clothing and had had no chance to wash the ones she'd worn here. She refused to sleep in a nightgown for fear of being snatched out of bed in the night while being that close to undressed. So she took off her bloody clothes and put the ones she'd arrived in back on.

Randi pointed to a bank of metal lockers with numbers written on them. "There are clothes in there for us to wear. The numbers are sizes. You can pick out more clothes."

"No," Jordan said. "I'll wash mine."

"I can help," Randi said, but Jordan shook her head, and so Randi went back into the dormitory.

Jordan got a bar of bath soap, took her clothes to a sink and began washing out the blood, one piece at a time, until they were all as clean as she could get them. Then she hung them over the back of some metal folding chairs to dry.

By the time she got back to her bed, she was sick from the pain and shaking from exhaustion. She eyed the pain pills, longing for the freedom to just take one and sleep away this misery, but she didn't dare.

Instead, she crawled between the sheets of her bed, then pulled up the covers and closed her eyes. Even though the lights were still on in places, and she could still hear the girls' voices as they played a game of Monopoly, she dozed, but fitfully. Her head continued to throb, her mouth was so sore and swollen that it even hurt to lick her lips, and her nose was too swollen to breathe through.

Aaron Walters was sitting cross-legged in front of his meditation altar, staring at the huge chunk of crystal before him. He wasn't into scrying, but he used it to focus.

He'd done all of his affirmations and still couldn't get into a state of receptivity. Not once since he'd become aware of his gifts had he ever failed to connect, until today. He'd lost his mojo by letting a girl and her father back him down, and he needed to rectify that tonight. Even though it was nearly midnight, he rang for Archangel Robert, and from the confused sound of Robert's voice, he'd been sound asleep.

"Yes, Master?"

"I apologize for disturbing your rest, but I need you to send for Archangel Jud and have the men bring him to my study."

"Now, sir?" Robert asked.

"Yes, now," Aaron said.

The men walking Jud across the compound were his friends—his equals—until now. Their presence behind him felt threatening, and with good reason. Being called to the Seraphim's quarters was always a little nerve-racking, but being called there at midnight, accompanied by escorts to make sure he went, was never going to be a good sign. He'd been expecting it all evening, but when it hadn't happened he'd gone to bed, only to be awakened a few hours later, and the timing of the demand visit made him uneasy.

The security lights lit the way, but he felt the ominous presence of the enclosure and the thick forest surrounding it. As he walked, he could hear dogs baying somewhere far away on the mountain and guessed someone was hunting.

He was thinking about what the Master might invoke as punishment when a large bird came out of nowhere, swooped down a few yards in front of him and grabbed what looked like a rat in its talons before flying away. When Jud heard the frantic, high-pitched squeal of the animal in its death throes, he shuddered. He knew just how that felt.

He glanced behind him, frowning at the escorts, and then began climbing up the steps. Halfway up, the door opened; Archangel Robert was standing in the doorway.

"This way, please. The Master awaits you in his study." Then he pointed at the escorts. "You will wait here." So they relaxed their stance and watched as the door closed between them.

The sound of their footsteps on the hardwood floors were drowned out by the thunder of Jud's heartbeat as he followed Robert through the house. It was a little too "dead man walking" for his comfort. When they reached the study, Robert knocked on the door, then opened it.

"Master, Archangel Jud is here."

"Thank you, Robert. I'm sorry your sleep was disturbed, but this won't take long," Aaron said, then pointed at Jud. "Enter."

Jud walked in, flinching slightly when the door shut behind him with a click.

"Sit down," Aaron said, waving his hand toward the chair on the other side of his desk.

As Jud sat, the fear he'd felt coming here was being replaced by a growing resentment toward the man they called Master, and when Aaron reached for his glass to take a drink of water, he suddenly focused on Aaron's hands. He'd never noticed how thick his fingers looked…how meaty his hands were—like a prizefighter's, and he'd used them on Jordan.

At that point Jud looked up and realized Aaron had been watching him the whole time. He'd neglected to put up his shield and now the Master knew he was angry. So be it. Jud stood up in defiance.

"If you expect me to sit here and wait for you to impose some sentence on me after you did what you did to my daughter, you're mistaken. Just spit it out."

Aaron's eyes flashed angrily. "So this is where Jordan gets her unruly behavior."

Jud just stood there, waiting.

"Fine. Have it your way," Aaron said. "You have forfeited your right to a bride, and in the face of this added insubordination, you will pack up your things tonight and leave Fourth Dimension, never to return."

"Fine with me. I'll get Jordan," Jud said.

"Oh no. Jordan stays. She's my insurance that you keep your mouth shut about our business here."

"No!" Jud roared. "I won't leave here without her!"

Aaron stood, so angry his voice was shaking.

"You drive away from here alive, or I can bury your body in the forest and let everyone think you left on your own. Your choice."

Jud gasped. The choice to leave her behind was horrifying, but leaving alive now might be the only way he could get her out later.

"I'll leave. But know this. If she cries, I will know it. If you hurt her again, I will know it. If any man touches her again, I will know it."

Aaron glared. "You won't know anything unless I want you to know it!" he said.

"You may be a psychic, but you're a stupid one," Jud said. "You can't control Jordan's abilities, and we both know it. So hear me now. If anything else happens to my daughter, I will come after you. If you lock her up. If you starve her. If you mistreat her in any way, I will know it! If you let a man touch her. If you kill her to get back at me...know that I will burn this place down around you." Then he pointed straight at Aaron's heart. "And that's a promise."

Aaron blanched, and for a minute he thought about killing Jud now, but if he did, he knew the girl would know. She was already furious with her father. Better to let her think he went off and left her behind.

Jud pivoted on one heel and left the office, slamming the door behind him. Robert heard the sound and came running.

"I've been banished," Jud said. "Make sure the security is off the front gate. As soon as I get my things, I'm out of here. Master's orders."

Robert's eyes widened in total shock. This had never happened before, and he didn't know what to think.

"Just turn off the security, dammit, or I'll drive right through the gates," Jud muttered and stomped out of the house, banging the front door behind him.

The men who'd escorted him there stared at him, uncertain what to do now.

"Get out of my face," Jud said and stormed past them.

Jordan hadn't been able to do much more than doze. Her headache had shifted to a dull throb. She couldn't breathe through her nose, but it had finally stopped bleeding. She was lying on her back, watching the moon shadows through the window beside her bed when she suddenly sensed her father's presence.

Startled, she sat up in bed, thinking he was somehow inside the dormitory, and then she realized he was in her head.

Don't block me. Listen. The Master banished me. I'm being forced to leave. Don't be afraid. Block everything but me. The Master won't hurt you. You won't be given to a man. You're too much trouble, but your powers are valuable to him, so you'll be safe. I'm going to get help. Despite what you think, I love you. I was blinded by a light that wasn't ever real. Stay strong.

Jordan leaped out of bed and ran to the window in time to see the lights of a car move across the grounds of the commune and then drive through the gates and disappear.

Don't leave me!

And the moment she thought it, she felt his pain. This wasn't happening! It couldn't be happening! She'd never been so afraid, but then she remembered his warning and shut down. She glanced around the dormitory. All the girls were still asleep. There wasn't anyone she could talk to, and there was no one to tell who would care what just happened to her, so she crawled back in bed and closed her eyes. She was in serious trouble, and the only advocate she'd had here had just driven away.

She couldn't breathe well enough to give in to tears, and the knot in her stomach was now as painful as the wounds on her face.

CHAPTER TWELVE

Special Agents Hank Raines and Luis Chavez took their seats on the plane an hour before sunrise. Once Hank had informed the deputy director about the abduction, they'd been told to find out everything they could on Jud Bien, and if he had so much as an unpaid parking ticket, to get an arrest warrant and take it with them. That man might be the "in" they needed to gain access to the compound, and if they could get inside, they could ascertain once and for all if it was linked to human trafficking.

To their dismay, Jud Bien turned up clean as a whistle. The only avenue they had left was to demand to see Jud and his daughter to verify her whereabouts for the mother. They were counting on the cult complying, so as not to upset the FBI and put them on the radar of the US government.

The plane would be landing in Lexington within a couple of hours, and after meeting up with agents from the Kentucky division, they would be taken to the team's location and could decide how to proceed from there.

After a fairly smooth flight, the plane landed just before

8:00 a.m. They exited the plane into the airport, quickly making their way to luggage claim.

As soon as they entered the area, they saw a man holding a sign with their names on it.

"There's our ride," Chavez said, pointing to the thirty-something man with blond hair.

"Welcome to Lexington," the man said. "I'm Sol Duran, an agent with the Kentucky division. My partner, Billy Richards, is waiting for us outside. I'll help you get your luggage."

After they'd collected their bags, they followed Duran out into the Kentucky heat and headed for a large, dark SUV waiting at the curb.

Billy Richards got out and introduced himself, then helped load their luggage into the vehicle. Raines and Chavez got in the back seat, and Duran and Richards took the front.

"How was your trip?" Richards asked.

"Hurried," Raines said. "Fill us in on any updates."

So Richards began talking as he drove away from the airport, with Duran filling in from time to time.

"We've had people keeping tabs on Fourth Dimension for some time," Richards said. "Everything there is secretive. Their security is satellite fed, which means there's no way for us to interrupt their feed to approach the compound without being seen, which also begs the question…how do they fund that? We have satellite images of the property inside the compound, and a few more images we got from mounting a camera on a drone."

"What did you see?" Raines asked.

"A lot of men but no industry at all. No gardening, no pretense at being self-sufficient. We've caught a glimpse of some young teens carrying babies around, but we've yet to see any adult women, although they're bound to be there because there are some babies."

"What would you say the age range of the kids might be?" Raines asked.

"My partner probably has a better grasp of that," Richards said, and Duran began to speak.

"I've studied the drone footage and the satellite images, and even have some video of people moving around the grounds. We estimate the children, who are all female, by the way, range in age from ten or eleven, up to early teens."

Chavez frowned. That smacked of child trafficking to him. "All girls? Really?"

Duran nodded.

Chavez frowned. "Okay...so you know girls are onsite, but have you seen any go out? Have you seen anything that would lead you to think this is linked to child trafficking?"

Duran shook his head. "Believe me, if we did, we would have already been in there. We don't have any indication that there's any buying and selling. What we do know is that they're all school age, but none of them go to school down in Shawnee Gap. However, with so much online schooling these days, we can't assume they're not being educated, and we don't have any legal reason to demand to inspect the place."

"What about supplies? Are there any delivery trucks coming and going? Any way kids might be smuggled in and out that way?" Raines asked.

"No. Their food is picked up by members of Fourth Dimension from the small store in Shawnee Gap. They order in bulk through the local grocer, drive down in three or four vehicles to pick it up and drive back up the mountain with it. They do this about twice a month," Duran said.

"What about recent arrivals?" Raines asked. "We want to verify if a new girl arrived within the past week. She would have come in with her father, a man named Jud Bien."

Duran nodded. "Our recon team got the tag number of a car that came in recently. It did check out as belonging to a man named Judson Bien, and it was reported he had a young female with him. That same evening, our team reported hearing glass breaking inside the compound and a lot of screaming."

"They heard it?" Chavez asked.

Richards nodded. "Yes. They have a parabolic mic, and were a couple of hundred yards from the perimeter when they picked it up."

Special Agent Raines frowned. "How do they get that close without setting off security alarms?"

"We don't know that it doesn't alert them inside in some way, but no alarms go off that can be heard from outside the compound," Duran said.

"Do you have anything solid that would get us a search warrant?" Raines asked.

"We keep trying to get a clear picture of the young girls' faces," Richards added. "Even one clear image would be good. If we could run it through facial recognition and match it up to any of the missing children in the national database, we'd be solid on a search warrant."

Raines sighed. "We're not here to step on your case. We are trying to do a follow-up on a parent abduction for a colleague. The mother of the missing girl was married to Jud Bien, and they shared custody after the divorce. Two years ago, he up and disappeared. They'd had no contact with him whatsoever, and then just a few days ago he showed up at their house, took their daughter when she was there alone, and without contacting the mother in any way, disappeared again. She did a little research on her own and found out her husband might have had a connection to Fourth Dimension, which is why we're here. She's frantic. She's scared for her daughter's safety. She knows Fourth Dimension is like a cult for psychics, and she claims her husband is one, and that her daughter has some abilities in that field. But she doesn't know what any of that means with regards to her daughter's abduction."

Duran frowned. "And that shared custody is still active?"

"Yes," Raines said.

"Ah...then the law has no legal grounds to go in and rescue her," Duran said.

"Exactly," Raines said.

"We'll do all we can to help," Duran said. "Not sure what yet, but maybe we'll get lucky and get some pics of the girls we can use. In the meantime, it's a long drive to get to Shawnee Gap, then up the mountain to our recon team. There's drinks and some snacks in the cooler in the back."

Hank Raines turned around, pulled the small hand-held cooler from the hatch behind the back seat, set it in the floor between his feet, and began handing out bottled water and cold-cut hoagies. They ate and talked as the trip continued, with the plan to get to their location by midafternoon.

Wyrick drove without stopping for almost five hours, then pulled in for a pit stop to refuel.

Charlie woke up as she was beginning to slow down to take the exit. He sat up and looked around. It was still dark, but as he glanced at the time, he realized he'd slept five solid hours.

"Where are we?" he asked.

"Sort of southeast of Lexington, Kentucky, in a place called Noland. We still have a ways to go to get to Shawnee Gap, and I'm not sure about availability of places to refuel, so I stopped here."

"Works for me," Charlie said. "I need to stretch my legs."

Wyrick drove through Noland until she saw a well-lit gas station that was open for business, and pulled up to the pumps.

"I'll fill up and drive the rest of the way. You go on inside. I'll join you shortly," Charlie said.

Wyrick patted her pocket to see if her credit card was still there and then tossed the keys to Charlie before she got out. But Charlie wasn't the only one with long legs. She stretched a couple of times to ease stiff muscles before heading toward the station, and was thinking about hot coffee and something sweet when she walked inside.

Within seconds, she was hearing a fight. Things were falling and breaking, and a woman was crying and screaming, "Stop, Troy, stop. Please don't hit me again."

Wyrick bolted past the front counter, following the sounds into the hallway leading to the bathrooms. There was a short, heavyset man straddling a woman's legs, hammering her with his fists and with some dishes on the floor near the woman's head.

Wyrick grabbed a broom leaning against the wall and swung it at the back of the man's head like a baseball bat. The broom handle snapped off about a foot above the bristles as the man dropped like a rock.

It took every bit of Wyrick's strength to pull him up and off the woman, and then she dropped to her knees beside her and made a quick call to Charlie.

He glanced down at his cell when it rang, but when he saw the call was from Wyrick, he moved out from behind the pumps, looking toward the station as he answered.

"What's up?" he asked.

"I need you in here. Bring your cuffs."

His gut knotted. "On my way," he said, then took the nozzle out of the gas tank and quickly hung it back up.

He didn't know what was wrong, but she never asked for help. He grabbed some cuffs from the console and ran into the store, then had a brief moment of panic when he didn't see her.

"Where are you?" he yelled.

"Back here by the bathrooms. Hurry, he's starting to come to."

Charlie was moving at a lope as he reached the hallway,

then came to a stop as he saw Wyrick on her knees beside a woman who'd obviously been beaten, and a man unconscious on the floor near a broken broom.

"I walked in on this," Wyrick said. "He was sitting on her legs so she couldn't move and beating the hell out of her."

Charlie saw the man's bloody knuckles and cursed beneath his breath as he cuffed him, then dragged him out of the hall.

"Stay with her," he said. "I'm going to use their phone to call 911 so it will go straight to the local police station."

Wyrick jumped up and ran into the women's bathroom, got a handful of wet paper towels, and then dropped back down beside her. The woman's eyes were swollen shut, so it was hard to tell if she was conscious enough to know what was going on.

"Honey, can you hear me?" Wyrick asked.

"Yes, hear you. Run. He'll hurt you, too."

"He's in cuffs, and my boss is calling the police. I have some wet compresses I'm going to put on your eyes. It will feel cold, but don't be scared, okay? Help is coming."

"Can't help. He'll do it again," she whispered and then started to shake.

"What's your name?" Wyrick asked as she laid the wet towels over her eyes.

"Evie. Troy is my ex-husband. I didn't know he was out of jail."

"Well, he's not going to be out long," Wyrick said, and then looked up as Charlie walked back into the hall.

"The police are on the way, and so is an ambulance. What happened?" he asked.

"Ex-husband. She didn't know he was out of jail," Wyrick said, then patted Evie's leg. "Evie, this is my boss, Charlie Dodge."

"Evie, I'm sorry this happened. Why did he do this to you?" Charlie asked.

"I testified against him in trial. I didn't know he was out."

"He won't be long," Charlie said, echoing Wyrick's earlier words. "I hear sirens. Just hang in there, Evie." Then he glanced at Wyrick and shook his head. "I turn my back and you get yourself into trouble. What the hell am I going to do with you?"

Wyrick could think of at least a half dozen things, none of which she would ever divulge.

"While you're deciding my fate, stay with Evie a second. I need to pee."

She jumped up and ducked into the women's bathroom.

Charlie heard a moan behind him and turned around. The man was trying to get up. Charlie shoved him back down on his ass.

"Don't fucking move," Charlie said.

"You're hurting me!" the man yelled.

"Then sit the hell still," Charlie said.

Wyrick came out of the bathroom just as a trio of patrol cars skidded into the station with lights flashing and sirens screaming.

The officers ran inside with their guns drawn, and then the gas station was full of people, and an ambulance had arrived on scene.

Evie was transported to the local hospital, while a second set of EMTs treated Troy's head wound on the scene before he was taken into custody. While Charlie and Wyrick were giving their statements, the owner of the station arrived.

Horrified by what had happened to his employee, he began cleaning up the blood in the hallway and then stayed to finish out her shift.

As soon as Charlie and Wyrick were released, they went back to the Jeep. Charlie finished fueling it up, and then they drove away, heading toward a little café the owner had recommended.

"Want to eat inside or get it to go?" Charlie asked.

"Inside, please. This might be our last chance to eat real food for a while."

Charlie grinned. "MREs are real food, too."

Wyrick rolled her eyes.

"I want biscuits and gravy on a plate, not stirred up in a pouch."

Charlie laughed, and after the tension of what had just happened, laughing felt good.

Jordan was awake and sitting on the side of her bed when the other girls woke up. As always, they began getting ready to go to breakfast.

One girl was crying as she got dressed. She'd dreamed of home and awakened to her reality.

Barbie was trying to get her long blond hair pulled up into a ponytail, and Randi was bemoaning the loss of her makeup back home.

Katie, the girl Jud had chosen as his bride, was in a state of panic, and Jordan knew why.

Sympathetic to Katie's fears, she got up and went to where Katie was dressing and tapped her on the shoulder.

Katie turned around, eyeing Jordan's swollen mouth and the purple bruises spreading across her face.

"Thought you might like to know that Jud was banished from the group last night," Jordan said.

Katie gasped. "What do you mean?"

By now, all of the girls were listening.

"The Master kicked him out for defending me. He's gone," Jordan said.

"Then why did he leave you behind?" Randi asked.

Jordan felt the weight of that answer like an ever-tightening noose around her neck. Just saying it made her voice shake, but her mother had taught her that once a trouble was shared, the fear of it lessened.

"I am their insurance. If Jud tells what he knows about this place, the boss man will have me killed."

The girls all crowded around her, wanting details.

"How do you know this?" Randi asked.

Jordan shrugged. "I know stuff, that's all."

Katie's eyes widened. "You mean, you're like them...the men? You're psychic, too?"

Jordan didn't answer. "What I am doesn't matter. I told you so you wouldn't be thinking you were going to have to marry him."

Katie's shoulders slumped. "They'll just give me to someone else."

Jordan shook her head. "They don't know it yet, but when the Master hit me, he disrupted the order of things. He showed a violence they'd never seen before. And when I show up at breakfast looking like this, it's going to cause more uncertainty among them. You'll see."

Barbie sidled up closer. "What if they lock you up again? What if they won't let you go?" she whispered.

There were tears in Jordan's eyes, but they heard the conviction of her truth.

"I will die where I stand before I'll ever be alone with those men again."

Katie looked at Jordan, and then put her hand on Jordan's arm.

"I'll stand with you. I'll stay behind with you," she said.

Not wanting to be outdone, Randi added her hand to the pledge.

"I'll stand with you, too," she said.

Then one by one, all of the girls pledged not to leave her behind, and by then Jordan was crying. It was the first time she'd let them see her fear. But she'd become the symbol of strength they had all needed, and they'd given her their allegiance. A new world order had just been established in Fourth Dimension. The men just didn't know it yet, but they soon would, because Archangel Thomas and his helpers were on the way to the girls' dormitory.

Thomas knew the moment he unlocked the door and walked in to bring the girls to breakfast that something had changed. They were already lined up and silent, rather than sitting about chattering and laughing as usual.

Then he saw the new Sprite lined up with them and a wave of shock rolled through him. He'd heard rumors about the Master losing his temper with her, but the violence with which it had happened was frightening.

"I'm sorry, Jordan, but Master hasn't changed his orders. You're supposed to stay here," he said.

She didn't argue with him, which was a relief, but when she stepped out of line, all of the girls went with her.

"Girls, get back in line now," he said.

"We're not hungry," Randi said.

Thomas didn't know how to proceed, but it was apparent the girls had ignored their orders to shun Jordan, and the symbolism of what just happened was impossible to miss. She wasn't just one of them now. They were protecting her.

He glanced at the men with him, saw the shock in their eyes, as well, and then sternly announced, "We aren't going to start mass insubordination. Line up, all of you, and we will proceed to breakfast."

"Jordan, too?" Katie asked.

"Yes, Jordan, too," he said.

The girls lined back up again with Jordan right in the middle, and then Thomas led the way out with the girls in single file behind him, and the two guards bringing up the rear.

The dining hall was full. Families were at their tables feeding babies as they fed themselves. Archangels were sitting about in the normal groups and enjoying their food as the girls filed in.

It took a few moments for them to realize the new Sprite was with them, and then silence fell when they saw her face.

But it was the look of anger and disdain on her face as she stared back at them that made them turn away. They looked at each other in shock and disbelief, and then down at their food, but their appetites were gone.

The girls sat at the one long table, separated from the others by their status as food was brought to them. But when they gave Jordan her plate, she got up and headed back to the kitchen with it, even as one of the men began following her, demanding she go sit back down.

She stopped and then handed him her plate.

"Then you take a bite of everything on my plate to prove to me it's not been poisoned or drugged."

The man frowned. "That is not our way!"

Jordan pointed to her face. "Jud Bien has been banished from Fourth Dimension for defending me after this happened, and the Master made him leave me behind. So if you think I feel safe in any way, you are crazy. Look at me. Is this your way? My father is gone and I am now a hostage, and you, by your presence alone, are complicit of abetting kidnapping. My mother is a lawyer, and this is a federal offense. I eat nothing unless someone else tastes it first. And if I die, you're all guilty of murder."

Aaron Walters walked into the dining hall just in time to hear her say *you're all guilty of murder*. He heard their gasps, saw the shock on their faces and braced himself when all eyes turned to him.

"I will taste her food," he said, waving his hand in a grand gesture of sacrifice.

Jordan turned around, then opened herself up to his thoughts and felt a moment of victory. The Master of Fourth Dimension was afraid.

"You can't possibly believe I would put anything into my mouth that you've touched. You've already done enough to me," she said.

One of the Archangels came out of the kitchen. "If it pleases the Master, she may come into my kitchen and put food on her own plate."

Aaron waved his hand and walked out of the dining hall. As things stood now, his morning greeting would fall on deaf ears. He should have done away with both of the Biens, but it was too late now. The damage had already been done.

Jud had driven away from the compound with a knot in his gut and the image of his daughter's brutalized face before him. He couldn't think about the hell he'd brought down on them for trying to figure out how to save her, but he knew he couldn't do it himself. He had to call his ex-wife. She was a lawyer. She would know someone who could make all this right. Whatever it took. Whatever he had to do. If it meant spending the rest of his life in prison, it would be worth it.

Around 3:00 a.m. he realized he'd missed the highway he meant to take and wound up in Berea, Kentucky. He stopped at a Red Roof Inn, and when he got into the room, he dumped his bag on the floor, kicked off his shoes and rolled over onto the bed. He didn't have the guts to call Tara just yet and talked himself into resting first.

He closed his eyes, and the next thing he knew, it was daylight and nearly noon. The events of the night came flashing back as he got up and staggered to the bathroom. He stripped and showered before putting on clean clothes, then sat down on the side of the bed and took out his cell phone.

He was about to unleash a maelstrom of epic proportions down on Aaron Walters's head, and for the first time in over two years, he called home.

CHAPTER THIRTEEN

The drive from Lexington to Shawnee Gap was longer than Agent Raines expected it to be, and he'd quit listening to the chatter back and forth between the others over an hour ago. He spent the time scouring social media and checking his messages to see if there'd been any new intel on Jud Bien or his daughter. But since there was none, the original plan was all they had.

When Richards suddenly announced, "We're here," Hank looked up from his phone. All he saw was a narrow dirt road in front of them and trees on both sides, as thick as feathers on a duck's back.

"Where's here?" Hank asked.

"We're about five miles up the mountain from Shawnee Gap, and about a mile from the compound," Richards said.

"Claustrophobic as hell in here," Hank muttered, thinking what this would be like after sundown.

Then, all of a sudden, they'd driven out of the trees and into a small clearing. The sight of two more government-issue SUVs parked in front of an old two-story cabin settled some of his initial discomfort.

"Home, sweet home," Richards said.

"What is this place, anyway?" Raines asked.

"One of our safe houses. The proximity to Fourth Dimension is purely a coincidence," he added, before he pulled up and parked.

The front door opened, and two armed men walked out.

"The tall one is Barry. The one in camo is Willis. There are two more agents on duty here, but they're probably up a tree somewhere," he said, then got out as they came to greet him.

"Guys, this is Special Agent Raines, and Special Agent Chavez. Help me unload their gear and then we'll talk."

A short while later, the men were sitting at a table drinking warmed-over coffee, listening to Raines explain the parental kidnapping and the plan to try to get inside the compound.

When Charlie and Wyrick drove into Shawnee Gap, it was immediately obvious how little the town actually was. It had two blocks of Main Street, including a grocery store, a post office, a café, a gas station and about twenty or thirty houses that they could see.

Charlie pulled up to the curb of the post office and parked, then turned to Wyrick. She had her laptop up and was checking a GPS setting for the Fourth Dimension compound.

"Where do we go from here?" Charlie asked.

Wyrick pointed. "We take that blacktop road that forks off this highway and goes up the mountain."

"By any chance would you have contact information on Special Agent Raines? We may not have to look for a place to set up camp if we can settle in at their location."

"I have his cell phone number," Wyrick said, then picked up Charlie's phone and punched in the numbers. "Do you want it on speaker phone?" she asked.

He nodded.

So she hit Call, then put the phone back in the docking system as it began to ring.

CHAPTER FOURTEEN

Hank Raines was reading daily reports from their stakeout when his cell phone rang. He glanced at caller ID and then frowned.

"Holy shit."

"What's wrong?" Chavez asked.

"Charlie Dodge is calling me."

"Who's Charlie Dodge?" Duran asked.

"A private investigator out of Dallas. He's the one who found that Dunleavy dude who went missing up in Denver," Hank said, then answered.

"Hello. Special Agent Raines speaking."

"Agent Raines, this is Charlie Dodge. I'm—"

"I know who you are, Mr. Dodge. How did you get this number, and what do you want?"

"We're good at stuff like that," Charlie said. "And I thought I'd give you a heads-up that my assistant and I are in Shawnee Gap and about to head up the mountain. Tara Bien hired me to find her daughter, and I think you're on a similar trip. Is there any chance we can talk about this?"

Hank was shocked. "How did you find out where Fourth Dimension was located?"

Charlie chuckled. "I told you. We're good at stuff like that. So do we have permission to approach?"

The group had been listening in on the conversation, and Willis gave Hank a thumbs-up.

"Tell him to start watching the blacktop road about five miles up. We'll send a welcome party to guide him in," Willis said.

"I heard that," Charlie said and disconnected.

"Well, now," Hank said, "I've always wanted to meet this man. He said he had his assistant with him. If that's the infamous Wyrick, I can't wait."

"What's so special about him?" Willis asked.

"Her," Hank said. "Word is that she makes the Dallas PD nervous, which makes me curious."

Willis frowned. "Hey, Barry. Let the guys know what's happening so they can guide them in."

"Will do," Barry said and left the room.

"You heard the man," Charlie said as he backed away from the curb. "We have a welcome party waiting for us five miles up."

"And us without a hostess gift. How embarrassing," Wyrick said.

Charlie grinned. A sense of humor was something she was short on, but when she did make jokes, they were spot-on and sarcastic.

As soon as he drove onto the blacktop, he marked the mileage so he'd know when he was getting close, then started up the mountain. He was curious as to what the FBI really knew about Fourth Dimension, and not sure how they were going to receive the information Wyrick got from Peter Long when they interviewed him in prison.

Regardless of what they could tell the Feds, they couldn't act on it without solid proof, but he and Wyrick were not bound by the same restrictions.

Wyrick was tired of the car and ready to be out of it for a while. Knowing they were almost at their destination was a relief, but with a few more miles to go, Wyrick spent the time on her laptop, checking out all of the feelers she kept on Universal Theorem, making sure they'd backed off from stalking her. When she didn't find any indications that they were back on her trail, she logged in to the office site and began answering email.

"I'm reading the office email and business is booming," Wyrick said. "Too bad we're not there to capitalize on the inquiries."

"What do you mean?" Charlie asked.

"A man belonging to one of Dallas's finer families wants you to dig up some dirt on his daughter's college boyfriend."

"I do not tail cheating spouses or dig up dirt. Respond with your usual tact," Charlie said.

Wyrick fired off a four-sentence paragraph and hit Send.

"Done," she said.

"That was fast," Charlie said. "Did you remember the tact?"

"I said, thank you," Wyrick muttered, and kept reading and typing until Charlie began to slow down.

When he did, she looked up. Two armed men dressed in camo were standing in the middle of the road.

"It appears we are overdressed," she said, then logged out as Charlie stopped and rolled down the window.

"Sir, may we see some identification?" one of the men asked.

Charlie flashed his driver's license and his private investigator's license.

"This is Wyrick, my assistant. Special Agent Raines is expecting us," he said.

The man leaned down for an eyes-on-the-passenger look.

"Ma'am," he said, and then took a step back and gave Charlie the instructions. "Drive forward until you see a narrow one-lane road to your left. Turn there and drive until you come out into a clearing. Raines will be waiting for you."

"Thanks," Charlie said and accelerated past them.

Wyrick was watching them in the side mirror. She blinked, and the next time she looked they were gone.

"That's creepy," Wyrick said. "One second they were standing in the road and now they're not. How did they do that so fast?"

Charlie shrugged. "They're just good at not being seen, and speaking of seeing things, here's our road."

He turned left, slowing down to maneuver through the old ruts and potholes at the entrance.

"This place is creepy. It wouldn't take five minutes to get lost up in here," Charlie said as he accelerated slightly up the narrow lane.

Wyrick eyed the forest as they passed through it, glancing often in the side-view mirror. The farther they drove, the less visible the road was behind them, making it look as if they were being swallowed up by the trees.

Then, all of a sudden, they drove out into the clearing.

"Maybe we won't have to pitch tents after all," she said, more than happy to see an old but well-preserved two-story cabin.

Then the front door opened and several men came out onto the porch.

"The tall one is Hank Raines," Wyrick said. "I recognize him from his picture. The one beside him is his partner, Luis Chavez. I don't know who those other two are."

"You mean there's something you don't already know?" Charlie said. "Well, hell, now I'm gonna have to fire you."

"You can't. You don't know the passwords to your own

bank account," Wyrick muttered as Charlie pulled up and stopped.

Charlie grinned. "Play nice with these dudes. We need them."

"I don't play with anyone, but I will remain cordial," Wyrick snapped.

"Good enough," Charlie said.

Wyrick grabbed her laptop as they got out of the Jeep and proceeded toward the cabin.

Hank watched them approaching, thinking their personal appearances were just as impressive as their reputations. For a big man, Charlie Dodge moved with an easy stride, but it was Wyrick who intrigued him. He hadn't expected her to be so tall, or so bald...or without boobs. He saw all this within seconds, and then shifted focus as the duo came up the steps in unison.

Charlie extended his hand. "Special Agent Raines, thank you for seeing us."

"You gained the audience when you said the magic words *Fourth Dimension,*" Hank said. "This is my partner, Luis Chavez. Joining us are Agents Willis and Barry." He led the way inside, where they were introduced to Richards and Duran, whom Wyrick promptly ignored.

The first thing that caught her attention was a mounted elk head hanging over the fireplace. The glassy-eyed stare was distracting, and the massive rack of antlers was obviously what got the poor beast killed. She doubted the Feds had anything to do with the trophy's presence, but out of sympathy for the elk's demise, she glared at them anyway.

Agent Willis was curious about the woman's appearance, and when he saw her staring at the elk head, he offered a little insight.

"That's our mascot, Randy. He came with the cabin. We

thought about calling him Rudolph for obvious reasons, but since he's an elk instead of a reindeer, we went for Randolph, instead."

Willis was smiling as he waited for her reaction to the joke when she turned her head.

"Were you speaking to me?" Wyrick asked.

Willis frowned. She sounded just like his ex-wife.

"Uh… I saw you looking at the elk head and thought I'd fill you in on—"

Wyrick interrupted. "We're looking for a kidnapped child named Jordan Bien. Unless you can fill us in on anything that has to do with her, I have no desire to discuss trophies or trophy hunters."

The room was suddenly silent, save for the shuffling of feet.

Hank Raines stifled a grin. She was living up to her reputation nicely, and poor Willis had just bombed out on trying to start a conversation with the first woman he'd seen in a month.

"Mr. Dodge, if you or your assistant would like to freshen up, there's a bathroom just down that hall to your left. Barry has—"

Wyrick walked out of the room.

"…just started a fresh pot of coffee," Hank added, then looked at Charlie. "Was it something I said?"

Charlie shrugged. "Hard to say, but I'd guess she's just a little road-weary. She took down a wife-beater back in Noland when we stopped to refuel. Delayed us some in getting here."

The agents were stunned.

"What do you mean, took down?" Chavez asked.

"I was outside filling up the Jeep. She heard screams as she walked into the gas station and found a man down on the floor beating the hell out of his ex-wife. She broke a broom over his head, then had to drag him off the woman's body before she could text me for help. Basically, I cuffed him as he was coming to, then waited with her for the cops and ambulance."

"Damn," Chavez muttered.

When they heard her footsteps out in the hall, they stopped talking.

"Okay, boss, what's the plan?" Wyrick asked.

"I think it's time for us to pool our information," Charlie said.

Wyrick followed the men to the long wooden table, then sat down and opened her laptop.

"Fresh coffee if anyone wants some," Barry said.

Charlie glanced at Wyrick, who was already pulling up notes. She shook her head no without looking at him.

Dammit. How does she always know what I'm going to ask? He sighed, then went to get a coffee for himself. When he saw the cookies on the table, he picked up a handful on his way back and set them down near her, just in case.

Wyrick saw them, taking note they were chocolate, and picked one up, took a small bite, and then leaned back in the chair, waiting for the rest of the men to join her.

"You're welcome," Charlie muttered.

Wyrick turned her laptop toward him so he'd have access to the notes she'd just pulled up.

"You're welcome," she said, and when she heard his sigh of disgust, she leaned back and ate the rest of the cookie.

The men took seats at the table, waiting for Charlie to begin, and so he did, beginning with the backstory of Jud and Tara Bien, then the abduction and Tara's desperate attempts to find out where they'd gone, and how she figured out Jud might have taken her to Fourth Dimension.

At this point, Hank interrupted.

"Okay, now I have questions. Was Tara Bien given the location to this site?"

"No," Charlie said. "Wyrick found it."

All eyes turned to the woman sitting beside him.

"Would you enlighten us as to how you made that happen in such a short time?" Hank asked.

"I google a lot," Wyrick said. "I'm good at it."

They were waiting for details, but when she didn't offer them, he pushed for more.

"Could you please elaborate on that?" Hank asked.

Wyrick glanced up at Charlie.

"It's okay. Tell as much as you want," he said.

She shrugged. "It's all a process of common sense and elimination. There were tons of people on psychic websites wanting to join it, but I began searching for names of people who'd left it. I finally found a link to a federal prisoner named Peter Wendell Long, who'd been convicted of kidnapping his niece to take to Fourth Dimension. I told Charlie. He wanted to interview him, so he made some calls to the federal prison in Phoenix where Long is incarcerated, and I flew him there."

Hank glanced at Charlie. "You have your own plane?"

"No. Wyrick owns the chopper, among other things. Working for me is her hobby," he said.

Wyrick glared at him. "I'd hardly call you a hobby. More like a reclamation project."

Charlie grinned.

The men laughed.

Hank was intrigued, but went back to the subject. "So you interviewed Peter Long?"

Charlie nodded.

Hank frowned. "We interviewed him numerous times, but he refused to divulge anything about the group. How did you get him to talk?"

"He didn't," Charlie said.

Chavez frowned. "Then how the hell did you find this location?"

Charlie shrugged. "Where I go, Wyrick goes. She had

previously given me a list of questions to ask him, so I asked. He didn't answer any of them, but I kept going down the list of questions."

"What were the questions?" Chavez asked.

"First I asked if he would just give us the name of the state. Then I asked if Fourth Dimension was in a city or a rural area, and asked for a description of the place. Then I asked for the name of the closest town to it. He answered none of them. The last question was the only one he responded to, and it made him angry. I asked if the group had anything to do with human trafficking and he got very angry…said it was nothing like that, that the group was pure and had good intentions, or something to that effect. His anger ended the interview. They took him back to his cell and we left."

Hank Raines had been watching Wyrick's face the whole time Charlie was speaking. He'd never seen anyone mask all emotion in quite the same way. But she knew something. He could feel it.

"So what am I missing here? He didn't tell you anything and yet here you are. You want our help, then don't give us but half the story."

"The rest of this is for Wyrick to tell, because I came out of that interview with no more info than when I'd gone in," Charlie said.

Wyrick had known this was inevitable and was willing to give up this much of herself so they could save the girls.

"I have a number of skill sets. Research is just one of them. Another one is something like intuition on steroids. With every question Charlie asked, Long immediately thought of the answers. He was picturing them in his mind every time, and I saw them…heard them…however you want to describe it. So the first thing I got was Kentucky, then heavily wooded areas…and the town Shawnee Gap. It wasn't until Charlie asked about human trafficking that I saw the rest of it."

"So it is human trafficking?" Hank asked.

"No. They're not selling anyone," Wyrick said. "They're using them for breeding, with the intention to raise a race of people with psychic powers. And the only way these men get their own bride is to donate a female member from their family bloodline for someone else."

The men took the news like a punch to the gut.

Raines felt all the blood drain from his face, and took a quick sip of his coffee, hoping to settle the sudden nausea bubbling at the back of his throat.

"We have satellite and drone photos of young teens with babies. So are you saying those babies are theirs?" he asked.

Wyrick nodded.

Hank got up and rummaged through some files on a nearby desk and then pulled out some pictures and slid them across the table at Charlie and Wyrick.

"The little girls…the ones who are walking in a line here. Tell me about them."

"Those are the donations. They bring them young, before they've reached puberty, because they want them pure. And they're not allowed to be a wife to one of the men until they've had their first menstrual period, which means an early maturing ten-or eleven-year-old qualifies for breeding, and if there are girls holding babies, it's unlikely any of them are older than fourteen or fifteen."

"Sweet baby Jesus," Willis said, and got up and walked out of the room.

Hank was still struggling. "And you know this because you saw it?"

"I believe we've already spoken to this fact," Wyrick said.

Hank frowned. "Charlie…you believe this, too?"

"I'm gonna try not to take this as an insult on her behalf since you just met her," Charlie snapped. "But she is the pivotal reason we found Carter Dunleavy so quickly when he went missing. I've trusted her with my life more than once, and she's never missed the mark or let me down. She found my lost ass in a Florida swamp a year or so back. I had a dislocated shoulder and a hundred-and-four-degree fever. It was as close to dead as I'd ever been. I didn't have anything to signal anyone with, and the battery was long gone in my cell phone. I finally came out of my fever enough to tie my shirt to a tree branch hanging over a bayou. Hours passed, and just when I was about to give up all hope, she was there. I cannot describe the sense of relief I felt when I saw that chopper flying treetop level down that bayou and her at the controls. I don't remember much after that," Charlie said.

"Damn," Hank said. "Ma'am, my apologies."

"I don't need them," Wyrick said. "What do you need from us to get a search warrant?"

"We've been hoping for some photos of the girls that were sharp enough to use for facial recognition. If we could match any of them to the ones in the missing children database, we could get the warrants we need."

Wyrick immediately thought of her remote control plane. It was a prototype she'd made during chemo treatments for something to do, thinking it might be the next generation of drones, but then she'd gotten well and packed it away. She wondered why they hadn't used drones, then Charlie asked the question for her.

"What about using drones? What about giving cameras to the men you have on stakeout?" Charlie asked. "Trees are everywhere. Climb one and wait for the opportunity."

Barry had been noticeably silent until now.

"Don't think we haven't tried, but drones couldn't tell us any more than we already know from satellite imaging. And we climbed the tallest trees we could get to without being seen, but the trees are so damn thick we couldn't get a clear view of much of anything. And if we moved closer, even with a telescopic lens on the camera, the angles are all wrong. Whoever designed that compound knew how to maintain secrecy."

Wyrick needed to do some research before she said anything else. "I need a place to work," she said.

"You can use this table," Hank said.

Wyrick edited her first comment. "A private place to work."

Hank waved that away. "There are a couple of spare rooms upstairs. You're both welcome to use them while you're here."

"May I use your Wi-Fi signal, or do I need to use my satellite feed?" Wyrick asked.

Once again, the men were speechless.

"You have your own satellite?" Chavez said.

"Not exactly. Just an agreement that I can use one in particular at my discretion," Wyrick said. "I assure you it's all on the up-and-up."

"Damn, Charlie, you must be one generous employer," Hank said.

Charlie shook his head. "She's in a whole other tax bracket of her own."

Wyrick didn't want them digging into her background, and gave them just enough to satisfy their need to snoop.

"I have businesses. One of my more lucrative ones is designing and creating computer games. Now, about that Wi-Fi?"

"Yes, feel free," Hank said.

"Are your bags in the car?" Barry asked.

"Yes," Charlie said, and when Wyrick started to get up, he stopped her. "You can have the rest of my cookies. We'll get the bags, and you're welcome."

She ignored the offer until he went out the door, then she folded the rest of them up in the paper napkin to take upstairs.

Tara had gone out to get the mail and was on her way back inside when her phone began to ring. She pulled it out of her pocket, praying it would be Charlie with news, but it came up caller ID unknown.

"Hello?"

"Tara, it's me, Jud."

She gasped and then started screaming. "You sorry bastard! Where's my baby? Where's Jordan? I want to talk to her now! Put her on the phone!"

He winced. "I deserve every name you can call me, but just listen to me. I don't have her anymore, and I need your help."

And as he began to explain, Tara realized every horror she'd ever imagined her daughter suffering wasn't even close to the truth, and now she was crying and shouting.

"You took Jordan to some cult in the mountains of Kentucky so you could get married? That makes no sense."

Jud sighed. "It was all for the good of humanity," he said. "I had to bring a Sprite to get a Sprite."

"What the hell are Sprites? And what does that have to do with you getting married? You're lying to me. Where's Jordan?"

"Sprites are the girls waiting to be married. They have to be from the male's bloodline in hopes of passing along the psychic DNA to their children, and—"

"You took our baby to marry her off to some man? You did not do that! I can't believe you would be that crazy! I can't believe you could be that heartless! I don't know you anymore. You are a certified idiot and a criminal, to boot! Oh God. Oh my God," Tara moaned and then started sobbing.

Now Jud was crying. "I'm sorry. I'm so sorry," he kept saying.

Tara was shaking so hard she kept dropping the phone, and then she finally got it on speaker and left it in her lap.

"You're not sorry. You are a selfish bastard...a pervert! You gave our daughter away to a cult so you could marry someone else's child? And then they kicked you out and you left her there? Is that right? Is that what you did?"

"Yes, that was my original plan, but then I was sorry. It wasn't how I thought it would be. And when I argued with the Master, it angered him. He ordered me to leave, and refused to let Jordan go with me. I didn't want to leave, but I was afraid if I didn't he would kill me, and then Jordan would still be there and no one would know where she was. She is his insurance that I won't tell. He threatened to kill her if I talked about Fourth Dimension, but I had to get help. You're a lawyer. I thought you would—"

Tara swallowed back angry tears, then took a deep breath.

"Just shut up and listen. I already hired help. His name is Charlie Dodge and he's on the job. Take down this number and call it. Tell Charlie who you are and then do every fucking thing he says, or I will find you and kill you, myself. Do you understand?"

"Yes, yes, I understand," Jud said.

"You got our baby into this, now you get her out. And don't let her down or I'll send Charlie after you, and you don't want that to happen. I'm going to call him right now and tell him to expect your call. Give me three minutes."

"Yes, yes, I will, and I won't let you down. I promise," Jud said. "I'll get Jordan out of there or die trying."

CHAPTER FIFTEEN

Charlie was walking back into the cabin when his cell phone rang. He dropped the bag he was carrying to answer it, and then saw who it was from.

"It's Tara Bien," Charlie said.

The agents all stopped.

Wyrick heard Charlie from the other room and joined them as he answered.

"Hello, Tara, this is Charlie."

Tara was still crying, trying to breathe between sobs.

"Jud just called me. He took Jordan to Kentucky to that cult—to Fourth Dimension. He got kicked out and they wouldn't let him take her. He took her there as some kind of donation to the cult, so he could marry someone else's child. He's turned into a monster. They're crazy. They're all crazy. Their intention is to breed a race of psychics. He said Jordan is in danger. He's going to call you in a couple of minutes. I don't know where you are, but find him. He can help you get Jordan out of that place. He knows where it is, and is willing to do anything."

"We know where it is, too," Charlie said. "We're already here and we're with the FBI. Is Jud still in Kentucky?"

"I don't know," she said and then started crying harder. "I'm taking the next plane I can get to Louisville," Tara said.

"No, Lexington is closer, but I don't think that's a good idea."

"Not one part of this was a good idea, and yet my daughter became a victim of this madness anyway. I will let you know when I land. It may be tomorrow before I can get a flight out, but I'm coming. I'll be in touch."

She hung up in his ear.

Charlie looked up. "Hank, I think you're about to get the physical evidence you need to get warrants. That was Tara Bien. Jud just called her in a panic. He got kicked out of the group, and they kept his daughter for insurance. He is willing to do whatever it takes to get Jordan out."

"Ah man...this is bad news for the kid, and good news for us," Hank said. "But will he verify what Wyrick told us?"

"He already confessed it to his wife, and just told her he'll say or do anything he needs to do to get Jordan out."

"Find out where he is," Hank said. "We'll pick him up and get him here. No need giving him a chance to change his mind and back out."

Charlie nodded. Then his phone rang again.

"It's him," Charlie said and then answered. "Charlie Dodge."

"Mr. Dodge, my name is Jud Bien, and I need your help."

"I just spoke to Tara," Charlie said. "Where are you?"

"Berea, Kentucky. Where are you? Where can I meet you?" Jud asked.

"You're in Berea? Where are you staying?" Charlie asked, knowing the Feds would jump on the location.

"I'm in a Red Roof Inn, but I'll drive anywhere to meet you, just tell me where."

"The Red Roof Inn?" Charlie repeated. "Just stay there. You'll be met and brought to me. Understand?"

Hank gave him a thumbs-up and left the room on the run.

"Yes, yes, I understand," Jud said. "Thank you. I'll do anything it takes to get my daughter out of there and back home with Tara. I'm sorry. I'm so sorry."

After all the drama about her concern about the safety of her food, Jordan couldn't eat much. The pain and swelling in her face and jaws were severe, and when they went back to the dormitory, she was hurting so badly that she crawled onto her bed and lay down. She hadn't been there long when she saw the other girls getting brooms and mops. She got back up.

"What's happening?" she asked.

"It's cleaning day," Randi said.

"What do I do?" Jordan asked.

"I think you should rest. You don't look so good," Katie said.

"I agree," Barbie added. The rest of the girls echoed the decision and sent Jordan back to bed.

She didn't have it in her to argue anymore. The standoff at breakfast had taken energy she didn't have.

"Maybe you should take one of those pain pills," Randi suggested.

Jordan shook her head. "I don't trust anyone not to kill me," she said, then rolled over on her side and closed her eyes.

Katie unfolded the blanket at the foot of Jordan's bed, covered her up and patted her shoulder. "Mother always said sleep was good for healing," she said, then teared up just saying the name.

Wyrick set up a little workstation in the bedroom she'd been given, and had been going through satellite images on her own when she glanced at the clock, then went looking for Agent Raines.

"I have a question," she said.

"Yes, ma'am. Ask away," Hank said.

"Those pictures you showed us. The ones of the girls walking across the compound in a line. Are there set times that takes place?"

"I would guess mealtimes, but we can check the time on the photos we captured. Come with me," he said and took her into their com center.

He sat down at a computer, logged on and pulled up a file.

"May I?" she asked, as she stepped up behind him.

"Yes, these don't need security clearance to view," he said.

Wyrick thought of the level of security clearance she'd had at Universal Theorem but kept silent. The less they knew about her connection to that place, the better off she and Charlie were for getting what they needed.

"Okay, here are quite a few," Hank said. "8:04 a.m. 8:10 a.m. 8:00 a.m., and so it goes, so these would be breakfast, and it appears they do have a set time for that meal."

"What about lunch? Check that out for me, please," Wyrick asked.

Hank scrolled through photos and then stopped. "These are all during the noon hour. There's 11:55 a.m. And 12:05 p.m. 12:10 p.m. 12:02 p.m. Do you need to see dinner times?"

"No, but I have one more question. What happened when you flew drones over the compound?"

"I was told they were too high up to get anything but the layout of the compound, which is what we already had with satellite images. Why do you ask?"

"You wanted pictures of the girls' faces to run through the missing children database, and I brought something that might help make that happen," she said.

Hank smiled. "Thank you, but what we use is state of the art. I doubt you'd have anything—"

"Your doubt is misplaced," Wyrick said, before leaving to go back upstairs and knock on Charlie's door. "If you're asleep, wake up," she said and knocked again.

Charlie came to the door, buttoning up a clean shirt. "What's up?"

"I need the keys to the Jeep. There's something in it I need," she said.

He pivoted in the doorway, ran back to get his car keys and then headed downstairs. Wyrick ducked back in her room to get her laptop and followed him.

"What's going on?" Willis asked as he saw them coming down the stairs.

"Just getting some stuff for Wyrick," Charlie said.

Hank came out of the com center and followed them out.

Charlie unlocked the Jeep.

"What all do you need?" he asked.

Wyrick pointed to a box and a small bag. "Those, and bring them to the porch."

Barry came out from behind the cabin with Chavez beside him.

"What's going on?" he asked.

Willis shrugged.

Charlie put everything down on the table, then watched as Wyrick began pulling stuff out.

"Now what?" he asked.

"I have a new kind of drone," she said. "We're going to get pictures of the girls' faces with it."

"No," Hank said. "That will alert them to the fact they're under surveillance and might cause them to move to another location."

"Only it won't," Wyrick said. "I need someone to alert me as to when the girls are being marched across the compound."

"I can verify that for you with my men on recon," Hank said.

"It's almost twelve," Wyrick said. "I'm putting this in the air. You said we're a mile from the compound, so the timing is going to be tight. Just tell them to let you know when the girls are coming out and I'll send it up."

Willis ran inside to the com center to deliver the message as she pulled out the plane. When she did, the men stared and moved closer. Except for the inner workings of the camera, both the case it was in and the plane were nearly invisible.

"What is that, plastic?" Hank asked.

"Sort of," Wyrick said and dug through her bag until she found a small plastic pouch full of gold and silver confetti. She turned the plane upside down, opened a little hatch in the bottom and then handed it to Charlie.

"Hold this for me, please," she said, poured the confetti into the belly of the plane and closed the hatch. She pulled up a program on her laptop, clicked a few keys, and then took the plane from Charlie and handed him the laptop. "Okay... you guys can see what the camera sees in real time as it's recording."

Then she grabbed the plane and her controls, and moved out into the yard, with Hank right behind her.

The men weren't convinced in any way that this was a viable option as they watched the plane take off, and it took them a few seconds to realize it was silent.

"It's not making any noise," Hank said.

"Solar powered. The better to sneak with," Wyrick muttered.

Her gaze was on the little screen in front of her as she aimed the tiny plane up the mountain, using the open road below it as her guideline.

All of a sudden Willis came running, carrying a walkie-talkie.

"Some men inside the compound are on their way to get the girls," he said.

Wyrick kept her eyes on the screen, seeing the ground and
the trees beneath the small plane, but still no walls. Remembering the layout of the compound from the aerial photos
she'd seen, she aimed the plane just slightly to the left and almost immediately saw it coming up.

The walkie-talkie squawked again. "The girls are coming out."

"Just what I wanted to hear," Wyrick said, and flew the
plane over the wall.

"There they come," Charlie said, as a long line of young
girls came out of a building in a single file. He was trying to
catch sight of Jordan Bien, but from the angle of the camera
he couldn't see their faces.

Wyrick lined the plane's flight path right over the girls'
heads and pressed a button on her controls.

"Wait...what's that?" Barry asked, as they began seeing
sparkles drifting down over the girls.

Charlie grinned. "I'll be damned. It's the confetti. And
look! The girls are looking up, just like you wanted them
to do."

At that point, Wyrick turned the plane around and flew it
back over the girls, knowing the camera was catching every
upturned face in different expressions of delight.

They could all see the guards' confusion as the confetti
began floating through the air, but by the time they thought
to look up, the plane was over the wall and on the way back.

Hank was embarrassed that the woman had accomplished
this so easily. He wanted access to that plane and her controls.

Then Charlie looked up and pointed.

"Hey, Wyrick, here comes your plane."

"I see it," she said, but before she could move, Hank was
already running toward it. She frowned, and when she saw
the expression on his face as he started back with it, she went
to meet him and took it out of his hands.

"I want to check this out," Hank said. "We need this to—"

Wyrick's eyes flashed angrily. "We? We as in the federal government? Oh hell no. I already hold the patents on every aspect of this, along with a patent on the formula for the material with which the plane is made. You people aren't getting your hands on it. All you ever want to do is turn things into weapons."

Hank had no comeback for her accusations and watched her walk away.

Still pissed, Wyrick packed up the plane and controls back in the box and took it into the cabin.

"I'll be right back," she said and took it up to her room. She started to leave, then changed her mind and got the bag with her clothes out of the closet. She dumped everything on her bed, then opened the box and put the plane and the controls in her clothes bag. She put a couple of shirts on top of it, then put the rest of her clothes in the box. Then she placed the bag back in the closet and left the box at the end of her bed before going downstairs.

"Everything okay?" Charlie asked as he handed her back the laptop.

"Yes. Just give me a few minutes and I'll get everything we need."

"We need the footage from the camera," Hank said.

Wyrick was already into her system, her eyes focused on the screen as she worked.

"You need to know who the girls are," she said. "Give me a few minutes."

The agents looked at each other and frowned. And since Hank was the one who'd given them permission to be here, he felt obligated to set their boundaries.

"I think the two of you have mistaken your role in this," he said. "We allowed you to come here to exchange information, but you do not have permission to—"

Charlie interrupted. "I don't need your permission to go in after Jordan Bien. But after I found out what was really happening in that compound, I made a vow to myself that I was bringing the rest of the girls home, too. You people have had months to deal with this and knew nothing of what was happening until we got here. I have no idea what security levels you're all at, but I can promise you, Wyrick's security clearance tops it. I know her value and honor it. And I know her honesty, and value that more. So back the fuck off and let her do what she does best. Or… I can just make a call to the nearest news station and drop a truth bomb about the workings of Fourth Dimension in their laps, and see how long it takes you to act then."

None of them liked being called down, but they couldn't argue with the truth of what he'd said.

"I'm going to see if they've picked Jud Bien up yet," Barry said and disappeared into their com center.

Wyrick was oblivious now to the undercurrents around her.

Her fingers were flying over the keys, pausing only to click the mouse as she moved from window to window.

But Hank wasn't satisfied. "Dammit, Charlie. There's a reason we play by the rules in our world. What she's doing might nullify the evidence we collect to use against them in court."

Wyrick paused and glared at them, sarcasm dripping from every word.

"Technically, none of the film from my camera belongs to the FBI. Technically, what I'm doing, I'm doing for my boss, who came here at the behest of a client. Technically, everything I'm doing, I'm doing for him, so if he wishes to share evidence with you, that's his business. And technically, your satellite images of the compound show you were spying on them. And technically, Charlie Dodge has a license to spy on people, too. So do you want to take down that cult and save those girls, or do you want to go to sleep tonight knowing those little girls are being raped by grown men and forced to have their babies? Are you afraid to allow us to help for fear someone else will get the glory? If that's your vibe, Chicken Little, why don't you go ahead and wait for the sky to fall? Or wait a few minutes."

Then she glanced at Charlie. "Boss, it's your call."

"Do your thing," he said, and gave Hank Raines a look that was unmistakable to misinterpret. Charlie was not only surprised by the Feds' attitudes, but they were pissing him off.

Wyrick began separating the faces of the girls on the film into individual photos. Each time she had a new photo, she uploaded it into the national database for missing children.

The girls didn't appear to have been starved or beaten, and they looked clean and healthy. It said nothing for the fact that they'd been turned into what amounted to slaves, but that would soon be rectified.

But then everything changed when she enlarged the next girl's face. The swollen lips, the black eye and bruising all over her face were shocking.

"Charlie, we just found Jordan Bien," she said.

Charlie headed straight for the table where Wyrick was working, and when he saw the photo, he groaned.

"What the hell did they do to her?" he asked.

"What happened?" Hank said and immediately circled the table to look for himself. "Oh my God. Do they all look like that?" he asked.

"No," Wyrick said.

"And this is why delay is not possible for the girl we came to save," Charlie added.

Wyrick continued to upload the rest of the pictures into the database, but as soon as she was finished, she leaned back.

"I'm having withdrawals. Does anyone here drink Pepsi?"

"I do," Willis said. "May I bring you one?"

"Yes," Wyrick said. She was thinking about getting a candy bar from the stash she'd brought with her, when her computer signaled a hit by shouting, "Hallelujah!"

"What was that?" Hank asked.

"The sweet sound of success," she said, pointing to the screen. "There's your first identification. A girl named Barbara June, aka Barbie, Lawson."

Hank's eyes widened. "That was fast. How did you—"

"May I link to your printer?" Wyrick asked.

Hank sighed. "Just a second and I'll get you the—"

"No need," Wyrick said, slipped into a new window and found the printer. She added the connection to her setup and hit Print.

As she continued to get more hits, she kept printing them out. When the last one came through, she hit Print and then threw up her hands.

"Okay, boss, that's the last one," she said.

A few moments later, Barry came out of the com center carrying a sheaf of papers.

"Uh…these just came through the printer, but I don't know who —"

"They belong to Charlie," Wyrick said.

As soon as Barry handed them over, Charlie spread them out on the table.

"How many did you identify out of the photos that went through the database?" Hank asked.

"All of them," Wyrick said. "But keep in mind, I didn't have any way to identify the others who are already married, and Jordan isn't in the database for obvious reasons."

The agents crowded around, eyeing the photos.

"It usually takes longer to get IDs through the database," Barry said.

"What's that supposed to mean?" Charlie said.

Hank shrugged. "Identifying all of the girls that fast is—"

"I don't make errors," Wyrick said, then stood up, her face devoid of expression as she took her laptop and walked out of the room.

Charlie was furious.

"You're assholes. All of you. Or is it because a woman just showed you up? Do your damn job and don't get in her face again. You want to be pissed at someone? You can be pissed at me. You want to make digs about someone's abilities, challenge mine. But while you're trying to decide who has the biggest balls, let me know when you get Bien picked up. I got hired to find him, and I'm the one he's willing to talk to. The glory of taking down this cult is all yours, and you would be doing me a favor if our names were never mentioned. We came after one girl, and her father is going to help us get to her. The rest of them are yours to rescue and run before the cameras, but you don't get access to Jordan Bien. You don't get to parade her through the media. Understand?" He pointed at the photos. "There's the evidence you need to get your warrants," he said and walked out, leaving the printouts behind.

They could hear the solid thud of his footsteps as he strode across the wooden floors and then up the stairs.

"He's pissed," Willis said.

"Ya think?" Hank muttered as he gathered up the printouts. "Chavez, you and Willis get the warrants we need. After those are in our hands, we'll call in for backup. We have to have total surprise on our side to make this happen without giving them time to hurt anyone, or destroy their records."

Chavez and Willis both left the room in tandem, leaving Barry behind with Hank.

"Is there any news on Jud Bien?" Hank asked.

"I know we sent people to pick him up. We haven't heard anything back yet, but I'll check," Barry said and left.

Jud had never unpacked, but now that he knew he was going back, he decided to shower and change while he was waiting. He'd forgotten to ask where they wanted him to meet them. If he was supposed to be outside, or waiting in his room, then remembered he was dealing with people who found criminals for a living. They'd find him soon enough. He showered and shaved, then changed into clean clothes before heading downstairs to check out.

It was just after 12:00 noon, and he hadn't eaten since last night, so he stopped in the main lobby at a coffee bar for a sweet roll and some coffee, and sat down to eat.

People-watching had always been something he enjoyed, but today he saw all of them as having one thing in common, one that he was about to lose—his freedom. And it was no more than he deserved.

He continued eating, finished off his coffee and was thinking about going to get another cup to go when he began hearing what sounded like a helicopter over the motel.

His first thought was that some kind of Medi-Flight chopper was passing over, but it kept getting louder instead of fading away, and that was when it hit him.

They're here for me.

He tossed his cup and napkin in the garbage, then picked up his bag and walked outside.

Police cars were everywhere, blocking off traffic so that the chopper could safely land in the hotel parking lot. He watched as it landed, then saw a couple of men get out of the chopper and start toward the hotel.

FBI. He recognized the look.

His heart started pounding as he shifted his suitcase from one hand to the other. Then a half dozen policemen came out of their cruisers, accompanying the agents.

In that moment, he realized how far away from decency he'd fallen, and that his life was never going to be the same. He had the feeling he was going to pee himself, and then remembered Jordan, and the feeling went away. His fear was nothing compared to what he'd done to her, and he could only imagine how frightened she was now on her own.

The agents stopped in front of him.

"Sir, may we see some identification?"

Jud took out his driver's license. "I'm Jud Bien. I'm the man you came for."

They took the wallet out of his hands, patted him down for weapons and then cuffed him. He hadn't expected that, but when he thought about it, he guessed they didn't want to take the chance that he'd change his mind and run.

"Come with us," the agents said and then took him by the arms to lead him toward the chopper.

Within minutes he was buckled in and they were in the air. He looked down as they were flying away and saw his car.

He looked at the agent beside him. "What will happen to my car?"

The agent stared at him a moment before he answered. "I have no idea. We're just following orders."

"How long will it take to get to Shawnee Gap?" Jud asked.

"A little over an hour as the crow flies," the agent said, and at that point, Jud leaned back and closed his eyes.

He didn't blame him for staring. What he'd done was the antithesis of decency. It occurred to him then that he should have let Tara know he'd called, but he hadn't done that. He wanted her to know that he'd kept his word, and then let it go. Nothing mattered now except getting Jordan out alive.

CHAPTER SIXTEEN

While ruffled feathers and hot tempers were settling among Charlie and the agents at the cabin, the confetti that had fallen on the girls was causing something of a stir within the compound. The girls were still giggling and picking it out of each other's hair as they entered the dining hall. Normally, they entered in silence and ate their meals the same way, so their giggles were surprising enough to raise eyebrows among the rest of the diners.

The only other people who were aware it had happened were the two Archangels who'd been a distance behind them, but when Thomas turned around and saw the girls still excited as they sat down, and poking around in each other's hair, he frowned.

"What's going on here?" he demanded.

"Something fell out of the sky on them," one of the Archangels said. "It looked like glitter."

Thomas frowned. "Glitter fell on them?"

"It was in the air and drifted down on their heads," he explained.

"And you saw this?" Thomas asked.

"I saw it in the air above their heads and then it fell in their hair," he repeated.

"Let me see!" Thomas demanded and went from girl to girl, poking through their hair and seeing the same bits of gold and silver confetti.

When he got to Jordan, he jammed his fingers straight into the thick dark length and right into the cut on the back of her head before he remembered she'd been injured there.

"Ow! That hurts!" Jordan cried and covered the back of her head with both hands.

"Sorry," Thomas said. "I forgot you're injured."

The casual way he said it, like it really wasn't a thing to be concerned about, not only hurt her feelings but made her mad. And because she was supposed to stay seated, she defied the rules again and stood, making him look at her face.

"I look like this and you forgot? You call yourselves Archangels, but you're all devils to me. You think being psychic makes you too special for rules and laws. It's glitter. It blew in our hair. We had nothing to do with it."

"Sit down and be quiet," Thomas said and yanked her by the arm.

Her head was still throbbing where he'd poked her, and when she let go of it, there was blood on the palm of her hand.

She shoved her hand in his face.

"You made that cut on the back of my head start bleeding again." And then her voice broke. "Why can't you people just leave me alone?"

She dropped back onto the bench, her shoulders slumped in a moment of complete defeat.

Thomas sighed. Even if she was a pain in the ass, he guessed she was scared, especially since her father was no longer on the premises. "I'm sincerely sorry," Thomas said. "I did not intend to hurt you."

"You pulled my hair," Katie said.

"You pulled mine, too," Randi said.

"It hurt when you poked my head, but I was afraid to tell you," Barbie whispered.

Thomas frowned, then turned around and walked out of the dining hall to report the incident to the Master.

Jordan Bien was not only a problem for Fourth Dimension, but she was influencing the other girls enough that they were beginning to defy the rules, too.

Aaron was on his way out of his residence when he saw Archangel Thomas coming toward him, and he could tell by the look on his face that he was troubled.

Aaron stopped. Clasping his hands together in a gesture of what was meant to be tranquility, he rested them on the curve of his belly.

"Master, there was an incident involving the Sprites," Thomas said, approaching.

Aaron frowned. "How so?"

"They arrived in the dining hall with some kind of shiny confetti in their hair. They said it fell out of the sky. I didn't believe them until one of my helpers verified he'd seen it falling, too."

"Were they harmed?" Aaron asked.

Thomas sighed. "Not by the confetti, but I looked at every girl's hair to verify the substance, and I guess I was too rough with Jordan Bien. I caused her head to start bleeding again."

Aaron frowned. All that did was remind everyone he was the one who'd caused the initial wound.

"How did she react?" Aaron asked.

"In pain, defiant, and then somewhat defeated. But some of the other girls then complained I'd been too rough with them, too, claiming I'd pulled their hair. Jordan is a bad influence on the girls. This is the second time they've stood up for her."

Aaron frowned. "I'll check the security cameras. In the meantime, please send someone to get me some samples. There should be evidence of it on the ground where they were walking. And in the future, try not to antagonize that girl. Without her father in residence, I believe she will eventually calm down."

"Yes, Master," Thomas said and hastened to obey the orders.

Instead of going to lunch, Aaron went back to look at the security footage. His houseman met him at the door.

"Master, is something wrong?"

"I need to check the security cameras. Please ask one of the cooks to send my meal to the house."

"Yes, Master," Robert said.

Confident his orders would be carried out, Aaron headed for the security center. He unlocked the door and went straight to the bank of computer screens, one for each camera on the premises, and went to the screen overlooking the Sprites' dormitory. He rewound it to the time line as the girls were first emerging. He was watching their faces for signs of some kind of deceit but saw nothing out of the ordinary. Just the usual, quiet demeanor he expected from them.

It took a couple of seconds for him to see something glittering in the air above their heads, but he couldn't tell where it had come from. Even though he rewound the footage a few more times to specifically watch the sky instead of the girls, all he saw were a couple of birds flying past the camera. There was nothing out of the ordinary to explain what had happened.

Satisfied that it was something that had been blown in by the wind, he moved to a hidden camera he'd had installed in the Sprites' shower and rewound the recording to this morning. Since he'd taken a vow of celibacy to serve as Master, he often satisfied his sexual lusts by viewing the nubile young bodies all soapy and wet. He was considering it again, when he heard Robert call out that his food had arrived. Regretting the missed opportunity for an orgasm, he settled for a meal instead and quickly left the room, locking the door behind him as Robert appeared in the hall, carrying a tray.

"I'll eat my meal on the back verandah, and I'd like a glass of iced tea to go with it," Aaron said.

Robert carried the tray through the house and placed it outside as ordered.

Aaron followed, his mouth watering from the aroma of meatloaf and vegetables. He unfolded a large cloth napkin and draped it across his lap, then lowered his head and blessed his food before taking the first bite. As always, he savored the texture of what was in his mouth as much as he did the taste of the spices that seasoned it. A bite of meatloaf, then the velvet texture of mashed potatoes, followed by the slight crunch of buttered carrots—for Aaron, each was a delight on its own. He'd never associated the concept of his carnal appetite as a mirror trait to his appetite for food. They were just part of who he was.

Robert emerged from the house with an ice-filled glass and a pitcher of cold sweet tea and set them down on the table.

Aaron waved him away. "I'll pour, and thank you, Robert. That will be all. Go along to the dining hall and enjoy your lunch. And tell cook the food is delicious."

Robert smiled. "Yes, Master, I will."

Jud had been watching the panorama of the geography below the chopper for some time now, wondering where he was being taken to meet Charlie Dodge. But when he began recognizing the old highway that ran through Shawnee Gap, he was surprised. The chopper appeared to be following it like a map.

A few moments later he saw a black SUV in the highway

ahead, and when the chopper began to lower altitude, he realized they were going to land.

"Why are we landing here?" Jud asked.

"The trees… There's no place else to drop you off," the
agent said.

"Oh. Right. Are you going to remove the cuffs?"

"That's for the others to decide," he replied.

Jud's stomach did a little flip-flop as the chopper's descent
turned into a sudden drop, and moments later, they were
down.

He was fumbling with the seat belt when the door slid
open, revealing two armed men in camo. The agent beside
him released the seat belt, freeing him for the men to pull
him out of the chopper.

"My bag!" Jud cried.

Someone tossed it out of the chopper. One of the men
grabbed it midair and then they rushed him into their vehicle.

The windows were dark, and as they put him into the back
seat and were buckling him in, the chopper lifted off and
quickly flew out of sight.

Hank went upstairs to let Charlie know they'd picked Bien
up and were on their way there. But when he knocked on
Charlie's door, he didn't answer. He didn't want to confront
Wyrick again, but he was given no choice and knocked on
hers, instead.

When Charlie opened the door, he could see Wyrick at
work near the window.

"Just wanted to let you know they picked Bien up. It won't
take much over an hour for them to get here."

Charlie nodded. "We'll need that satellite photo you have
of the compound."

"Right. I'll pull it," Hank said. "We made sandwiches.
Thought you might want something to eat."

"We'll be down in a bit," Charlie said and closed the door.

Hank sighed, then turned around and went back downstairs. He hated the hard feelings hanging between them but felt justified in everything he'd said and done.

Charlie was just as bothered by the tension between them, but his allegiance was to Wyrick and the girl they'd come to rescue. The last time he'd been this antsy, they'd been looking for a little boy. Lost kids didn't sit well with Charlie.

Wyrick had linked a second computer to her laptop and was using both of them to dig through the security setup at Fourth Dimension. She was looking for ways to shut it down without triggering an alarm, and to disable the electric fencing surrounding the compound. She'd overheard Hank Raines talking to the other agents about getting some men over the walls at the back of the compound before the main force came in through the gate, and she needed to make sure everything was offline before that happened. Hopefully, Jud Bien would be able to answer some of the questions. Otherwise, it was likely to be a long night.

She was so focused on what she was doing that she didn't even hear the knock on her door until Charlie got up to answer it. She heard Hank Raines's voice, then something about Jud Bien, then sandwiches. When Charlie shut the door, she stood up.

"They invited us to eat?"

"Unless you'd rather have one of the MREs we brought," he said.

"Shut your mouth," Wyrick said, which made Charlie grin.

"I'm going back to my room to wash up," Charlie said. "I'll meet you downstairs...unless you don't want to go back into enemy territory unescorted."

Her snort of disgust made him chuckle.

"I have real enemies in my life," Wyrick said. "The only problem the bunch downstairs has is too much testosterone."

Charlie knew she was right. As soon as he got in his room, he tried to call Tara to let her know they'd picked up her ex. But when she didn't answer, he sent her a text instead.

A few minutes later, he walked into the kitchen and noticed Wyrick had changed from the dark T-shirt she'd been wearing to a white tank top. He sighed. She'd pulled out the big guns her own way by making them see her in a whole new light. That dragon tattoo where her breasts used to be was an in-your-face statement impossible to miss. And the fact that they could easily see the beast coiled around her body, as well, made it better.

Wyrick heard him coming. She knew the measured stride of his steps like she knew her own heartbeat. And she knew he'd get why she'd changed shirts. She just didn't want to look at him and see empathy, so she kept building her sandwich, making sure there was mustard on both pieces of bread before she added any cold cuts.

Willis looked up, then offered Charlie a beer.

Charlie took it, nodding his thanks, and then moved to the island where everything was laid out. He caught the men staring at Wyrick more than once as he was fixing his plate, and by the time he carried it into the other room and sat down at the table with them, he knew she'd made her point. Their behavior toward her had shifted from treating her as an outsider to all-out admiration for the badass she was, and she was silently basking in it.

Right now they were all in a holding pattern, waiting for search warrants and arrest warrants. Identifying the children being kept there had been the break they needed to legally get in. But it was the safety issue that concerned them most. There wasn't an agent in the entire division of the FBI who didn't remember Waco, Texas, and the disaster with David Koresh and the Branch Davidians. No one wanted another debacle like that to happen.

Most of them were through with eating and were beginning to clean up when Hank Raines's phone signaled a text.

He checked it, then looked up.

"We have Jud Bien. They should be here within the next ten minutes to fifteen minutes."

Wyrick got up from the table and carried her things into the kitchen, dumping paper plates and cups. She then headed down the hall to the bathroom to wash the smell of mustard off her hands.

Charlie took his things to the trash, and then walked to the windows at the front of the main room to watch for their arrival. He was braced for the next step in their quest to get Jordan Bien home.

Wyrick had just turned off the water in the bathroom and was drying her hands when she realized she was hearing footsteps overhead. It took a few moments for her to realize someone was in her room and she knew it wasn't Charlie.

The plane! They were still determined to get their hands on it, to examine the material she'd used that made it virtually invisible in flight.

She slipped out and quietly moved up the stairs. Just as she reached the top landing, she saw Willis come out of her room carrying the box, then go down the hall to another room and slip inside.

She waited, motionless. *Wonder how long it's going to take him to realize he's been had?*

A few seconds passed, and then all of a sudden he came flying out of his room and darted back into her room.

Wyrick took off toward her room, then stopped a few yards short and waited, her hands on her hips, her feet apart.

Seconds later, Willis emerged and then stopped.

"Uh, I was—"

"I guess my underwear didn't fit?"

A dark flush spread up his neck onto his face.

"So when the Feds don't get what they want, they just steal it? Is that how it works now?" she asked.

"I follow orders," Willis said.

"Well, here are some new ones," Wyrick said, jabbing her finger sharply into his chest. "Don't fuck with my stuff again unless you want Charlie Dodge in your face. And you can pass that along to the boys in the band."

Willis didn't have an argument that would hold water. He didn't take orders from civilians, but she'd just caught him trying to steal her property. What bugged him most was that she'd expected it and set a trap they fell for. There was a lot beneath the surface of this woman besides that crazy dragon tattoo, that was for sure. He didn't answer her but walked past her without arguing.

She went into her bedroom and locked the door, then dumped her clothes out on the box, got her bag from the closet and switched everything back to the way it originally was, then took the box with the plane into Charlie's room and put it in his closet.

Downstairs, Charlie heard the sound of running feet and turned. He saw Willis's face and the haste with which he was descending and wondered what was going on. Then a couple of minutes later, Wyrick came sauntering down the stairs.

He raised an eyebrow.

She shook her head.

He let it go—for now.

"Here they come," Hank said.

Charlie looked out the window as a black SUV pulled up to the house. He recognized the men in camo who got out, and then saw Jud Bien emerge from the back seat in cuffs.

He walked out onto the porch, making no attempt to hide his disgust. The agents unlocked the cuffs, and Charlie took Jud by the arm and walked him inside.

"Thank you for helping," Jud said.

Charlie glared. "I'm not helping you. I'm helping Tara get her daughter back. And just so you know, we already know what Fourth Dimension is about. We know all of it, so don't lie about anything. What we need from you is the layout inside the compound. How the security system is set up, and the daily routine. We also need to know where the married couples live, and their routines, as well. Understand?"

"Yes, yes, I understand," Jud said.

Wyrick slid into a chair across the table from Jud and opened her laptop.

The others sat down around the table, blocking him in on both sides.

But Charlie couldn't bring himself to sit at the same table with a monster, so he paced as he began to talk.

"I saw your daughter's face in a picture today. What the hell happened to her?"

Jud dropped his head. "She's been defiant ever since we arrived, and—"

"What did you expect?" Charlie asked. "You gave her up to a gene pool so you could fuck someone else's little girl, without a care for who drew her for a bride! I've seen a lot of things in my life, but your blatant disregard for your own daughter's welfare is unbelievable. That cult is illegal, unnatural and obscene. Are you the one who hit her?"

Jud gasped. "No, no, I would never hit her!" And then the moment he said it, he flashed on jabbing that needle into her neck to knock her out. "I didn't hit her, the Master did. She was disruptive, but I didn't expect her to ever be in danger of violence. That had never happened before."

"You don't call raping little girls violent?" Charlie shouted and then turned away, shoving his hands through his hair to keep from putting them around Jud Bien's neck.

"We marry them. We honor them. We take care of them," Jud said. "I defied orders when I stayed to take care of her and it got me kicked out. I'll do anything it takes to get her home safe to Tara. What do you need to know?"

Charlie pointed to the people in the room. "Except for my assistant, everyone in here is a federal agent. I don't know what they plan to do with you when this is over, but don't think your help is going to get you any special treatment, understood?"

"Yes, yes, I understand," Jud said and started to cry. "I'm sorry. All I can say is I lost my way after I joined, and I guess I lost my sanity, too, or I would never have been able to justify to myself that what I did was okay."

Charlie was short on sympathy, and while he already knew a lot of these answers, he wanted them on record and glanced at Hank.

"Are you guys ready to record?"

Barry adjusted the angle of the tripod, checked the camera one last time and gave Charlie a thumbs-up.

"For the record, what's the name of the cult leader? Who is the Master?" Charlie asked.

"His name is Aaron Walters," Jud said.

"Where is he from? Is Fourth Dimension his creation, or is there someone higher up?" Charlie asked.

"I think he grew up somewhere around here, but I don't know where. Just that Kentucky was the state where he was born. I know he's the Seraphim. We call him that, or we call him Master. He is the ultimate authority there. But I've heard some of the Archangels talking about the Master answering to someone else. Archangel Robert is his houseman. He once mentioned something about the Master getting monthly calls regarding the tests that are run there, and that he reports to that person as to what's happening within it."

"Damn it," Willis said. "We thought this cult was Walters's baby. So unless he talks later, we might never find out who's behind this, or if there are other places like this operating under other names."

Charlie's job was not about the bigger picture. "How many girls are married with babies?"

Jud paused, mentally counting. "There are six who are married with five children among them. Two of the six are newlyweds, having married within the last three months. One of the newlyweds recently lost the child she was carrying."

"Do they each have a home of their own?" Charlie asked.

Jud shook his head. "Not separate dwellings. There are two large buildings set up with apartments. They live in those. The men who aren't married live in another building, each with a private room of their own. The Sprites, which is what the unmarried girls are called, live together in a dormitory setting in a separate building. They have their own tasks to work at inside during the day."

Before Charlie could comment, Wyrick interrupted, and the shock in her voice was evident.

"You aren't saying they're locked inside?"

"It's for their own good," Jud said. "They're learning how to keep things clean and how to sew...to repair clothing. They have books to read and games to play. They're learning duties any wife would need to know."

"How old is the youngest?" Wyrick asked.

"I think she's ten," Jud said.

Wyrick flashed on her own life, a child kept away from everyone but the men who viewed her as a successful experiment in manipulating DNA. She had endured constant testing as they recorded her rapidly growing skills, and she felt sick to her stomach for those little girls in lockup.

Jud sighed. "Look. It isn't as bad as it sounds."

"Well, it is to them, and you're an idiot, so there's that," Wyrick said, then looked at Charlie. "The upside of this is that they're all together."

Charlie nodded. "Easier to keep them out of harm's way until it's safe to remove them."

Hank also had questions needing answers.

"Okay, Bien. We know what the girls do, but what about the married ones? When their husbands aren't with them, are they locked up, too?"

With each question Jud was forced to answer, he was beginning to see how off-kilter the world of Fourth Dimension really was. They'd all been so wrapped up in what they were going to accomplish for humanity that they'd completely lost sight of what they were doing to make it happen.

"Yes, the building where the married couples live does stay locked up, too. But there's a large common room where the mothers and babies can go to be together, and where the babies can play. The fathers have little tests they perform daily with the babies, to check for signs of innate psychic abilities."

Hank frowned. "So we have victims locked up in two places."

Charlie handed Jud a pen and slid a large black-and-white photocopy of the compound in front of him.

"Label every building, stating what it's used for. Label the place where the controls are for the security system. If there are motion detectors, mark their locations. If there are daytime or nighttime guards, tell me how many and where they are located. What, if anything, sets off the alarm system besides opening the gates? Write down everything you know and don't skip anything. Your daughter's life depends on us being able to take this place down without a shot being fired, or anyone being injured. I'm sure you have friends there, so you wouldn't want them hurt, either."

Jud turned the photo around so that the entrance to the compound was in front of him, and then began to write.

CHAPTER SEVENTEEN

After the hair glitter incident, the mood in the dining hall reflected the discomfort of all the diners. The young girls with babies secretly admired the new Sprite for her defiance, but, at the same time, were now afraid of conflict within the group because of their babies. Despite their young ages, the innate sense of a mother to protect her young was strong within all of them.

There were times in the early hours of the mornings, as they woke up with the babies, when they allowed themselves to remember life before. It made them sad, but they'd been within the group for so long that this life had become their new norm.

After the incident with Archangel Thomas, the Sprites had eaten their meal in silence and filed back to the dorm the same way.

The medic who'd initially tended to Jordan's injuries had gone back with them to check on Jordan, but when he started to approach her, she backed up.

"Don't touch me," she said, holding both hands out in front of her.

"I won't hurt you," David said.

"You hurt me the first time. You don't touch me again. It will stop bleeding on its own."

David was torn. He'd become a paramedic to help people, but his empathic abilities had been a deterrent rather than a help. He felt pain and trauma and their fear as if it was his own, and what he was feeling from Jordan was pure horror.

He'd helped deliver babies here, both alive and dead. He'd stitched up small cuts and tended to insignificant injuries since he'd joined three years prior. He'd felt the sadness of the new Sprites from time to time, but until this one, his contact with them had been minimal. This one had been the exception, and now that he'd locked into her world, he saw them for the children they were. They hadn't been given a choice to be part of the Master's grand plan. They were the sacrificial lambs for the greater good.

"I'm sorry," he said softly. "I'm truly sorry for your pain." He dug through his bag, pulled out a tube of antibiotic ointment and some small gauze pads and laid them on her bed, then stepped back. "Clean the place that's bleeding, then put some of this ointment on it. It will keep it from getting infected."

Then he left the building with his head down, his shoulders bent as if he'd suddenly taken on the weight of the world.

It wasn't until they were locked in and alone that the girls all crowded around Jordan again.

"Barbie, bring me a clean wet washcloth. Jordan, sit down and I'll see what Thomas did to make it bleed again," Katie said.

Jordan sat. Her head was bleeding and her body was bleeding. She didn't know how long a first menstrual period lasted, and she wanted her mother. She wanted the hugs and reassurances that everything happening inside her body was normal. She wanted to text her girlfriends about it. She wanted to cuddle up on the sofa beside her mom, with a bowl of popcorn between them, and watch their favorite movies together again. She wanted all of this to be a horrible nightmare from which she would awaken, still safe in her own room, in her own bed, but the horror of this place was wearing her down. She was losing her edge to fight.

And so she sat, her head down as Katie wiped away the blood.

"He knocked the scab off the cut," Katie said. "Probably with his fingernails."

"His fingernails give me the creeps," Randi said. "They're long like the way women wear them. My daddy's hands don't look like that," she said and then started to cry. "My mommy is a nurse. When she worked the night shift, Daddy always tucked me in bed at night. Uncle Ted, who brought me here, says they think I'm dead. Nobody can find me, because nobody is looking."

Jordan grabbed Randi by the wrist. "There are people looking for me. And when they find me, they'll find all of you, too."

The girls gasped, and then they all began to cry. The concept of their old life became the glimmer of hope they'd long since lost.

"You mean we could go home some day?" Barbie whispered.

"I mean we *will* go home. My mom knows what happened to me, because I sent her a text before Jud took me away. He didn't know that. But she knows why I disappeared, and she'll never stop looking for me," Jordan said. And with that affirmation, her will to keep fighting returned.

Katie finished cleaning the cut, dried it with one of the gauze pads, then applied the ointment.

"All done," she said. "You know, we're supposed to be memorizing a recipe from the cookbooks today."

"But we could play hockey instead," Jordan said.

"We aren't allowed to play," Randi said.

"We don't have hockey sticks or pucks, and you need to play on ice," one girl said.

Jordan stood. "But we have wood floors and brooms, and we have bars of soap. And we have all this room. Shove the beds against the wall and choose up teams. They locked us up in here, so this is our space. We can play if we want to."

The idea of play had almost been forgotten, but with Jordan in their presence, they felt powerful enough to do what they wanted—even play.

All of a sudden beds were being pushed out of the neat rows and up against the walls in jumbles, leaving a wide open space between.

They dragged twin mattresses from two empty beds to use for padding behind their goals. They propped one against the door and dragged another mattress to the far end of the room and stood it up against some chairs for the other goal.

They had eight brooms in total and a mop apiece for each goalie. Their teams consisted of four players each on the floor at the time, with others trading off. The puck was a new bar of soap, and by the time teams were chosen, the girls were in high spirits.

Jordan was excited now, too, and had set herself up as the referee.

"We're not on ice, so our face-off has to be a little different. One of you from each team come to center. If I drop the soap, it might break, so I'll just lay it in the middle of the floor. When I say, Go, you'll both have equal chances to gain control of the puck. No wild swings. No broken windows. And no pushing or shoving, because we don't hurt each other, agreed?"

They nodded eagerly, giggling with unconcealed delight that they were going to play. Everyone was in place, waiting.

Jordan put down the new bar of soap and stepped back.

"Go!" she cried, and within seconds, the girls came alive, some of them in a mad race to push the soap toward their goal, and the others doing their best to steal and push it the other way.

The other players were cheering on their teammates, and the laughter was contagious. The first slap shot was blocked by the goalie, and then the opposing team swept the bar their way and took off down the room with guards trying to steal. By the time the first goal was finally scored, they were red-faced and sweating, but their elation was impossible to miss.

One of the Archangels heard noise coming from inside the dormitory and went to see. As he got closer, he realized it was laughter; he slipped around to the back side of the building and peered in through the window. He saw Ella, his cousin's little girl, pushing something around with a broom, and two other girls trying to get it, and he saw their laughter, and their red, sweaty faces, and knew a moment of guilt.

They were playing. Just playing. And after everything else that had happened in the past couple of days, he wasn't in the mood to run tattle about this. He just walked away.

Unaware they'd been found out, the teams switched out players, and the next set began.

The game finally ended at a two-to-one victory. The girls were exhausted but happy, and no one really cared about the team win, because today, they'd all won back their right to childhood.

In their exuberance, they'd lost track of time, and when it dawned on them that the sun was slipping down below the treetops, they began the mad race to put the room back together before anyone knew what they'd been doing.

They'd just dragged the last bare mattress back onto the metal bedsprings when one of the girls called out.

"Here they come!"

But the beds were in their neat rows, the brooms and mops were back in the closet, and the bar of soap was tucked away with the rest of the supplies. The only visible signs of the game were the faint streaks of dry soap on the hardwood floor.

"We're good," Jordan said. "No giggling. No smiles. We follow their rules until we don't want to, got it?"

"Got it," they echoed and lined up as always, with Jordan in the middle, waiting to be taken to supper.

Aaron had been in his office all afternoon entering the test notes from the latest baby exams, and when he had finished, he segued to a little bookkeeping and paid some bills. He was logging out and getting ready to go to the dining hall when the phone rang. He glanced at the clock. 6:00 p.m. on the dot. He answered promptly, knowing this would be the Boss.

"Good evening, sir," he said.

"Good evening, Aaron. It's good to hear your voice."

"And yours, as well," Aaron said.

"So now that the new Sprite has arrived, how is she fitting in?"

Aaron frowned. He'd been dreading this because the discord would fall back on him for not being able to handle her. But lying to the Boss wasn't an option.

"She's not, sir. She's been defiant from day one, and continues in that behavior. We isolated her at first to keep from spreading unrest among the others, but that was unsuccessful because she destroyed property. She was then housed with the other Sprites, and they were given orders to shun her. They obeyed, but she continued to defy our rules. She was punished."

There was a long moment of silence, and when the Boss spoke again, the jovial tone was missing from his voice.

"How was she punished?"

Aaron's gut knotted. "I hit her several times for screaming at me. She fell. Her father witnessed it and went to her defense.

When he defied my orders and stayed with her, I was forced to null his membership. He is no longer with the group."

"What about the girl?" the Boss asked.

"She's still here and with her father's understanding that her safety depends upon him not divulging the rules of the path upon which we walk."

"I am not happy to hear this. You should have eliminated both of them."

"Given the circumstances, sir, I knew it would have undermined all we were doing here. We would have lost the trust of the others. They would then fear for their own family's safety."

"Yes, yes, I see what you mean. Still, I don't like loose ends. I need the name of the man who was cast out."

Aaron sighed. "His name is Judson Bien. I'll send you his file."

"Yes, thank you," the Boss said. "And what is the behavior of the Sprite, now that her father is gone?"

"The same. She didn't have much of a bond with him before, and it was broken when he took her from her mother. I tolerate the insubordination now, because I believe she will eventually settle, and because I sense her psychic abilities are already far beyond most of the adults here."

The Boss's voice shifted back into a more interested tone.

"Really? This is, indeed, good news."

"Yes, and by not forcing her to marry, we may avail ourselves later of all of her skills with her full cooperation."

"Yes! Yes! I like that. That is a good solution to a nasty problem. Don't worry about anything else. I'll see to tying up the loose ends. Enjoy your evening meal. We'll be in touch."

The connection was broken before Aaron could say goodbye. He was glad that call was over, but as he left to go to supper, he had to accept that giving up Jud's name meant the man was as good as dead.

★ ★ ★

Charlie and the agents spent the remainder of the afternoon at the cabin, going over the details of the compound with Jud. Even the men on recon had been called in to listen. Everybody had to be on the same page tomorrow morning for the raid to happen without incident.

Wyrick heard everything Jud had to say, and then went upstairs, spending the rest of the evening online.

She'd been working for about two hours when she finally located the name of the company and the contractor who'd built Fourth Dimension. After searching back records, she also located the blueprints. The contractor's name popped up several times in her search, in connection to previous projects he and his team had worked on. But it was the newest article on him that bothered her most. Less than a month after Fourth Dimension took possession of their new compound, the contractor and his work crew were dead. They'd perished in a private plane crash on their way to a new jobsite. For Wyrick, this was far too convenient to be an accident. It felt more like getting rid of witnesses.

After finding the blueprints, she began searching deeper into the files on the Fourth Dimension project and stumbled onto a schematic of the entire electrical and security system at the compound. Within seconds, alarms were going off in her head.

"What the hell?" she muttered.

She turned her chair to her PC and began searching through personal files of her own that she'd kept from when she'd still worked for Universal Theorem. When she found the file she was looking for, she sent it to the laptop, then pulled it up onto a split screen and began comparing the schematics of the security she'd designed for one of UT's off-site buildings to the security schematics of Fourth Dimension. The more she read and the more deeply she searched, the more convinced she became that they were the same. The implications of that were horrifying, and at the same time, made horrible sense.

She immediately sent Charlie a text.

You need to see this. In my room. Now.

Charlie was outside lounging around the firepit, swapping war stories with the two men who'd been on recon as the woodsmoke rose in thin shreds above the canopy of the forest.

The agents had previously served in Afghanistan in the early days of the war, and after learning Charlie was a former army ranger, their opinion of him as "just a PI" had shifted to one of camaraderie.

The sun was going down behind the treetops, and the air was finally beginning to cool from the heat of the day. Birds were going to roost, and the animals of the night were coming out of their dens, readying to hunt the mountain.

Hank was on the back deck grilling burgers for supper. The aroma of charring meat was enticing, and there was an ongoing argument between Willis and Barry about opposing football teams.

Charlie happened to glance up just as an owl flew across his line of vision. He leaned back to watch, sending a silent message as it flew out of sight. *Happy hunting, dude.*

"Burgers will be ready soon," Hank called out. "Is everyone here who's going to eat?"

"I'll go get Wyrick," Charlie said, and before he could get up, his phone signaled a text from her. He read it, then got up and went inside.

Jud Bien was in a chair in the living room, handcuffed and dozing, with a guard nearby. Charlie glanced at him as he passed, and then kept moving. He didn't know what had happened, but Wyrick wasn't one to flip out over nothing.

He took the stairs up two at a time, then hurried down the hall, knocking once before going inside.

"What's up?" he asked.

"There's something you need to know about the Fourth Dimension security system."

"What's that?" Charlie asked.

"I designed it."

He stared down at her in disbelief. "What? What the hell do you mean, you designed it?"

"The entire layout of the security system, as well as the safeguards and the intricate backups, are a replica of a system I designed for Universal Theorem years ago. The implication that Cyrus Parks is involved with Fourth Dimension is obvious. What if he's that guy Aaron Walters reports to? The one who calls for updates? If he is, and UT is funding this cult, I guess they're still trying to grow baby geniuses."

"Can you prove it?" Charlie asked.

"Maybe," she said.

"Holy shit," Charlie said. "Does this endanger the takedown in any way? I mean…is this something the Feds need to know?"

She shrugged. "Me knowing this makes it a cinch for me to take down the power, but telling them this will call attention to the fact that I once worked there, which might open up a whole new can of worms if the government gets on my ass and wants to confiscate me and my brain, too. What I can do when this is all over is find a money trail between UT and the compound and send it in anonymously to the right people. After that, it will be on them to prove and prosecute. Not you. Not me."

"Then we know nothing, and it's time to eat," Charlie said. "Burgers are on the grill outside. It's going to get a little cooler as the sun goes down. You might want to get a jacket."

As she began logging out, Charlie remembered something he was going to ask.

"Hey, I saw the box with your plane in my closet. What's up with that?"

"Agent Raines tried to confiscate it after I brought it back. We had words. I took it to my room, guessing they might try something."

"So you hid it in my room, instead?" he said.

"No," Wyrick said, and then told him what had happened, right down to catching him in the act. "The plane is in your room now. I didn't think they'd have the guts to try it twice."

"Son of a bitch," Charlie said. "So that's why he came down so fast. I'll be having a word with him."

"No need," Wyrick said as she dug a hoodie from her bag and pulled it over her head. "He's already embarrassed that I set them up to fail and they fell for it."

Charlie frowned. "Well, I have a need. What was Hank's reasoning for wanting it in the first place?"

"Military weaponry. Let's go eat. I'm starved."

They came down together without talking, and as they walked through the kitchen to the back deck, they passed Jud, who was now sitting at the counter, under guard, already eating his meal.

Jud didn't look at them, and they didn't speak to him.

The storm door squeaked as they walked out.

"Needs oil," Wyrick said.

"When I was a kid, the hinges on the screen doors at our house always squeaked. Mom wouldn't let Dad oil them because that's how she knew we were coming and going."

Wyrick's eyes widened, and then she smiled. "I love that."

Charlie knew better than to acknowledge the friendly moment and destroy the rare moment of camaraderie, so he didn't respond.

The scent of woodsmoke was stronger now, and the soft

undertones of laughter from around the firepit were inviting, but Charlie had a bone to pick with Hank, and he wasn't
breaking bread with anyone until he'd had his say.

Hank turned around as they walked out.

"Hey, Charlie, how do you like your burger cooked?"

"Medium," he said.

"What about you, Wyrick?"

"Kinda like I leave my enemies. Crispy on the outside.
Bloody on the inside," she said.

Hank sighed. "Look. I know you're pissed, and rightly so.
But—"

"There are no buts in outright theft," Charlie said. "Drop
the subject. We have a job to do, and when it's over, we're
gone. With all of our belongings and none of yours. It would
be a smart move if you returned the favor. I don't know what
the laws are about punching federal agents in the face, but I'm
willing to chance it if I have to."

The sudden silence among the men was telling. No one
asked what was going on, which meant they'd all known it
was going to happen, and for Wyrick, it meant they wouldn't
quit until they got what they wanted.

She didn't like being watched, and she didn't like being vulnerable, so the solution for her was to remove the temptation.

"I'll be right back," she said and went back inside, then up
to Charlie's room, and opened the box.

The controls were nothing out of the ordinary, something
anyone could build. They wanted the plane and the formula to
make it disappear in full sunlight without flashing refractions.

She took the plane, leaving all the rest behind, and came
down the stairs at a jog, with it dangling from one hand. She
was out of the cabin and halfway to the firepit before any of
them realized what she was holding.

Charlie knew the set of her shoulders and the length of her
stride meant trouble, and then she tossed it in the fire.

"Shit!" Hank said.

Willis jumped to his feet to grab it, but it was already too late. The gray woodsmoke turned black as the plane began to melt. There was a sudden whoosh as it became a fireball, and then it was gone.

Wyrick came back up the steps, grabbed a cold drink from an open ice chest and a handful of chips. She took them to an empty chair beside the deck rail and proceeded to eat.

Hank couldn't bring himself to look away. He couldn't believe that just happened.

"You're burning her burger," Charlie said. "I wouldn't want to piss her off again today, if I were you."

Hank jumped, then scooped her burger from the grill onto a paper plate, took a bun from the warmer and added it to the plate, and handed it to Charlie.

"If you don't mind, please pass this to your assistant."

"Sure," Charlie said and took it to the table where all the fixings were set up. "Your burger's ready."

Wyrick set her pop on the deck rail and met him at the table without comment. She was adding condiments and sides when Charlie's phone rang. Wyrick glanced at his phone and thought, *Tara Bien is in Kentucky now*, and then added a piece of cheese to the hot meat patty before putting on the other half of the bun.

Charlie glanced down. "It's Tara Bien," he said.

Wyrick already knew that and took her first bite. Even as she was chewing, she was thinking about her awakening facet of precognition. It was weird and unexplainable, like all the rest of what she knew how to do.

Charlie answered. "Hello? Tara?"

"I've just landed. I'm in Lexington. Talk to me. Did you find my baby?"

"Yes. We'll bring her out tomorrow."

"Oh my God! Thank you, Charlie. I need to be there. Tell me how to get there," Tara said.

"No, ma'am, you do not need to be here. I can't be worrying about your safety and hers, too. Understand?"

Tara's voice was shaking. "I need to hold her, Charlie. I need to see her face and know she's alive and well."

Charlie wasn't about to tell Tara what had happened to her daughter's face. She'd find that out soon enough.

"I understand. And as soon as she's with me, she can call you. That way you'll know she's safe. Okay?"

"Oh God, Charlie. I can't stand this. I don't know what's been happening to her. This has forever changed the woman she was meant to be, but broken or not, I want my baby back."

"Get a hotel. Eat some dinner. Try to rest. I'll call you tomorrow. In the meantime, tell no one where you are or what you're doing. Understand?"

"Yes, yes, I understand. No one knows where I am except you."

"Okay, then. I'll be in touch."

He disconnected, dropped the phone back in his pocket and began fixing his burger.

"So the mother is in Kentucky?" Hank asked.

"Lexington," Charlie said. "We'll deliver Jordan to her there."

Hank glanced down the length of the deck to where Wyrick was sitting.

"I'm sorry," he said.

"Don't tell me. Tell her. She's the one you betrayed. She got the evidence you wanted to get search warrants, and the first thing you did was try to steal the way she did it. Doesn't speak too highly of the Feds, if you ask me," Charlie said.

Hank laid down the spatula and started walking toward her. He didn't expect her to look up, but she did, and then she just kept chewing and watching him, like a big cat watching its prey. He'd never been this intimidated in his life—not even when he'd met his wife's father for the first time.

"Wyrick, I owe you an apology. I'm sorry. My behavior was unconscionable. I got carried away by the marvel of what you'd created and kept envisioning all of the ways that it could be applied for the greater good and—"

Wyrick held up her hand.

"Just stop right there. Claiming something—anything—and telling people it's for the greater good is how people die and wars begin. You did it. You got caught. Now you want me to absolve you of all guilt. Kiss my ass, Special Agent Raines. You overcooked my burger, but I'm too hungry to care."

Then she took another bite and looked at him, then past him, as if he'd suddenly become invisible, like that plane.

He turned and left her there.

Long after the meal was over and everything had been cleaned up, Hank was still thinking about what Wyrick had said. Today had changed him in some way, and probably for the better.

The team met one last time before they called it a night, to go over all the details of tomorrow's raid.

They had search warrants and they had arrest warrants. They would have an FBI SWAT team standing by to scale the walls just before daylight, and more agents to enter from the front. They were ready to take down Fourth Dimension and get some missing children home.

CHAPTER EIGHTEEN

Tara Bien was emotionally spent by the time she collected her luggage and checked in at the Embassy Suites by Hilton on Newtown Pike. As soon as the bellhop left and the door was locked between her and the world, she sat down on the side of the bed and started weeping. But not the deep, gut-wrenching sobs from all the days of not knowing where her baby was, or if she was still alive. These were tears of relief. Charlie Dodge had found Jordan, and God willing, tomorrow they'd be reunited.

When she finally got herself together, she ordered room service and ate as much as she could of the food when it was delivered. Then, later, as she was getting ready for bed, she pulled a worn brown teddy bear from her luggage and hugged it to her like she used to hug her baby girl, remembering all the nights she'd tucked Jordan into bed with the little bear as she was growing up.

Brownie Bear Bien had been waiting for Jordan when they brought her home from the hospital as a baby. It seemed only fitting for Brownie Bear to help bring Jordan home again.

★ ★ ★

Charlie was in his room getting ready for bed. He'd felt a need all evening to check on Annie, and finally found a moment alone to call Morning Light. After a brief conversation with the nurse on duty, the call ended. The report was as good as it could be, which was a relief, but the emotional distance between him and Annie was vast, and he was the collateral damage left behind.

He stared at the floor for a few moments and then reminded himself why he was there. He couldn't save his girl, but they could damn sure save some others, and 4:00 a.m. came early.

He showered, shaved, then set the alarm on his phone and crawled into bed. The moment he closed his eyes, he flashed on Wyrick throwing that plane into the fire. She'd destroyed one thing to keep people from turning it into something else, and that was what they were going to do tomorrow with Fourth Dimension. Regardless of the humanitarian implications of Fourth Dimension's initial project, it had turned into something vile, and it was time to take it down.

Jud was stretched out on the living room sofa and staring up at the ceiling. The agent they'd left on guard with him was sitting in a chair on the other side of the room, reading by lamplight. Every so often he would glance up from his book, look at Jud, check his phone for messages, then go back to reading. There were guards outside, but they had nothing to do with Jud's presence. Jud had now been placed under guard for two reasons. The first was that they didn't trust him, since he was, or had been, a member of the cult they were about to take down. And the second being, by his coming forward, he had become their chief witness against Fourth Dimension.

The lingering scent of the woodsmoke and grilled meat was still heavy in the air. For Jud, everything seemed so ordinary but for the handcuffs on his wrists. Tomorrow would mark the end of life as he knew it, and after that his days were numbered. They would know he was the one who'd given them up, but it was okay. A life for a life. It was in the Bible.

Then, all of a sudden, a sad, hopeless feeling swept through him that wasn't his, and he knew it was Jordan. He sensed her sleeplessness and felt her fear, and even though there was a risk in sending it, he had to let her know she wasn't alone.

Jordan showered with the other girls, then hand-washed the clothes she'd worn that day, hung them up to dry and, as was her habit, changed into her other set of clean clothes. She had yet to take pajamas out of her bag, and even went to bed in her shoes, in case she got a chance to run away. She slept on top of the bedclothes, with the extra blanket as her only cover.

She still held on to the mental image of Wonder Woman's strength, sword and shield for courage. Jordan's defiance was her sword, and staying clothed was her strength and shield. She didn't have Wonder Woman's Lasso of Truth, but she had the truth of her mother's love.

Tired from the impromptu game of hockey, the girls had long since fallen asleep, while Jordan still stood at the window nearest her bed, looking up at the stars. They were so beautiful, but so far, far away.

Her eyes welled as she sent a message into the Universe. *Find me. Help me.*

And then she heard a voice.

Be ready.

She froze.

Oh my God, oh my God.

Breath caught in the back of her throat and then she blocked every thought she had as she turned away from the window and quietly crawled onto the bed. She covered up and tried to find a comfortable position, but she couldn't sleep. She didn't have to be told how important it was not to focus on the message her dad had just sent her. There were too many people here who would know it.

At 4:00 a.m., a convoy of black SUVs passed through Shawnee Gap and took the blacktop off the highway heading straight up the mountain. The only witness to their passing, a lone pickup truck going through town in the other direction.

At the five-mile count, the lead car took the turnoff from the blacktop onto the narrow road leading through the trees and to the cabin—their rendezvous point.

Everyone in the cabin was up and moving around downstairs. Some were eating cereal, some settling for toast and coffee, but all of them were unusually quiet. The imminence of the raid was affecting them all in different ways.

Wyrick knew her part. She would stay behind to man the computers and cut off the power, giving them access to the compound. Also, she would be wired to be in constant contact with Charlie throughout the raid.

Charlie had one role. Rescuing Jordan and the other girls with her. Armed with his Glock and wearing a bulletproof vest, he was out on the back deck with his second cup of coffee and third piece of toast. He was focusing on the mental image of the distance from the gate to the girls' dorm in his head, and the short span of time he would have to get there and get them down in case of gunfire.

The men inside were hyperaware of Wyrick's presence but gave her space. No one knew, not even Charlie, that she'd stayed up all night looking for a money trail between Universal Theorem and Fourth Dimension. And she'd found it— funneled through three separate offshore accounts and into a numbered account in a Swiss bank. How she'd found it would never be admissible in court, but that would be someone else's problem to solve. Just giving the Feds the information that the link was there would be satisfaction enough for her. It was her payback against UT for taking something she'd created and using it to enslave children.

And then, all of a sudden, the mood in the room shifted from the tension of waiting to a surge of adrenaline, when they heard the sound of approaching cars.

"They're here," Willis said. Charlie heard them and came in the back door just as Hank walked out the front.

The drivers parked around the perimeter of the clearing, and then agents began emerging from the cars in rapid numbers. All armed.

All dressed in black.

All moving toward the cabin in total silence until they reached the porch where Hank was standing.

One man stepped forward.

"Good morning, sir. SWAT Team Hostage Rescue reporting for duty. And we have a man here to transport your witness."

Hank turned back toward the open doorway. "Chavez, get Bien."

Moments later, Jud came out, his hands cuffed in front of him and walking with his head down. Chavez handed him over.

"Take good care of Daddy Dearest," he said.

The agent didn't know all the details of what was going down, but he knew this man had been a part of it, and that it was a nasty.

"Will do," he said and led Jud to the car with the prisoner cage. He put him into the back and buckled him up, then got in and drove away.

As soon as they were gone, Hank addressed the new arrivals.

"Good morning, officers. We'll go over the plans inside."

They entered without speaking, filling the large room to capacity and then some.

Uncomfortable being squeezed in around so many males, Wyrick retreated to the stairs to listen.

Hank introduced himself, then Charlie.

"The civilian to my left is Charlie Dodge. Army ranger turned private investigator out of Dallas. He and his assistant, Wyrick, who's standing on the stairs, were hired to find a missing girl, and tracked her to this compound. They have been vital in helping get us the proof we needed for search and arrest warrants. Among other things, Wyrick will be in charge of cutting off the power to the compound."

Wyrick accepted their stares with her usual disassociation as the meeting continued.

Hank showed them the map of the compound, assigning teams to take down different areas at the same time. Once they all understood where they were to go and what to do, he continued on to the aftermath.

"We will have a number of prison buses waiting down in Shawnee Gap to transport the men out, as well as commercial buses for the removal of the girls after the compound is secure. The prisoners will be transported to Lexington for booking, and the girls will be taken to one of the larger hospitals in the same city," Hank said, then glanced at his watch. "Twilight will begin a few minutes after 6:00 a.m. It's five fifteen now. Since the road ends at their compound, we can't just drive up there and hop out because of the security cameras. And we can't turn them off too soon or they'll be alerted. We'll have to go a mile uphill through the trees to get to the compound, and once we're in place, Wyrick will cut the power. After that, everything has to happen in split-second precision. The SWAT team will go over the walls into the back side of the compound, while the rest of us go in through the front gates. You each know your targets. Knock on the doors, take the men down and keep the girls inside until we have every-one in custody and off the premises."

"Yes, sir," they echoed.

"May I interrupt?" Wyrick called out.

Hank turned. "Certainly."

"Whether you believe in psychic abilities or not, you need to remember that all of those men are there because they claim to have special abilities that allow them to know things other people don't. With that in mind, there is the real possibility that they will know you're coming before you get there…and at the least, might know before you have them all contained. So keep that in mind. Let me know the second you are all in place. I will cut the power. After that, speed will be your ally."

"Good point. We don't have to believe. But we have to act as if their abilities do exist," Hank said. "Let's do this."

Charlie started out the door, then turned around to look for Wyrick. She was watching him from the steps.

"Can you hear me okay?" he asked.

She tapped her earpiece and gave him a thumbs-up.

"Can you hear me?" she said.

He nodded.

"Good. Then pay attention to what you're doing," she said and headed back upstairs to where she was set up.

"This is not my first war," he muttered as he jogged to catch up.

Then Wyrick's voice was in his ear. "Just make sure it's not your last."

She had both computers up, and the screens open to what she needed to do. The power wouldn't go off with one sin-gle keystroke. She had to take it down one layer at a time, beginning with the power generator and the alarm backups first, so that when the mainframe to the power went off, there was nothing but silence. It shouldn't take more than fifteen or twenty seconds, but it had to be done in proper order.

And so she waited.

★ ★ ★

The men had spanned out about three feet apart, moving uphill at a steady pace while maintaining radio silence. Their dark face paint and black clothing blended in with the night and the forest through which they were walking to the point that, from a distance, they were little more than a ripple of shadows.

Some were carrying climbing gear with their weapons, and they all had handcuffs and zip ties to immobilize the men once they were in custody.

According to Jud Bien's accounting, there were about twenty girls there, six who would be on the married side of the grounds, while the fourteen others would be in the dormitory reserved for Sprites. He'd also stated that there were thirty-four men in residence. He'd been the thirty-fifth, but with his expulsion, the number was one less than before.

They knew the likelihood of at least three men being in the kitchen at the dining hall, in early stages of preparing breakfast for the camp when they arrived, so the men coming over the walls from the back of the compound were to get to them first.

It sounded good. It sounded like the perfect plan, except for the warning Wyrick had given them. If those men were real psychics, they might be armed and waiting to pick them off.

They reached the outer area of the compound just after 6:00 a.m. Twilight was a breath away as night gave way to the light of day.

Hank sent the climbing team to the back of the compound, then looked for Charlie and signaled him to let Wyrick know they were ready to go.

Charlie gave Hank a thumbs-up, then spoke into his mic. "We're here. Shut it down."

"Shutting down now," she said, her fingers flying across the keyboards as, one by one, she shut down the power sources to the backup generator, the backup power to the security systems, the backup power to the motion detectors, and then the gas feeding into the compound. The last to shut down was the mainframe to the electrical grid.

And then it was done.

"It's down. You're in," she said.

Charlie gave a signal to Hank, and Hank delivered the message to his men.

"It's a go," he said.

When the climbing team rushed the walls and no security lights came on, they knew they were in the clear. They were over and inside the compound in less than a minute and a half, while the others began approaching the main gate.

Aaron Walters was in the habit of early-morning meditation, and was already in a state of waking up when the image of men in black clothing swarming the compound flashed through his thoughts. He sat straight up in bed and tried to turn on the lamp, then thought the bulb was burned out until he realized the ceiling fan over his bed wasn't turning, and the nightlight in the bathroom was out.

He flung back the covers and ran to the windows. All of the security lights were off, as were all the lights in the dining hall. The power had gone off and no warnings had sounded! And then he saw the figures of two men in black clothing slip into the kitchen from the back.

At that moment, the hair stood up on the back of his neck. They were being invaded, and the only person who could have given them the information to take them down in this way was the man he'd just kicked out. Jud Bien!

"You bastard! You fucking bastard! I told you what would happen if you betrayed me!" Aaron cried, then grabbed one of his white robes and pulled it over his head, slid his feet into slippers and snatched the set of master keys from a drawer.

He got the handgun from his nightstand and ran through the house, then out the front door, racing toward the Sprites' dormitory.

The sky was growing lighter by the second. He didn't have much time. This might be the end of Fourth Dimension, but Jordan Bien wasn't going to live to see another day.

Aaron wasn't the only one who'd sensed what was happening. Jordan had been antsy for the better part of two hours, walking quietly from window to window, sensing the imminence of danger.

When she suddenly flashed on men—lots of men—coming through the forest toward the compound, she knew instantly that the evil here was ending today. What she couldn't see was if she'd survive to go home, or if this was the day that she would die. But after all she'd been through, this was not the day to quit fighting. She began waking up the girls.

"You need to get up and get dressed, and hurry," she said.

"What's wrong?" Randi asked as she rolled out of bed.

"What's happening?" Katie asked, fumbling around for a light.

"No! Don't turn on the lights!" Jordan cried. "Get dressed in the dark. I think the police are going to raid the compound this morning. I think today is the day we are saved. Now hurry, and stay as quiet as you can. No lights. No noise. We'll know within a few minutes what's going to happen."

The girls dressed in a panic. The idea of going home was now entangled with the danger it was going to take to get there.

Jordan took up a stance at the window overlooking the grounds. To her far right was the entrance gate. To her far left was the dining hall. She was trying to see past the glare of the security lights when they suddenly went off. The whole compound was in darkness.

Jordan ran to the bathroom and flipped the light switch, but it didn't work.

"They've cut the power," she said.

The girls began murmuring and whispering as they ran to the windows to see for themselves. The night sky was already disappearing, but seeing the security lights off was a shock.

And then one of the girls cried out.

"The Master is coming! I see his white robe!"

"He's coming after me," Jordan said, bolting for the other end of the building and into the janitor's closet. She fumbled around in the darkness until Randi suddenly appeared with a flashlight.

"Here!" Randi said, giving Jordan the light she needed to find the old mop with the wooden handle that she was looking for.

She ran with it into the showers and began to swing it as hard as she could at the long metal sink, trying to break off the head of the mop.

The sound of broomstick against metal reverberated like a gong, and she struck it again and again until the mophead broke off and went flying into the shower, leaving the ragged wooden shards at the end of the handle in Jordan's hands.

"He's almost here!" Katie cried.

Jordan ran back to the front of the building.

"All of you, get behind me and crawl under the beds. He just wants me, but if he's mad enough and crazy enough, he may try to kill all of us."

They'd long since given up to Jordan's authority, and now obeyed without hesitation, running headlong into the shadows, then going belly down onto the old wooden floor, crawling beneath the beds.

Wyrick could vaguely hear what was going on through Charlie's headset, but it was more than enough to set her teeth on edge. Being here when he was there was worse than she could have imagined.

She needed to calm down in case there was something else they needed her to do, and made herself focus. Within seconds, she saw a man in a white robe, running through a house with a gun in his hand, and when he opened the front door and stepped out onto the porch, she was in his head and seeing what he was seeing.

"Charlie! Charlie! Can you hear me?"

"Yes, we're just moving through the gate. What's wrong?"

"Aaron Walters—he knew! Somehow he knew. He has a gun and he's going to the girls' dormitory to kill Jordan. Big man in a long white robe. Hurry! Hurry!"

It was Charlie's worst fear.

"They know!" Charlie cried. "Walters is on the move!" He pushed his way through the officers and went in with the first wave.

The sky was turning pearl gray as he entered the compound, and he was only a few steps in when he saw a white-robed figure running toward the building where the girls were housed.

"That's Walters! He's mine!" Charlie said and took off running, while the others dispersed in different directions.

CHAPTER NINETEEN

Aaron was so intent on vengeance that he didn't see the men coming in the front gate. But he was halfway across the yard when he caught a glimpse of men in black running between the buildings at the back side of the grounds. He kept thinking, *This isn't happening, this is all a bad dream.* He couldn't go to prison. The Boss didn't like failures. But he was out of breath now and there was a pain in his side. It didn't feel like a dream. It felt real, and just in case it was, he kept running.

By the time he reached the dormitory, his hands and legs were trembling from exertion he wasn't used to, and he began fumbling for the keys.

He jammed the first key in the lock, but it didn't turn, so he tried the next, and then the next. By now, the twilight had added hints of a pink to the awakening day, and there was a yellow haze appearing at treetop level. Sunshine…putting a halo on the morning.

He chose another key and pushed it in the lock. It turned, and the door was suddenly swinging inward and he leaped over the threshold and came to a stop just inside the door, trying to acclimate his sight to the shadows in the room.

★ ★ ★

Jordan flinched as the door swung inward, and now only yards separated them. She stood alone in the middle of the room with a long stick held across her chest in a gesture of defense, and when he saw her, he laughed, and it was a horrible sound.

"I told your father what would happen if he betrayed me, and I am a man of my word. You die first, and then the others."

Jordan was shaking, but she wasn't going to die with a bullet in her back. She pulled back the mop handle like a spear, pointing the jagged edge toward him and started running toward him, screaming.

Charlie had tried hard to intercept Walters before he reached the building, but he was too far away, and he was still a good twenty yards behind when Walters finally got the door unlocked and leaped inside.

"Oh hell no," Charlie said and grabbed his gun. He'd never shot a man in the back before, but if he couldn't stop him one way, he'd stop him another.

He'd forgotten Wyrick could hear him, so when he heard a girl inside beginning to scream, Charlie shouted.

"Aaron Walters! Drop your gun or I'll shoot!"

His shout startled Aaron enough to make his first shot go wild, and as he was turning around to take aim at Charlie, Charlie cleared the threshold in one long leap, taking Aaron down. The gun went flying as Charlie landed on top of him, then drew back his fist and knocked him unconscious with one blow. Charlie had a brief glimpse of a young, long-legged girl running toward Aaron as he'd come through the door, but now that Aaron was down, Charlie rocked back on his heels and looked up.

The girl had come to a halt, the spear still raised in a gesture of defense. Her eyes were wide and fear-filled, and yet there she stood, still in attack mode.

"Jordan's here. We got her, Wyrick. We got her," he said.

Then Wyrick's voice was in his ear.

"You did it, Charlie. All I did was turn out the lights."

Charlie quickly cuffed Aaron, then stood.

"Jordan Bien, my name is Charlie Dodge. Your mama hired me to find you. I came to take you home."

Jordan dropped the spear, took a few steps forward, then fell into Charlie's arms, shaking so hard she could barely stand.

Charlie felt her trembling and kept patting her back over and over, talking to her in a calm, steady voice.

"It's okay, honey. It's okay. This nightmare is almost over for all of you, but right now, I need you to get to the back of the building and stay down. It's not safe to bring any of you out until the FBI has all of the men in custody, okay?"

Jordan glanced down at the Master. He'd been her monster in this hell, and Charlie Dodge had taken away his power. She let go of Charlie and stepped back, watching intently as Charlie retrieved the gun, but it wasn't until he pulled a long zip tie from his pocket and shackled Aaron legs together at the ankles that she began to realize this was over. The demon who'd taken away their freedom had just been cuffed and hobbled.

Outside, the sounds of shouting and then a random burst of gunfire could be heard as Charlie moved Jordan to the back of the room with the other girls.

"All of you, stay down," he said. "The FBI is here arresting all the men. They don't want to bring you out until everyone is in custody. I'm going to stay here with you, okay?"

They nodded silently but never took their eyes off him as he sat down.

At that point, Charlie radioed Hank. He answered, sounding a little breathless, but calm.

"This is Raines."

"Aaron Walters, the man who called himself the Master, is in the girls' dorm, handcuffed and unconscious. When you get a minute, send some men to come get him. He came in here armed and with full intent on killing my girl and shooting up the place. He scared the shit out of all of them."

"Are they okay?" Hank asked.

"They are now," Charlie said.

"Good job. Sending men," Hank said.

Charlie glanced at the kids all huddled beneath the metal beds and staring up at him, in a state Charlie would have called shell-shocked.

Jordan was sitting on a bed, facing him, transfixed by his presence and the safety he represented.

It didn't take long before thirteen little girls came crawling out from beneath the beds, in varying states of shock and disbelief.

"Are we really going home?" Katie asked.

"Yes, baby. You're really going home," Charlie said.

They looked at each other and then at Charlie again, but instead of celebrating, they reached for each other and held hands, still in disbelief that this would truly be over.

Jordan was afraid to speak and find out she'd just been dreaming, that none of this was real and they were still lost to the world. But the longer she sat, the more reality sank in.

Then she thought of her father's message.

"Is Jud with you?"

Charlie was a little surprised that she referred to her father that way but answered without hesitation.

"No. The Feds took him into custody after he gave us the lowdown on how to get inside."

She sighed. At least he'd kept the promise to come back for her.

"Where's my mama?"

"She's in a hotel in Lexington, waiting for me to take you there. She wanted to come here today, but I wouldn't let her. I did, however, promise that I'd let you call her the minute I had you safe, so how about we do that now?"

Jordan nodded, her heart pounding as she watched Charlie make the call, then get up and hand her the phone.

"It's ringing," he said.

Jordan took it, her hands trembling so hard she almost dropped it, and then she heard her mother's voice.

"Hello? Charlie?"

Jordan swallowed past the lump in her throat.

"Mama, it's me."

Her mother's cry of joy shattered the last of the wall Jordan had kept tight around herself, and now she was trying desperately not to cry.

"Are you okay? Are you safe?" Tara asked.

"Yes, I'm safe now. Charlie is here beside me."

But it wasn't until she realized her mother was crying and talking all at the same time that she felt her own tears coming. She took a breath, listening to the sound of her mother's voice, but couldn't respond. Unable to stand it any longer, she handed the phone back to Charlie and buried her face in her hands, releasing in deep, choking sobs every horror she'd endured and every fear she'd had that this day would never happen.

Tara stopped talking the moment she heard it, and a thousand things went through her mind as to what was happening. She was almost in hysterics, screaming Jordan's name over and over, when Charlie got back on the phone.

"Tara! Tara! Jordan is okay. I think it was the sound of your voice, and maybe the relief of being safe that undid her. Just give her a minute and I'll put her back on the phone, okay?"

"Yes, okay. It's my fault. I asked too much, too soon. She doesn't need to talk until she's ready. Just so you know, I'm at the Embassy Suites by Hilton. The street is Newtown Pike. Just tell her it's all okay and I love her."

"I will," Charlie said. Putting the phone in his pocket, he moved to sit beside Jordan and pulled her close.

"Your mama said everything is okay and that she loves you. And she's right. It is okay, honey. It's okay to cry. Cry out every ugly thing you've seen and every bad thing that happened to you, and let it go. You beat them. You survived this place. All of you did. You aren't victims. You are survivors."

Wyrick was back at the cabin with her head down between her arms, listening to Jordan's gut-wrenching sobs and shedding silent tears with her. If she pretended, she could almost believe that Charlie was talking straight to her, his lips against her ear, whispering to her, telling her to cry it out, reminding her that she was no longer a victim, but a survivor.

The relief of finding Jordan was sweet, and being able to get the other girls out in the same process was huge. But there was much yet to do. Since the men had left the cabin on foot, getting back to their vehicles was on them, as well.

But not for Charlie. She let go of the self-pity that she'd wallowed in, pulled herself together and asked him another question.

"Are the prisoners contained?"

"I'm with the girls, but from what I can see from the window, I think most of them are. I still see movement at the married couples' building, but it appears they're mostly waiting for buses to come pick up the prisoners."

"Then I'm packing us up. Give me the go-ahead when they begin loading up the men, and I'm heading your way."

"The car keys are in my shaving kit in the bathroom," Charlie said.

"Noted," Wyrick said, and then she was gone.

★ ★ ★

The girls had gathered around Charlie, like little chicks trying to get beneath the old hen's wings. He was big and strong, and he'd taken the Master down in front of their eyes. They kept glancing at the Master's unconscious body, afraid he'd wake up and become the Master again, issuing orders everyone was expected to follow.

Jordan had been watching him, too, and when she sensed he was coming to, she got up and walked toward him.

Charlie frowned, then stood and followed her. When he noticed her hands were doubled into fists, he got it. She needed to see him powerless.

"Are you okay?" he asked.

She nodded but stayed in place, watching the Master waking up in a whole new world. There was a trickle of blood running from the corner of his mouth. And when his eyelids began to flutter, she shifted position so that her face would be the first thing he saw.

Aaron's whole face was throbbing, and he kept tasting blood. He didn't know what had happened, but he knew he wasn't in bed. He moaned, then reached for his nose. That was when he realized he was in handcuffs, and he remembered!

When he opened his eyes, the first thing he saw was Jordan, standing over him and staring down at his face. Then he saw the man beside her.

"You broke my nose," he mumbled.

"Hurts, doesn't it?" Jordan said.

Aaron glared but wouldn't respond.

"Believe me, it gets worse before it gets better," she added, then kicked the sole of his shoe before walking off.

Aaron shouted. "Damn you, Jordan Bien! Everything was fine until you came along!"

Charlie grabbed Aaron by the hair. "Shut your mouth. You aren't fit to say her name!"

"Ow, ow, you're pulling my hair. Police brutality! Police brutality!" he shrieked.

"I'm not a cop," Charlie said and then abruptly let go, taking satisfaction in the thump when Aaron's head hit the floor.

Aaron groaned. He'd never felt this helpless in his life. And to make matters worse, he knew the two armed men walking in the door had come for him. Their disdain was obvious as they looked at him. Disgusting. They thought of him as disgusting. The beautiful dream was over.

"Charlie Dodge. We came to relieve you of your prisoner."

Charlie handed them the gun. "This is his. He shot at one of the girls, but the shot went wild. He intended to kill them all, and you have thirteen witnesses who heard him say it. You might need to cut the zip tie around his ankles so you can walk him out. He's way too big to carry."

"He's fat," Barbie said and then clasped her hands over her mouth. "I'm sorry. That's not a nice thing to say."

"Since he came with the intent to shoot everybody here, you are certainly entitled to your opinion of the man, honey. Don't worry about it," Charlie said.

The agents cut the tie, dragged Aaron Walters up to his feet and hauled him out and across the compound, then dropped him into the dirt with the rest of the men they were in the process of arresting.

The men who'd called themselves Archangels were now belly down in the dirt, their arms spread out like the wings they would never earn, waiting to be cuffed, while others were already in restraints and sitting cross-legged in the dirt.

When the Master was brought into their midst and dumped on his ass in the dirt, they looked at him in shock, and then quickly looked away. Their vision of creating a superior race had ended in a most convincing way.

Some of them had given up without a fight, while a few had tried to run, but the only way out was the gate where the SWAT team was coming through, and so it became their trap instead of their exit.

The couples in the married units were unsuspecting of what was happening until the team kicked in the main door. The noise brought the husbands out into the common room, in shock at the swarm of armed men coming at them, shouting.

"FBI! FBI! Get down on the floor, get down on the floor now!"

They went belly down and were immediately cuffed, and then the SWAT members began dragging them out into the courtyard.

Suddenly one of them stopped.

"This is only five. They said there are six married couples. We're missing a man."

The child wives were standing in the open doorways of their apartments, watching what was happening in disbelief, while the babies in their arms were shrieking in their ears.

"Ladies, we're missing one man. Could you tell us where he is?"

One of the girls stepped out of her doorway and pointed.

"Archangel Larry and his wife, Maria, live in the last apartment on the right."

"Thank you, ma'am. Now, all of you please stay inside your apartments until we have him in custody. And stay inside this building until we have removed the men from the compound. When it's safe, we'll come back for you," he said.

The girls nodded, then watched as a half dozen agents took off toward the last apartment at a jog.

SWAT was concerned. The fact that one man had not come out when the others did was concerning. They didn't want a hostage situation on their hands. As soon as they reached the apartment, they pounded on the door.

"FBI! Open up! You're under arrest!"

They heard voices inside, then the sounds of a man and woman arguing, the sound of something breaking, then silence.

The leader grimaced.

"We're going in."

They kicked in the door and swarmed into a foyer, only to find themselves facing a man with a toddler held against his chest with one hand, and a gun aimed at them with the other.

"FBI. Drop the gun! You're under arrest for kidnapping!"

"I'm not going to prison!" the man shouted, and then he did the unthinkable. He turned the gun to his own baby's head and started screaming. "I'll shoot him, so help me God, unless you let me pass!"

Just then, a young girl came running into the room with a rifle, and before they could stop her, she put the barrel to the back of her husband's head and pulled the trigger.

Blood spattered all over the screaming baby, and then it was falling head over heels toward the floor.

A quick thinking agent grabbed the baby in midair, while another one stepped over the dead man's body and took the rifle out of the mother's hand.

She was pale and shaking, and swaying on her feet.

"I couldn't let him kill Andy. Larry always does what he says. He would have done it."

Her arms had both new and fading bruises, and her nose was bleeding, but it was the lack of expression on her face that was most telling. The baby was screaming and reaching toward her, but she didn't seem to be able to move.

"Is Andy okay? Did he hurt my baby?" she asked.

"Your baby is fine. Your husband never fired his weapon."

"Is he dead?" she asked.

"Yes, ma'am," the agent said.

"Thank God," she said and then fainted, while the baby continued to scream.

Two of the young wives were suddenly standing in the door.

"Give us the baby," one of them said and then pointed at the girl on the floor. "Bring her to us."

The agents handed the baby over, and then carried Maria to them, leaving the dead body for the coroner.

The wives had gathered in one apartment, and a couple of them were already stripping the crying baby and carrying him to the sink to wash off the blood. Their own children were on the floor or in playpens, crying along with him.

Maria was already regaining consciousness as the men laid her on the sofa.

"Ma'am, you're safe here. All of you stay together. We'll be back for you when the men are gone," the agent said, and then the men left to notify headquarters they had one casualty.

All of a sudden the girls were alone, and the entrance door that was always locked was standing ajar.

"That was the FBI," one of them said, shifting the toddler in her arms to her other hip.

The others nodded.

"They're coming back for us," she said, as if repeating the agent's words would make them real.

Another one walked all the way across the common room to the open door. They'd never been allowed to leave on their own, and now the door was open. She glanced out and saw all of the Archangels, who'd been taken into custody, sitting in the middle of the compound.

She came running back.

"The men are all handcuffed and sitting on the ground. I'm going to pack. I think we're being rescued. I think they're going to take us home," she said.

"What if our families don't want us now? We haven't been to school since we were taken. We have babies. I'm scared. What if home isn't there anymore?" Maria said and started to cry.

Within twenty minutes of Archangel Larry's demise, prison transport buses began arriving. And as soon as one was full, the next one pulled into line, and then the next and the next, until thirty-three men were all loaded. Number thirty-four was being left behind for a coroner to haul away.

Each bus had a driver and two guards on board, both of whom stood at the front with their weapons at the ready, staring into the faces of the men handcuffed to the seats.

None of the men had ever been arrested before, and the shock of what just happened had taken them down to a level of submission that was a mirror image to the females they'd kidnapped. It was karma at its finest.

When they loaded Aaron Walters onto the bus, the Archangels stared at him.

"Why didn't the security alarms go off?" one asked.

"You are the all-knowing one, Master. Why didn't you warn us?" another asked.

"I didn't see them coming until it was too late," Aaron said.

"They've been watching us," another man shouted. "I told you months ago there were people in and out of that house in the woods."

"And I told you why!" Aaron shouted back. "It's a vacation rental. What else would you expect? People come and go."

"You didn't believe me," the man persisted. "They were Feds. I know because two of the men who helped arrest us were the two men I kept seeing at the store in town."

Aaron wouldn't listen, because accepting that truth meant his psychic skills were flawed.

"It's not about that! We were betrayed!" Aaron said. "Jud Bien did this."

They were silent a moment, and then one man spoke up from the back of the bus.

"You shouldn't have hit his girl. Everything was okay until you hit his daughter."

Aaron dropped his head and closed his eyes. *I should have killed them both and none of this would have happened.* He didn't say it aloud, but some of them heard it anyway, because that was how they rolled. It had been a wonderful dream, but their utopia had just come to a very unsettling end.

Once they began loading up prisoners, Charlie radioed Hank.

"How much longer until you move the girls out?" he asked.

"Thirty minutes, more or less," Hank said. "Tell the girls to pack what they want to take with them."

"Will do," Charlie said. "Okay, girls, you heard him. Pack up what you want to take with you. They'll be coming for us in about thirty minutes."

Jordan went straight to the front of the room where she'd dropped her spear, and picked it up.

"You don't need that now," Charlie said. "You're safe. I promise."

She shook her head. "I don't feel safe. I'm taking it with me. I might need it again." She walked back to get her bag, then ran to the bathroom and grabbed a handful of tampons and stuffed them in her bag.

Charlie didn't argue with her about anything. He'd seen soldiers mustering out with a look of panic on their faces as they handed over their weapons. He understood fear, and as he watched the girls disperse, he knew going home would be harder than they thought.

As soon as they were all out of earshot he shifted focus.

"Wyrick?"

"I'm here."

"Hank said thirty minutes or so and they will start loading up the girls."

"Then that will be my ETA, as well. Are we going to need to stop somewhere to see to Jordan's injuries?"

"No. Nothing is critical. We'll leave all that to her mother. Tara is going to need to do that for her own peace of mind, as well as for Jordan."

"Be there shortly," Wyrick said, then quickly changed clothes and began packing. She dropped the flash drive with the proof of Universal Theorem's backing for the cult into her pocket, then carried her bags and the computer gear into the hall.

Charlie's things were next, so she went into his room, got his duffel bag out of the closet and began gathering up his things. She found the car keys where he said they'd be and dropped them in her pocket, then carried his bag into the hall. She made one last trip back for the remote controls to the plane she'd burned, and began carrying things down to the Jeep.

It took four trips to get everything, and as soon she was finished, she ran back into the kitchen for some bottled water, before heading out the door.

The drive back through the trees wasn't as creepy as it had been going in. But once she reached the blacktop, she was forced to wait for the convoy of prison buses to pass. They glanced at her there and then looked away, unaware of the part she'd played in taking them down.

Just as she was about to pull out onto the road, two large charter buses appeared on the way up. She guessed they'd been sent for the girls. One had a blue-and-purple sunset painted on it, and the other had a cowboy motif, complete with the silhouette of horses racing across a prairie. As ornate as they were on the outside, she could only imagine how nice they would be on the inside. They were the perfect vehicles to bring lost girls home.

As soon as they passed, she pulled out behind them and followed them up. Security was tight at the gate, and even though the SWAT team knew who she was, they still stopped her.

She rolled down the window as one agent approached. "I'm here to pick up Charlie Dodge and his missing girl," she said.

The agent nodded. "Yes, ma'am. Thank you for helping us pull this off, and just for the record, you were right."

"About what?" Wyrick said.

"Some of them did know this was happening before we came into the compound. We had to run a few of them down, so thanks for the heads-up."

As Wyrick looked up, she saw Hank Raines moving past the gate and thought of the flash drive.

"I have something Agent Raines needs. Would you ask him to wait a second?"

The guard radioed Hank, who turned and saw her, gave her a thumbs-up.

"Am I allowed to pass?" Wyrick asked.

"Yes, ma'am. Girls' dormitory is to your left as you—" He stopped. "But I guess you already know that. Proceed."

Wyrick put the Jeep in gear and drove to the entrance, then stopped.

"I have something for you," she said and dropped the flash drive in Hank's hand. "It's proof of who was bankrolling the cult. Get it into the system fast, because once they find out about this raid, they'll scrub every bit of evidence."

"How on earth do you—"

"Get this to someone now or it's useless later."

Then she took her foot off the brake and drove into the compound as Hank dashed toward the SWAT team com center in their van. He came in running and handed the drive to one of their techs.

"Upload this info and send it to Agent Vickers. Tell him to upload this into the files on this case and begin immediate verification."

"Yes, sir," the officer said and plugged it into port in his computer as Hank left the van.

CHAPTER TWENTY

For Wyrick, it was odd seeing everything in the compound from this angle, since she'd only seen it from satellite images and blueprints. But she knew where she was going, so she drove straight toward the building and got out of the Jeep.

The sun was shining. The sky was blue and cloudless, but the energy of this place was dark and ugly. She shuddered slightly as she walked up the steps. The door was ajar, so she entered without ceremony to a room full of metal beds set up in barracks-style rows.

She saw Charlie at the back of the room, surrounded by a ragtag bevy of young girls, and headed toward them, bracing herself to be the curiosity they needed.

Charlie had recognized the sound of his Jeep as she drove up, and knew she'd arrived, but when she stepped inside, she was but a tall, dark silhouette framed in the light of the doorway. He took a moment to appreciate her long legs and the sway of her body with her stride, but the girls were curious and already staring, and introductions were in order.

"Girls, this is Wyrick. She's my assistant and a very important part of Dodge Security and Investigations. She helped me find Jordan, and was also the one who made this rescue possible."

Wyrick had dressed for the road in a clean white T-shirt, skinny-leg blue jeans that made her long legs look even longer, and hot pink tennis shoes—her concession to the flash that was part of her public face.

She stopped near where they were sitting, and within seconds, one of the younger girls began quizzing her.

"Did you have to shave your head 'cause you had lice? Mama shaved my brother's head once 'cause he got lice."

"No. I had cancer. The medicine made my hair come out," Jordan said.

"Will it grow back?" the little girl asked.

Wyrick smiled. "No. But I'll never get head lice."

The little girl nodded, satisfied with the logic.

The girls' curiosity was obvious, but Wyrick felt Jordan checking her out, and stayed open just enough to let her search, while she did a little searching of her own.

Once she was satisfied Jordan hadn't been raped, she resurrected her walls. Seeing Jordan's injuries close-up brought back too many bad memories of her own, so she shifted mental gears as Jordan suddenly stood up.

"It's nice to finally meet you," Wyrick said.

In three steps Jordan was in front of her, then wrapping her arms around Wyrick's waist. When Jordan laid her cheek against the dragon tattoo and closed her eyes, Wyrick flinched. This was a familiarity allowed to none, but she knew Jordan had seen the tattoo, and her need to hug Wyrick was mixed up with a desire to be one with the dragon. That, Wyrick understood, and so she held her.

"Is he strong?" Jordan whispered.

"Very," Wyrick.

"As strong as Wonder Woman?" Jordan asked.

"In his way," Wyrick said.

"Thank you for helping Charlie find me," Jordan whispered.

From Wyrick's height, she could see a nasty, healing gash in the young girl's head—one more wound to add to what had already happened to her face.

"You're welcome, honey. But after we found out how many others were with you, we knew we had to help save you all."

The girls gasped, and then looked up at Charlie.

"Did you really?" Randi asked. "You knew we were here and came for all of us?"

"We sure did," Charlie said.

When the girls began pounding Charlie with questions, Jordan moved back, but kept staring at Wyrick.

"You're like us, but more, aren't you?"

Wyrick shrugged. "Everyone is different. Some have more of one thing. Some have more of another."

"Except you have all," Jordan said.

Wyrick shrugged. "I had what I needed to find you. And that's all that matters." Then she shifted into female mode and raised her voice. "Girls. Everybody go pee whether you need to or not. I think there will be bathrooms on your buses, but go anyway, just in case."

Used to following orders, the girls got up together and headed to the bathrooms.

Still sitting, Charlie observed the changing expressions on Wyrick's face as she watched them go, then was surprised by what she said after she caught him staring.

"We didn't save Jordan. We just came to pick her up," Wyrick said.

Charlie frowned. "What do you mean?"

"Wonder Woman saved her. She kept that image in her mind the whole time she's been here…fighting against bad people. Staying strong even when she was scared."

"Well, hell. That explains what I saw her doing, but I didn't understand then," Charlie said. He got up, grabbed the broken mop handle Jordan had on her bed and tested the jagged points with the tips of his fingers.

Wyrick saw the ragged shards. "What do you mean?"

"As I was coming in the door after Walters, I caught a brief glimpse of Jordan running toward him with this pulled back like a spear. She wasn't running from a man with a gun. She was in attack mode, willing to fight to save herself and the girls."

Wyrick glanced out the window over Charlie's shoulder, then pointed.

"They're loading up the married ones."

Charlie turned to look. "Hey, girls, better hurry. They'll be here any minute."

The girls began coming back carrying garbage bags. Since they'd all been kidnapped, none of them had been given the opportunity to bring clothes of their own when they arrived. Jordan was the only one who'd arrived with a bag, because she'd been duped into thinking it was a sleepover and had packed accordingly.

"Does my mama know where I am?" Randi asked as she plopped down beside Charlie.

"Not yet, but she will," he said.

Randi sighed. "I'm sad for Missy, though."

Jordan had never heard that name. "Who's Missy? One of the married ones?"

Randi shook her head. "She was, but she died a week after she was married. They told us one morning at breakfast, and then we had oatmeal. Like it didn't really matter. They didn't have a funeral for her or anything."

Charlie was immediately on alert.

"Is she the only one who died here?"

Randi shrugged. "I don't know. I've only been here two years. There were already girls here when I came."

"What did they do with her body?" Charlie asked.

"They wrapped her up in a quilt and carried her out the front gate," Katie said. "Some of the Archangels had shovels. We guessed they buried her in the woods."

Randi nodded. "We watched them carry her out. We didn't know what happened, and we were scared for a long time that we would die, too."

"Jesus wept," Charlie muttered. "Wyrick, stay with them. I need to talk to Hank." He bolted out the door and radioed him again. Hank answered quickly.

"This is Raines. The men are on the way, Charlie."

"Did you know that one of the married girls died?"

There was a moment of silence, and then Hank sighed.

"No. How did you find out?"

"The girls told us. The name of the girl who died was Missy. It was a week after her marriage. They announced her death at breakfast, then the girls saw them carrying a quilt-wrapped body out of the compound, and some of the men were carrying shovels."

"Well, that complicates things," he said. "Thanks for the heads-up. I'll notify the proper people."

Charlie came back into the building with a grim look on his face and sat back down beside Randi.

"Did you tell them?" she asked.

"Yes, I did," Charlie said.

A single tear rolled down Randi's face. "Missy was nice to me. I'm sad she doesn't get to go home."

Jordan thought about the dead girl. She'd wondered more than once if she would die here, too. If it hadn't been for Mama sending Charlie and Wyrick, she might have. She shifted the bag between her feet and kept her spear across her lap.

A couple of minutes later, a half dozen officers entered the building.

"We're ready to load up," they said.

The girls started to get in line and then remembered Jordan wasn't going with them. They looked back at her and started crying.

"We'll never see you again, will we?" Randi asked.

"You'll always be in my heart," Jordan said and got up from the bed, and one by one began hugging each one goodbye.

"You saved us," Katie said.

"You were the bravest of us all," Barbie whispered.

Jordan shook her head. "No, not the bravest. You were all here far longer than me. You are all brave and strong. You just didn't know it. We can't lose each other. Not really. We have Snapchat and Instagram. Right?"

"What are those?" the girls asked.

Jordan was shocked, and then remembered how long they'd been here, and how young they were when they came.

"Uh, it's social media. You'll find out soon enough when you get home. You all know me. All you have to do is friend me or follow me. You'll figure it out."

"We love you, Jordan. You're our hero. Don't forget us. Don't forget us," they cried. "We'll never forget you."

And then, without being told, they lined up as they'd always done, and for the last time, followed a man out the door.

Jordan turned around, a stricken look in her eyes.

"I'll carry your bag," Charlie said, as Jordan picked up her spear. He headed for the exit, with Wyrick and Jordan following.

Just before they reached the doorway, Jordan stopped, then turned and looked at the empty room. The closet doors were standing open, bedspreads were rumpled on all of the beds, and she could see a couple of wet towels on the floor in the room beyond.

"Charlie, wait!" she cried.

He stopped. "What's wrong? Did you forget something?"

"I will never forget," she muttered. "But will you take a picture of this for me?"

"Of the room?" Charlie asked.

"Yes."

"Absolutely," he said.

"Just wait a second," Jordan said as she tightened her grip on her spear and ran back into the middle of the room.

When she turned to face the camera she was in a warrior's stance of defense. The bruises and swelling only added to the fierceness of her expression. She stood with feet apart, head up, holding the spear upright beside her.

"Now take it," she said.

The hair stood up on the back of Charlie's neck as he raised the camera, centered her in the middle of the shot and started clicking. Even after she started walking toward him, now carrying the spear horizontal to her body, he was still taking pictures.

"Want me to send them to your mother?" he asked.

"No. Mama's not ready to see this yet. Send them to my phone," she said and gave him the number.

"You aren't ready, either," Wyrick said. "But you'll know when you are."

Charlie picked her bag up again. "Let's get out of here," he said.

Moments later, they were settling Jordan into the back seat of the Jeep. Wyrick dug a pillow and a blanket out of their camping gear, and handed them to her, along with a bottle of water.

"Sleep if you can. It will make the trip shorter."

Jordan clutched it all in her lap like an unwrapped gift, staring out the windows as they drove past the girls getting on the buses. The girls waved and she waved back.

A car from the coroner's office came through the gates,

followed by an old hearse. They'd come to claim Archangel Larry's body.

When Charlie stopped at the gate and got out, Wyrick wondered what he was doing until she saw him taking pictures of the empty compound, and then she understood. One more picture for Jordan.

This is how justice is supposed to work. All the good people get rescued. All the bad ones go to jail.

Once Charlie was back behind the wheel, he glanced up in the rearview mirror.

"Are you ready to talk to your mother now?"

Jordan nodded.

He pulled up Tara's number and made the call, then handed her the phone. As he drove, he heard the tone of Jordan's voice change from the warrior she'd had to be, to the young girl she still was. Jordan's life would go on, and God willing she'd find a way to get past the betrayal of her father's actions. But she was a survivor, and those kinds of people never quit.

The media had gotten wind of the raid at Fourth Dimension, and by the time the prison buses reached the city jail in Lexington, the streets were swarming with news vans and journalists, all waiting for the sight of the cult members.

All they'd been told was that missing children had been located on the grounds. They had yet to learn why they'd been taken, and knew nothing about a breeding program or the dead ones.

When the men, thirty-three in number, began filing out of the buses, handcuffed and shackled, on their way inside to booking, cameras began rolling.

The reporters didn't yet know Aaron Walters by name, but by virtue of the fact that he was still wearing that long white robe, filthy now from the dirt and the blood, he became the face of the cult. The mastermind of evil.

* * *

Cyrus Parks was at the main office of Universal Theorem, getting ready for a meeting, when his cell phone rang. He glanced at caller ID. Kenneth Fields was the head of their DNA lab, so he answered.

"Ken, can I call you back? I'm just getting ready to leave for a—"

"Turn on CNN. Hurry."

Cyrus grabbed the remote from his desk and hit Power, and when the picture flashed, it took him a few moments to figure out why a bunch of men coming out of prison buses had anything to do with him. It wasn't until he heard a reporter say Fourth Dimension that it hit him. And then he saw the man in the white robe.

"Dammit!" he said. "Dammit all to hell!"

"What do you want us to do?" Ken asked.

"We don't have a choice," Cyrus said. "Destroy the evidence. Shred the reports on the babies. Delete the files from all the computers."

"All of it?" Ken asked.

"All of it," Cyrus said, and after he hung up, scrolled through his contacts and made a call. It rang twice and then was answered.

"Yes, sir?"

"Have you located Jud Bien?"

"The last location was at a hotel in Lexington, Kentucky. His car is there, but they said he checked out and was picked up shortly afterward in a chopper. He hasn't been seen since, and there are no records of any purchases he's made or withdrawn any money."

Cyrus groaned. The Feds had him. "Just stand down until I can make some inquiries. I'll be in touch."

"Yes, sir," the man said, and the line went dead.

Cyrus needed details. He wondered where Bien's daughter

was now, and then guessed she'd be returned to her mother. Aaron said she was gifted. He'd planned on using her skills in that project, but with this on the rocks, she no longer mattered to him in the same way. Maybe it was best to just let her be. It was obvious that Jud was the one who'd given them up, and so it would be Jud who had to pay.

As for Aaron, he had become a liability. When the Feds began grilling the fat bastard, Cyrus didn't trust him to stay quiet. He canceled his meeting and began making calls. There were too many fires from this unexpected event that needed to be put out before it became a conflagration.

And…he had to get rid of the money trail. He picked up the phone and buzzed his secretary.

"Yes, sir?"

"Reschedule my meeting. Something came up."

Jud Bien didn't know his destination; he only knew they were taking him to a safe house. They'd been on the road about two hours now, and he'd been dozing off and on most of the way. When the driver's cell phone suddenly rang, it startled Jud awake, and when he heard the driver ask about casualties, he sat up. They were talking about Fourth Dimension!

He grabbed hold of the steel cage between them and leaned forward.

"My daughter! Is my daughter okay? Has she been rescued?"

The driver gave him a thumbs-up and continued the call, but that was all Jud needed to know.

"Thank the lord and Charlie Dodge," he said, then fell back against the seat and closed his eyes.

The Archangels had all been booked and jailed into one holding cell, and were now contemplating a future in prison. There were federal charges against them for kidnapping and sexual assault, as well as a multitude of lesser charges, and if anyone found out about the girls who'd died in their custody, there would be charges for that, as well.

And they were all giving the Master among them a wide birth. Seeing him sitting in the dirt back at the compound had taken some of the shine off his status.

As for Aaron, trading his white robe for prison orange had been a come-to-Jesus moment. Being locked into a holding cell with all the others added more stress to the situation.

The noise level in the cell was bordering on chaos. The Archangels loudly bemoaned their fate, and many were having trouble blaming Jud Bien. They were sympathetic to a father defending his daughter, and kept casting angry glances at Aaron.

When the news began to spread among them that Larry was dead, and that his wife, Maria, had killed him when he aimed a gun at his own baby, it shifted their perspective again.

Larry was one of the more gifted among them. He had mad skills in clairvoyance, and the Master had always held him in high esteem. But he'd also been a mean one. Too bad psychics couldn't read themselves. Larry might have made better choices today.

Aaron was trying to get a read on his future, but between the noise in the holding cell and the pain in his head and face, he couldn't focus. Every time he closed his eyes, all he saw was that girl standing over him, taunting him at the reversal of power. He felt his nose and then his rapidly swelling eye and realized that what he'd done to her had come back to him, as well. He'd always heard that old axiom, but never really believed it until now. It was a hard and lasting lesson with no escape.

The SWAT teams removed the married girls first, loading them and their babies onto one charter bus furnished with food, water and diapers, and then loaded the Sprites onto the remaining bus, furnished in a similar fashion, minus the diapers.

As Wyrick predicted, each bus had a bathroom and two female agents on board to accompany them.

The first bus was noisy. The girls wept off and on, as did their babies. Going home with children made them unsure of a welcome. There was nothing the agents on that bus could say to reassure them, because they knew it was a valid fear. It all depended on people's prejudices.

The second bus was quiet. The Sprites had been brainwashed by cult rules so thoroughly that without Jordan as the spark, the fire of their tiny rebellion had gone out. Like the other girls, they didn't know what to expect. What should have been a mood of rejoicing in both buses had become a fear of the unknown.

Agent Patty Barrow, a thirteen-year veteran of the force, began to explain a little about what they had ahead of them.

"The FBI is contacting all of your parents to let them know we're taking you to a hospital in Lexington first."

"When we arrive at the hospital, will we have to get shots?" Barbie asked.

Barrow gave Barbie's hand a quick pat. "They won't give you medicine unless you're sick, honey. They just want to make sure the men didn't hurt you."

"She means they're going to see if we're still virgins," Randi said.

"Well, we are, because they wouldn't have wanted us there if we weren't," Katie said.

The agents looked at each other, and then back at the girls.

"What do you mean, they wouldn't have wanted you?" Jergans asked.

Katie folded her hands in her lap and begin reciting what sounded like a want ad for a job.

"We have to be pure, and getting our first period is when you're ready to get married and make babies for them."

"What do you mean, make babies for them?" Jergans asked.

Katie scratched at a spot on her neck and then swiped the hair out of her eyes. "Oh, that's why they chose us. To make psychic babies for them."

Both agents were in shock. These girls were still so young, none of them even in their teens, and to hear them talking about marriage and sex and making babies, like it was as simple as making cookies, was horrifying.

Barrow turned toward her partner. "Does headquarters know all this?"

"I don't know, but I'm about to find out," Jergans said and moved to the front of the bus, away from the girls, to make the call.

As the charter buses and their federal escorts neared the city limits of Lexington, they were met by a half dozen units from the Lexington Police Department. Three cruisers guided the Feds and the charter buses through the city to Albert B. Chandler Hospital on Rose Street, with the other Feds and three more cruisers following.

"Where are we now?" Katie asked, looking out the window.

"This is Lexington," Barrow said.

"No, I mean, what state?"

"Oh, we're still in Kentucky."

When the girls all began talking and whispering among themselves, Barrow was curious as to why.

"What's up?" she asked.

"We didn't ever know where we were," Randi said. "We just knew we were in the woods."

"Where are you from?" Barrows asked.

"La Jolla, California," Randi said.

Barrows began pointing to each of the girls, asking where they were from.

"Pine Bluff, Arkansas."

"Santa Fe, New Mexico."

"Pryor, Oklahoma."

"Baltimore, Maryland."

"Boston, Massachusetts."

And on and on, until there was no one left but Barbie.

"And where are you from, honey?" Agent Jergans asked.

Barbie started to cry. "I don't know. I used to live in Grapevine, Texas, but Mommy and Daddy were moving when Gerald took me away. I can't remember where we were going. I don't know where to find them."

Mel Jergans couldn't stand it. She plopped down beside the fragile little blonde, pulled her into her lap and started rocking her where they sat.

"It's okay, it's okay. I promise. The FBI is as good as Santa Claus at finding where kids live. We'll find them easy as pie."

"Really?" Barbie said.

Mel nodded. "Yes, really. And look! See that big building there in the distance. The really, really tall one? That's the hospital where we're going."

All of the girls got up and moved to that side of the bus to look out as Mel kept talking.

"When we get there, you will each have a counselor assigned to you. She will stay with you through your exams. And you will each tell your story of being taken away, and what happened to you, and how you were treated. Understand?"

They nodded and quietly returned to their seats. This was a whole new aspect of rescue they hadn't foreseen. It was all a little scary, but they knew how to live with fear.

CHAPTER TWENTY-ONE

Jordan was curled up in the back seat with a pillow beneath her head and the covers pulled up to her chin. She'd been asleep for more than two hours, so Charlie and Wyrick had purposefully chosen not to talk. The broken mop handle was on the floorboard, pulled up against the seat where she was sleeping.

They knew she was dreaming, because she kept mumbling. The few times they'd heard distinct words they were shocked, but they now knew how Jud Bien had gotten her all the way to Kentucky without tying her up. He'd stabbed her in the neck with a needle full of drugs. Later, she began crying, mumbling something about blood and rats and snakes.

Wyrick had seen Charlie angry plenty of times, but not like this. His jaw was clenched, his fingers curled around the steering wheel tight enough that his knuckles were white.

She finally dug through the carryall between her feet and then pulled out a Hershey's bar, tore off the wrapper and broke it in half.

"Take it," she said.

He took it without comment, but Wyrick didn't need

thanks. She just wanted that scary expression in his eyes to go away. They ate in silence, savoring the sweet chocolate melting on their tongues, then licking the ends of their fingers when it was gone. When Jordan began to stir, she sat up, rubbing the sleep from her eyes.

"Do I smell chocolate?" she asked.

"Yes. Want some?" Wyrick asked.

"Yes, please!" Jordan said and held out her hand.

Wyrick dug through the bag again. "Snickers or Peanut M&Ms?" she asked.

"M&Ms, please."

"Catch," Wyrick said and tossed it into the back seat. "Do you still have water?"

"Yes, but if I drink it, I'll have to pee," she said.

"I can solve that problem," Charlie said. "There's a truck stop about ten minutes ahead. I'll stop there, okay?"

"Okay. Um, Charlie, how far is it to Lexington?"

"About an hour, more or less," he said, then watched as she tore into the bag of candy and popped a couple into her mouth, before turning his attention back to the highway.

The sweet crunch of the candy shell was so good Jordan closed her eyes as she chewed, relishing every bite. She ate about half the bag before stopping to take a drink.

"Does Mama know where we are?" she asked.

"I just sent her a text," Wyrick said. "I'll text her again when we're closer."

Jordan sat back and finished off the candy, eating one at a time to make it last.

A few minutes later Charlie exited the highway and pulled into the truck stop and then up to a pump. He killed the engine, then paused.

"I know this may seem like overkill, but humor me, okay? I'm still in protect mode, so let me fill up, and then we'll go in together."

Jordan's heart skipped a beat. "Am I in danger?"

"No, ma'am, you are not," Charlie said. "But your mama is already going to be ticked off at me for not telling her about you being beaten, so I don't want any new bumps or bruises when we deliver you. Okay?"

"Oh," Jordan said and relaxed.

As soon as Charlie got out, Wyrick added her reassurance.

"Honey, the reason Charlie is so good at his job is because he pays attention and takes extra precautions about everything. People hassle me a lot because of how I look, and if he is a witness to it, he makes them sorry."

Jordan frowned. "About how you look?"

Wyrick shrugged. "A woman with no hair and no boobs is an oddity, and there are plenty of jerks in the world who get their kicks laughing about it."

"That's terrible," Jordan said. "I'm so sorry. For what it's worth, I think you're amazing."

"Same to you," Wyrick said. "And since you're doing Charlie a favor, I need you to do one for me, too."

"Anything," Jordan said.

"When we get out, leave your spear in the car, and when you get home, get your mom to help you hang it on the wall in your bedroom or something. You don't need it anymore, and it doesn't need to become a false crutch. Do you understand?"

"Yes. I'll get Mama to help me," Jordan said.

Wyrick nodded, and then they sat in the quiet, looking out at the people coming and going, and at the white, puffy clouds drifting across a perfect blue sky.

"It's a pretty day, isn't it?" Jordan finally said.

Wyrick nodded. "A perfect day to be going home."

A few minutes later she saw Charlie replacing the nozzle at the pump and unlocked her seat belt. "Looks like Charlie's finished. Let's go."

They both got out and headed for the station with Charlie

walking a couple of steps behind. He followed them all the way to the bathroom area, then waited for them afterward until they came out.

"I need a Pepsi," Wyrick said and glanced at Jordan. "What about you?"

"Mountain Dew," she said.

Charlie swung by the cooler and got a bottle of sweet tea, then followed them up to the register, where they got in line to pay.

Because she'd been warned about people hassling Wyrick, Jordan was superconscious of the way people were looking at her. Most people were just curious; some looked a little longer than was polite, but nothing that felt upsetting to her, and finally they reached the counter.

She was watching Charlie insert his credit card in the pin pad when a couple of young men walked in. Jordan noticed them giving Charlie the once-over and thought nothing of it, but when their focus shifted to Wyrick and then to her, she felt challenged and stared back.

Charlie caught the men staring and took one step sideways until the only view they had was of his chest.

They looked up.

"Move on, boys. We're none of your business," Charlie said.

Wyrick took Jordan by the arm. "We're out of here."

When Charlie moved toward the door, the men stepped aside, but one kept staring to the point Jordan felt threatened. The instinctive need to back him off was overwhelming.

"Hey, Woodrow. Didn't your mother ever tell you it was rude to stare at people? And just so you know, your boss knows you're stealing from him, and Laverne is pregnant and is gonna tell your wife."

Charlie turned around and stared at Jordan in disbelief.

Wyrick rolled her eyes and hustled Jordan out the door, leaving the two men in shock.

The last thing she heard was one man saying, "How did she know your name?" and the other one saying, "I don't know, but I gotta call my wife."

Wyrick glanced at Jordan as they were walking back to the Jeep, but Jordan didn't seem upset. Charlie was the one freaking out.

As soon as they got back in the Jeep, Charlie started talking.

"Girl, I have to ask, how did you know his name?"

She shrugged. "I don't know. I just heard it."

"Is his girlfriend really pregnant?"

She nodded. "His wife is gonna be mad. Really mad. Him and Laverne didn't practice safe sex."

Charlie laughed out loud, which made Jordan blush.

"That's what Mama says," she added.

"Your Mama is one smart lady," Charlie said. "Buckle up. It won't be long before you're with her again."

Jordan was still struggling with how life would be now. Her friends would find out what her daddy did to her, and they'd talk behind her back.

But she was free of that place, and Mama was waiting, and that was enough. She took another sip of her Mountain Dew, and as she was pulling the blanket across her legs, she found a stray M&M in the folds.

"Score!" she said and popped it in her mouth.

Tara's hotel suite overlooked the city of Lexington, much as her office at the law firm overlooked the city of Dallas. She was used to skylines and traffic, of seeing thousands of people passing below her window on a weekly basis and thinking nothing of them other than part of the throng in which she lived.

It was a gorgeous, sunshiny day, a good day for a reunion, but she was full of angst. She had no idea what Jordan had been enduring, and fear of the unknown was the worst.

She jumped when her phone rang, thinking it might be Jordan again. But it wasn't. It was one of her clients, a wealthy

Texan named Dwight Goodall. She started to let it go to voice mail and then decided staying busy would be easier than waiting, so she answered.

"Hello, this is Tara."

Dwight's voice boomed in her ear.

"Mornin', Ms. Tara. I hope I'm not intruding."

"No, no, it's fine. What can I do for you, Dwight?"

"It's more like, what may I do for you?"

Tara frowned. "I'm sorry?"

"Well, you know I play golf with your boss, and a couple of days ago he mentioned a bit about your daughter going missing, and he also happened to mention something in passing about some kind of cult called Fourth Dimension."

Tara sighed and sat down on the side of the bed. "Yes, that happened."

"So, the reason for my call is, me and Janie were watching CNN just now, and they were showing prisoners being taken into the jailhouse in Lexington, Kentucky, and the reporter said the FBI raided a cult called Fourth Dimension, and those were the people they'd arrested."

Tara grabbed the remote and turned on the TV while Dwight kept talking. When she saw men coming off a prison bus in cuffs and shackles, she realized she was seeing men who'd been a part of Jordan's disappearance.

Then she realized Dwight was still talking; she made herself focus.

"So I got to thinking, you might already know about that raid, and that these men had been arrested. I was also thinking that if it was me, I'd probably already be in Lexington waiting to get my girl back. How am I doin' so far?"

Tara remembered Charlie's warning not to tell anybody where she was, but Dwight wasn't just anybody.

"You might be a good guesser," she said.

"So, I'm also guessing you might have flown there, and that she hasn't been returned to you yet."

"You're still on a roll," Tara said and heard Dwight chuckle.

"Anyway, Janie didn't think it was a good idea for the two of you to fly home on a commercial flight, in case the media was already doggin' the parents, and I agreed with her, so I'm offering the use of my private jet to fly you both home. All you need to do is tell me when you're ready to come back to Dallas, and I'll send it to Lexington to pick you up."

Tara gasped. "Oh, Dwight! That is the kindest and most thoughtful thing anyone has ever done for me. I have been worrying a bit about that myself, and I will definitely accept the offer. Can I call you back tonight to let you know when?"

"Yes, ma'am, you sure can, and we want to send our best wishes for your girl, too."

Tara was in tears. "Thank you. Thank you so much."

"Oh, honey, after all the litigation and court dates we've been through over the years, I am happy to be able to help. I'll be expecting your call. You have a nice day now, ya hear?"

"Yes, yes, I will, Dwight, and thank you."

She put the phone aside, returned to CNN and upped the volume, searching the faces as they kept looping the feed. The only one not dressed in regular clothing was a heavy-set, middle-aged man with long hair, dressed in a long white robe. She guessed that would be the leader, whoever he was. His robe was dirty, and his face was bloody and swollen. She hoped it hurt. Then she glanced at the clock.

Charlie Dodge had said about three hours or so, and that time line was swiftly approaching, and so was noon. She picked up the house phone and ordered some food, enough to accommodate Charlie and Wyrick, too, and then started pacing again, wondering which would be the first to arrive—the food or her girl?

Jordan had been reading road signs for miles, counting off the distance still between her and Mama. When they arrived on the outskirts of the city, she threw the blanket off her legs.

"Is this Lexington?" she asked.

"We're a ways from downtown, but yes, we're basically in the city limits now," Wyrick said.

Charlie glanced up in the rearview mirror at Jordan and smiled. "Won't be long now," he said.

"Mama's scared," she said and leaned back.

"That's just because she's afraid of all the things that could have happened to you," Wyrick said.

"Are you scared?" Charlie asked.

Jordan nodded. Tears were rolling down her face.

"I'm different. I'm not the me I was."

Charlie shook his head. "You're still her daughter. That will never change."

Jordan swiped at the tears and returned to her view out the window as they sped past houses and people.

"Charlie?"

"What, honey?"

"What will happen to Jud?" she asked.

"I don't know for sure, but since he helped the Feds take down the cult, he'll probably become a material witness when they get to trial and they'll make some kind of deal with him about his sentence," Charlie said.

Jordan was silent for a few moments more, and then she moaned beneath her breath and covered her face.

"What's wrong?" Charlie asked. "Are you sick? Do you need to stop?"

"No, no, not sick," she said, and then grabbed the blanket and pulled it up to her chin. "I saw Jud's face and I saw the Master's face, too. They're melting. Someone is going to kill the Master. They need him to be dead."

Charlie was once again stunned by how she just blurted stuff out, and was wondering at her skills, but Wyrick was the one who asked.

"Who's *they*, Jordan? Who wants Aaron Walters dead?"

"I don't know...some man. The Boss. They call him the Boss."

Wyrick typed *Cyrus Parks* on her iPad and showed it to Charlie.

"Is that man going to kill your daddy, too?" Charlie asked.

"No. He'll do it," Jordan whispered, her eyes open in a fixed and unblinking stare.

And then she pulled the blanket up over her face and didn't utter another word until they pulled up to valet parking at the hotel.

Charlie gave Tara a mental high five for opting out of a high-rise hotel. This one was a simple, five-story building, and he knew the setup. First floor lobby and shops, and the other four were all one-or two-bedroom suites with mini kitchens.

"Jordan, we're here," Charlie said.

She laid the blanket aside, picked up her spear, and when Wyrick opened the door, got out.

Charlie was carrying her bag over his shoulder as he went to talk to the parking attendant, then he and Wyrick flanked Jordan as they headed for the elevators across the lobby.

Jordan's injuries and the makeshift spear she was carrying drew some stares, but for the most part they went unnoticed. Once they reached the elevators, Wyrick pushed the up arrow. The doors opened and, as luck would have it, they entered an empty car. Wyrick pressed a button for the fourth floor and up they went.

Jordan was pale and shaking as they got out, and Wyrick reached for her hand and held it all the way to room 425.

Charlie knocked.

A few moments later, the door swung inward. Tara had no time to dwell on the wounds on her daughter's face.

"Oh, honey! Thank God, thank God."

"Mama," Jordan said, and still clutching her spear, fell into her mother's embrace.

Charlie closed the door behind him, then followed them into the living area.

Tara settled onto the sofa with Jordan tucked beneath her arm. She couldn't stop touching her and kissing her, and yet didn't know what to say without triggering an episode, so she kept to banalities.

"I knew everything happened really early this morning, so I ordered food and drinks. The bathroom is down there on your right. Please make yourselves comfortable."

"I need to go, Mama. I'll be right back," Jordan said, but when she got up, Wyrick held out her hand, and Jordan reluctantly handed over the spear.

"You don't need this anymore, remember?"

Jordan nodded. "But I need to keep it."

Tara didn't know what was going on, but she quickly agreed. "You can keep anything you want."

Satisfied, Jordan walked into the bathroom and closed the door, but the moment she was out of sight, the questions started flying.

"What happened to her?" Tara asked.

"She'll give you details when she's ready, but the bottom line is, your girl fought them the whole time she was there. The man who called himself the Master is responsible for her injuries. It was punishment for breaking one rule too many," Charlie said.

Tara immediately flashed on the man in the white robe and felt sick, knowing he'd done that to her baby.

"I saw him. On CNN. Being taken into jail with all the others," Tara muttered. "Would he have been wearing a long white robe?"

"That's him," Charlie said, and then pointed at the spear in Wyrick's hands. "I'm telling you this now so you'll understand. The raid was supposed to be a surprise, but Wyrick warned us it might be difficult to surprise psychics, and she was right. By the time we got into the compound, some were already aware of our presence. The man you mentioned is Aaron Walters, the leader, and he was already running toward the girls' dormitory when I first saw him. He knew Jud had given them up, which in his mind forfeited Jordan's life. I saw the gun in his hand as he ran toward the dormitory. I tried to catch up before he got inside, and as I took him down, the shot went wild. But as I was coming through the door, I saw Jordan running toward him with that in her hand, pulled back like it was a spear. And all of the other little girls were belly down on the floor beneath their beds. She was coming after him, not running away. She has a warrior spirit, and her psychic skills are way beyond what you know. Go easy with her. The old rules she lived by won't work anymore."

Tara's hands were over her mouth to keep from screaming. She didn't know how to process this. What the hell had they done to Jordan that would put her in a mindset to kill?

Wyrick saw the fear and wanted to temper it.

"Jordan and I made a deal," she said. "She gets to keep her makeshift spear, but only as a reminder of her strength. Not as the emotional crutch it could become. I suggested you two might find a way to mount it on her bedroom wall, and she agreed. I don't know how you're going to get that on an airplane, but I can promise you she won't leave it behind."

Tara sighed. "Then what happened to me this morning has become a double blessing. A wealthy client of mine has generously offered the use of his private jet to get us home. All I have to do is call him and his pilot will come pick us up."

"Problem solved," Wyrick said. And then the bathroom door opened and Jordan came out.

"Mama, I used your hair brush."

Tara shook her head. "Don't you always?"

Jordan grinned and then looked at the food. "I'm hungry. Can we eat?" And without waiting for an answer, she picked up a chocolate-covered strawberry and ate it in two bites.

Charlie laughed. "She does like chocolate. The smell of it woke her up on the way here."

"You should see us on Valentine's Day," Tara said. "We both make ourselves sick. Please, come eat. I ordered enough for all of us."

"I never turn down food," Wyrick said and was on her feet with a plate in her hand in seconds.

"I want to wash the road off my hands first," Charlie said. "Save some for me."

By the time he came back, the three females were head to head around the table, eating and talking about anything and everything, except what had happened, and where Jordan had been.

Charlie got a sandwich and a cold drink and sat down with them. It was a good outcome to a dangerous case, but they didn't linger. Jordan needed time with her mother, and it was time to go home.

For Wyrick, being able to sit and watch the love between mother and daughter was a beautiful thing. She couldn't help but wonder what she would have turned out to be if her mother hadn't been murdered and if she'd grown up like a normal kid.

But she let go of the thought before it turned into regret, and got up to get something sweet. The best meals always ended with desserts.

When it came time to leave, Jordan hugged Charlie fiercely.

"Thank you for rescuing me from the monsters, Charlie Dodge."

He tilted her chin, looking deep into her eyes. "You are an amazing young girl. Don't stop believing in yourself, okay?"

"Yes, okay," she said and hugged Wyrick, too. "Thank you and your dragon for finding me."

Wyrick cupped Jordan's face. "It's what we do."

Jordan moved back to the food array as Tara walked them to the door.

"Thank the both of you again for bringing my girl home. You have my address for the final bill, and if ever you have need of a lawyer…"

"Duly noted," Charlie said, and then they were gone.

They left the hotel without talking, retrieved the Jeep from valet parking, then began making their way out of Lexington.

"We'll find a stopping point somewhere and spend the night, then drive the rest of the way back to Dallas tomorrow morning," Charlie said. "That nonstop drive out here was hard."

"You're the boss," she said and then opened her laptop.

"Only when you let me," Charlie said, then saw her frown at the screen. "What's up?"

"Do you want to take a case involving a stolen cannon?"

He shook his head. "Nope. Reply accordingly."

CHAPTER TWENTY-TWO

Dinner was chocolate pie and sweet tea, because it was what Jordan wanted, but it wasn't long afterward that she began to crash. This morning had been a nightmare, but tonight she was safe in her mother's arms.

Tara saw past the bruises on Jordan's face to the exhaustion beneath and made a suggestion.

"Let's change into pajamas and get ready for bed. That way, if you fall asleep watching TV, you'll already be in bed. Okay?"

"Okay," Jordan said.

Tara began looking around. "Where did Charlie put your bag? I saw him… Oh! There it is at the end of the sofa. I'll take it to your room."

Jordan followed, but when Tara put it at the foot of the bed, she stopped.

"I never unpacked it," Jordan said.

Tara paused, then saw the look on Jordan's face.

"What do you mean, honey?"

"I packed two sets of clothes, plus something nice, think-ing we were going out for dinner, but after I was there, I slept in my clothes and left everything else in the bag. So I washed one outfit every night and put the clean ones on to go to bed, including my shoes, just in case I got a chance to escape. And, oh yeah... I started my period there."

Tara's eyes welled. "Oh, honey."

Jordan shrugged and looked at the bag again. "I figured it out. When we get home, I don't want to ever wear those outfits again, okay?"

"Absolutely," Tara said, swallowing back tears. "Do you want to shower first?"

Jordan nodded, then dug her pajamas out from the bottom of the bag and took them with her.

Tara was so sick at heart. Jordan's first step into becoming a woman, and she hadn't been there for her. But it was also the first revelations Jordan had made about her life there, and the safer she began to feel, the better.

God, please give me the strength to hear her, and the wisdom to know what to say.

After Jordan showered and changed, Tara took her turn.

Jordan was in between the covers with the air conditioner blasting, watching TV on Mute, when Tara came out.

"Can't find anything you want to watch?" she asked. "Maybe we can watch a pay-per-view movie. Want me to see what's available?"

Jordan glanced at the bed in the other bedroom, then up at Tara.

"Mama?"

"What baby?"

"Will you sleep with me tonight?"

"Absolutely, just let me call Dwight first about our ride home."

Jordan closed her eyes, listening to her mother's voice as they set up the time for the jet to pick them up. If her jaw wasn't sore, and if her lips weren't still swollen, it would almost feel like she was home…and nothing bad had ever happened.

When Tara turned out the lights, a nightlight came on in the bathroom. Nice touch, she thought. She went to the dresser, pulled out Brownie Bear and, scooting up next to where Jordan was sitting, tucked the old floppy bear in her arms.

"Brownie was waiting for you when I brought you home from the hospital. He's been waiting for you to come home again, so I brought him with me this time."

"Oh, Mama, thank you," Jordan whispered, then slid down between the covers until her head was in Tara's lap, with Brownie tucked beneath her chin.

Tara patted the crown of Jordan's head without thinking, but when she did, Jordan winced.

"There's a cut there, Mama."

Tara turned on the lamp and then carefully parted the hair until she found it, and in that moment she didn't even ask how it happened. That it was even there was a brutal reminder of what Jud had done to their child.

"I'm so sorry, baby. I'm so sorry this happened to you, but I am so grateful to have you back in my arms. I love you more than anything in this world, and we'll get through this together, like we've faced everything else. Okay?"

Maybe it was just knowing she was safe now…and maybe it was the little brown bear in her arms that gave her the courage to say it.

"Daddy stabbed me in the neck with a syringe full of drugs," she said and started sobbing.

Tara gasped. "What? No! Oh my God! That place turned him into a monster! I'm so sorry, baby, I'm so sorry."

After that, the truth began spilling out of Jordan in fits and starts, from when she first realized she was being kidnapped, then figuring out what Fourth Dimension was all about. One story after another kept coming, and Tara held on, crying with her now, as Jordan told how she defied the Master and the rules.

And about being locked in the old dorm with nothing to sleep on but a dirty mattress, and then killing snakes and rats.

Breaking out all of the windows.

Being locked up every day with the Sprites.

Refusing to eat for fear they'd drug her again.

Publicly defying the Master time and time again.

Sabotaging the mending, and getting beaten for it.

Jordan kept talking, vomiting out one incident after another until she finally cried herself to sleep, comforted by the feel of her mama's hand on her back.

Tara's eyes were swollen and her heart had broken a thousand times. It felt like she would never sleep again; she was so enraged she was shaking.

As soon as they got home, she was taking Jordan straight to their family doctor for a thorough checkup. Just knowing she'd suffered a head injury that knocked her out and she'd had no medical treatments for anything had Tara bordering on panic. At that moment, if someone had given her the opportunity, she would have put a gun between Jud Bien's eyes and pulled the trigger without one moment of remorse.

While Jordan had been reuniting with her mother, the other girls arrived at the ER and paired up with an advocate, then began undergoing physical exams that involved blood work and countless questions about their food and living conditions. As word began to spread about their presence there, the media who'd been at the prison began gathering outside the hospital in hopes of getting footage of them, as well.

Reporters tried more than once to sneak into the girls' exam rooms, snapping pictures and asking questions the girls didn't even understand. Their advocates did all they could to protect the girls' privacy, but it quickly got out of hand.

Hospital security was finally called; they stood guard at the entrance, making sure no one got in again.

But the biggest issue for the girls came when they were separated in the ER. Before, they'd done everything together, including sharing pain and fear; now they were apart and with strangers. They didn't know where the other girls were. They couldn't see them. They couldn't hear them.

Katie finally broke down in tears.

"I want to go home," she wailed, pulling the sheet up over her head, and then quit talking.

Barbie had thrown up twice from the stress.

And Randi was sitting in the middle of the bed with the sheet wrapped around her, refusing to lie down among so many strangers.

One of the younger girls had leaped from the bed and run into a corner, then squatted down with her arms over her head in sheer terror.

Another girl got out of the exam room and began running, crying and screaming.

The ER was used to broken bodies, but they didn't have medicine for what was broken within each child. It was the promise of all going together to get food that finally soothed them, and after the basic tests had been run and they were reunited, calm returned.

Federal agents and advocates escorted them down to the hospital cafeteria, and when the girls were given free choices to have whatever they wanted to eat, they couldn't decide. They hadn't been given a choice about anything, and there were so many options they didn't know how to choose. Finally, the agents began choosing for them, and the girls relaxed and were intrigued by getting to carry their own trays to the table.

Finally, they finished eating, and when the agents began getting them all together again, they all bunched up together, holding hands.

"Where are we going?" Katie asked.

"Next stop is the police department," Agent Barrow said.

"Why are we going there? Are we being arrested?" Randi asked.

"No, no. Absolutely not," Agent Jergans added. "This is where you get to tell your story. Remember I told you they would want to hear how each one of you was kidnapped and taken to the compound?"

Randi nodded.

"So this is where that's going to happen. Don't worry. Agent Barrow and I will be with you the whole time."

"Okay," Randi said, and then they were loaded back up on the buses and transported to a conference room at the main branch of the Lexington Police Department.

It was late afternoon before they finished. When they put them back up on the buses to take them to a hotel to spend the night, they were so overwhelmed by the day that they just sat in their seats and cried, and it was no wonder.

They had all been diagnosed with varying levels of PTSD. The mothers were anemic. The babies were underweight. And they were all suffering from a lack of Vitamin D from being locked away from the sun.

Tomorrow, the process of returning them to their families would begin. US marshals would begin showing up in the morning to transport children back to their homes. The Feds had been able to locate all of the families, even Barbie's parents, and the notifications had been made.

Upon arrival at the hotel, the girls were housed in separate suites, much as they had been separated at the compound.

The married girls and babies were in one, along with agents who would stay with them until they were officially assigned to the US marshals, and the Sprites were in another suite under guard, as well.

Foldaway beds and playpens had been brought into the mothers' suite. And more foldaway beds had been taken to the suite where the Sprites were. Their food of choice—pop, pizza and ice cream—had been delivered to both the rooms, along with baby food and milk for bottles.

The luxury of the suites, compared to the stark existence they'd been living, was obvious, but their greatest comfort came from just knowing they were safe and they were together, and could choose the food they wanted.

The Sprites were all bunched together on the beds watching television. It was the first time they'd seen a TV show since they'd been taken from their homes, and they'd turned into little zombies, watching one cartoon show after another, their laughter often bordering on hysteria from being unable to process the drastic changes.

There was a much different vibe in the other suite. Babies still cried and had to be fed. Diapers still had to be changed. And the unfamiliarity of the hotel made them cranky.

The young mothers were exhausted by the time they got the babies fed and settled down to play, but the pizza and the pop were still waiting, and they didn't care if the pop was no longer cold and the pizza was a little soggy. They just kept chattering about how good it tasted, and how long it had been since they'd had it.

Maria was the exception.

She'd turned fifteen years old this morning, and shot her husband on her birthday to save her child. For the rest of her life, her birthday would be a resurrection of the memory, and the reality of the day was beginning to set in.

She was crying as she ate but seemed unaware of the tears. She kept getting up to go check on her baby, even though he'd fallen asleep in the playpen, and couldn't seem to sit still. During a lull in the conversation, she finally uttered the greatest of her fears.

"In the Bible, it says it's a sin to kill someone."

There was a moment of shock, and then everyone began talking at once. With the truth of her sin finally uttered, Maria couldn't stop trembling.

But it was something one of the agents said that made the difference.

"Maria! You didn't kill an innocent person. You were protecting your child. Your baby is alive because of you. Understand?"

All of the girls were nodding in agreement and praising her bravery. Maria wanted this to be true, and kept searching their faces for some kind of silent judgment, but she saw nothing but empathy.

"Today's my birthday," she said. "I'm fifteen. One more year and I can drive."

Charlie stopped in Nashville for the night, then followed Wyrick's directions to the hotel she'd picked out.

"There it is," Wyrick said, pointing up the street to the Nashville Airport Marriott.

Charlie turned off the street and pulled up to the entrance, stopping in valet parking. They retrieved the bags they wanted for the night and went into the lobby to register.

The clerk smiled cordially as they approached the desk.

"Welcome to Nashville Airport Marriott."

"Thanks," Charlie said. "We need two rooms with king-size beds. The rooms can either be side by side or across the hall from each other, with morning checkout."

"Yes, sir," the clerk said and pulled up a screen to check availability. "We have two single kings that are side by side on the fifth floor. Will that be okay?"

"Yes," Charlie said, taking out a credit card and a photo ID.

Wyrick was so ready for some real food and a soak in a hot bath that she'd inactivated her normal sarcasm. By the time they were registered and in possession of their room keys, Charlie had already inquired as to restaurant and breakfast options.

Wyrick was good at navigating and research.

Charlie was the bomb at scouting out the best places to eat.

They shouldered their bags and walked to the elevators, rode up to the fifth floor, then headed down the hall to their rooms in a comfortable silence.

Charlie paused outside his door.

"How about you meet me out here in ten minutes, and we'll go to dinner before we hole up for the night?"

"I'm good with that," Wyrick said and went inside after swiping her keycard.

She could already hear Charlie thumping around in the adjoining room, so she dumped her bag on the bed and hurried to the bathroom to wash up.

A few minutes later they walked into Champions, the restaurant/sports bar on site. The place was big and inviting, with more than half the tables filled with diners.

The food looked good and smelled good, and with a total of thirty big-screen TVs tuned to continuing sports feeds, Charlie was happy.

Wyrick couldn't have cared less about sports, and as soon as they were seated, they checked out the finer points of their menus.

At that point, a young man appeared.

"Good evening. My name is Justin. I'll be your server tonight. What can I get you to drink?"

"Do you have Blue Moon on tap?" Charlie asked.

"Yes, we do," he said.

"I'll have that," Charlie said.

Justin eyed Wyrick carefully.

"And for you, ma'am?"

"Sweet tea and keep it coming," she said.

Justin smiled. "Yes, ma'am. I'll be right back with your drinks."

Wyrick reached across the table, snagged a couple of mini pretzel twists from a bowl between the salt and pepper, and popped one in her mouth.

Charlie began checking his phone for missed messages. His eternal fear every time he left town had to do with Annie, but there were none from Morning Light, so he ignored the rest and put the phone back in his pocket just as the server returned with their drinks.

"Are you ready to order, or do you need a few more minutes?" Justin asked.

"I'm ready," Charlie said. "I'll have the New York strip, medium rare."

"And you, ma'am?" Justin asked.

"Smoked chicken with barbecue dipping sauce."

"Want an appetizer?" Charlie asked.

"If you do," she said.

"I've had shrimp, but I've never had Boom Boom Shrimp," Charlie said. "I think it's time we try it."

"I'm good with that," Wyrick said.

Justin paused.

"Just a warning, ma'am. It's spicy."

When Charlie saw Wyrick's eyes narrow, he knew Justin was about to be schooled.

Wyrick leaned forward, both elbows on the table, as she checked him out from head to toe, then almost smiled.

"That's okay, kid. I like everything hot."

Charlie grinned.

Justin blushed, then stuttered. "Uh…yes, yes, ma'am. I'll get that out just as soon as I can," he said and went to turn in their order.

"You made him blush," Charlie said.

"He assumed I didn't have sense enough to read a menu," she said, then took a long drink of her sweet tea and popped another pretzel in her mouth.

Because Charlie was so entranced by whatever sports event he was watching on the TV screen behind her, she glanced up at the one in front of her, staring for a few seconds at the feed.

From where Charlie was sitting, he could see two different sports in progress. One was pro basketball, and another one was horse racing. Then, as he reached for another pretzel, he noticed the expression on Wyrick's face.

"What are you watching?" he asked.

"College baseball, I think."

"Do you follow it?" Charlie asked.

She shook her head. "No. I never played a sport, so I don't know any of the rules except for the obvious, like home runs are instant scores, and balls that go in the baskets are gold, and footballs caught in the end zones make crowds roar in the stadiums."

"I'll bet you would have been good at sports," Charlie said. "Your ability to focus is off the charts."

Wyrick hid the spurt of delight she felt from the praise. "I do enjoy running. They had an indoor track at UT. I ran at least a mile during my lunch hour every day."

This was something Charlie hadn't known about her.

"Really? What was your best time?"

She shrugged. "Oh, probably thirty or forty seconds over three minutes."

Charlie's lips parted, but it took him a couple of moments to process what she said.

"Three minutes and change. Are you serious?" he finally said.

She nodded. "Why?"

Charlie grabbed his phone and went straight to Google.

"What are you doing?" Wyrick asked.

A few seconds later, he looked up at her in disbelief.

"The world record for running a mile is three minutes and forty-three seconds, set back in 1999 by some dude with a name I can't pronounce. The women's world record is a few seconds over four minutes. You broke both of those records."

"Yay me," Wyrick said. "I'm starving, and here comes our spicy shrimp."

They waited as the server delivered the appetizer and the plates.

"Enjoy," Justin said and bolted.

"Looks good," Charlie said. "You first."

Wyrick picked up a small plate and put a couple of shrimp on it, then took a bite.

"Yum. Good choice," she said.

Charlie ate a couple, agreeing they were tasty, but he couldn't let go of what she'd told him.

"Could you still do that? Run that fast, I mean."

Wyrick sighed. He was beginning to push buttons.

"I don't know, Charlie Dodge. But it doesn't matter."

"Not even if you could go down on record as the fastest person alive?"

Wyrick leaned across the table and lowered her voice.

"I'm already the strangest and the smartest. I don't need to be the fastest, too, and I don't want my name in record books. It would please me greatly to be anonymous in this world."

He stared at her for a few moments, but he finally got it.

"Sometimes, Jade Wyrick, I forget how completely unique you are. I take what you do for granted daily, and I apologize."

She glared. "Jade belongs to my past and you know it."

"You're the one who brought up your assets, and what I said is called a compliment. Calm down and eat your spicy shrimp, dammit."

Wyrick let it go. She'd gotten back under his skin, which was where she felt safest.

With their appetizer finished, the conversation pretty much ended until their entrées arrived. By the time they'd waded through all that food, almost two hours had passed.

"Do you want dessert?" Charlie asked.

"No. All I want is a bubble bath and a bed."

Charlie frowned. Now he had the image of her deep into a tub of bubbles, with the red-and-black dragon's head just above the suds, peering at him with those fiery yellow eyes.

He signed the tab to the room, adding a hefty tip to celebrate the end of a case, and left the sports bar.

"What time do you want to leave in the morning?" Wyrick asked as they exited the elevator onto their floor.

"After breakfast," Charlie said.

She shuddered. "I can't even think about food."

"You will tomorrow," he said. "I'd like to be back on the road no later than nine. We'll go down to breakfast around seven thirty. How's that sound?"

"You're the boss," she said.

He rolled his eyes. They both knew that was a joke. But he was a gentleman, and so he waited until she was safely in her room before he went into his and locked up for the night.

As soon as Wyrick turned the dead bolt, she headed for the bathroom, stripping off her clothes as she went. It was a practice of hers to never welcome the night until she'd washed away the day.

The next day was the last leg home, only this time when they left Nashville, Wyrick was driving and Charlie was sleeping off a stack of pancakes and bacon.

She was rolling down the interstate, thinking about shopping for a permanent home in Dallas, when Charlie mumbled something about Annie in his sleep.

She glanced at him then, allowing herself five seconds to appreciate his broad chest and flat belly. And, since she wasn't into masochism, ignored everything else below his belt buckle.

It was midafternoon when the Dallas skyline appeared on the horizon, and Charlie was driving.

"We're almost home," he said. "I'll bet Tara and Jordan are already back. Hope the kid is able to settle in okay."

Wyrick thought about her own childhood for a few seconds, then put away the memories.

"She'll find a new level of being. That's what you do. All those little girls will struggle. Maybe the ones with babies, the most."

"Do you think the Feds will be able to pin any of this on Universal Theorem?"

Wyrick shrugged. "I don't know. Cyrus Parks is no fool. He's good at covering his tracks. I'm proof of that. I gave the Feds everything they'd need to prove UT was funding the cult, but they're going to be sadly disappointed if they didn't get their own information in time."

They rode in silence the rest of the way until Charlie reached his parking garage. He drove up to his level, then pulled in beside Wyrick's Mercedes and parked.

They got out and began unloading her things into her car.

"The office is still closed today," he said. "Go home and unwind. I'm going to check on Annie. See you tomorrow."

"Tomorrow," she said, and then jumped into the Mercedes and started the engine.

She backed out of the parking spot, then burned rubber on the concrete as she took off.

"That was entirely unnecessary," he said and then shifted focus. He still had camping gear to get back in storage, but everything else could wait until later. He was going to Morning Light. It was getting harder and harder to psych himself up to go, but as long as Annie still drew breath, she held his heart in her hands.

CHAPTER TWENTY-THREE

Charlie pulled into the parking lot at Morning Light and then grabbed the sack he'd brought with him.

Pinky, the daytime receptionist, looked up from the desk as he went inside.

"Hello, Charlie."

"Hello," he said and signed his name, then walked to the door for her to buzz him inside.

As always, it was the scents that got him first. Industrial-strength cleaning solvents, the very faintest hints of urine as he passed by resident rooms, and the odor of old bodies still hovering between a heartbeat and decay.

He went straight into the common room first, searching the faces of the residents scattered about. A few were in front of a television, watching a game show, but the TV was on Mute. For some, too much sound was agitating, so they left the shows playing, and the color and movement was enough to entertain them.

An elderly man was asleep in a wheelchair near a window. The garden beyond was awash in color, but the scene was wasted on him. And an elderly woman was pacing back and forth, from a table in the middle of the room to an empty chair near the wall, scolding a nonexistent person for misplacing her purse.

The knot in Charlie's stomach tightened as he continued to scan the room, but Annie was nowhere in sight. Then one of the aides saw him in the doorway and hurried to him.

"Hey, Charlie, Annie is in her room today."

Charlie frowned. "Has she been there all day?"

He nodded. "She does that a lot now."

"Thank you," Charlie said, then left the common room and turned left. Annie's room was the third one down on the right.

He paused outside the door, then took a deep breath and walked in.

Annie was lying on her bed, watching a show on a wall-mounted television, but it was also playing without sound. They'd dressed her in a yellow long-sleeve shirt and gray knit pants, and she was covered from the waist down with a fuzzy blue blanket. It could be ninety degrees outside, but sick people and old people were always cold.

He pulled up a chair beside the bed and sat down so he wouldn't appear to be looming, but her focus never shifted from the screen. Most of the bruising from her fall was fading, but the staples were still in her head, and for the first time ever, her hair was disheveled. She looked ten years older than she had the last time he'd seen her.

"Hey, baby," he said and tested the waters by putting his hand on her arm.

He blinked away tears when she didn't respond. It hurt to breathe.

Then there was a knock on the door and Rachel, the nurse who'd been with Annie in the hospital, walked in.

"Good afternoon, Charlie. They said you were here."

"Hi, Rachel. How's she doing since her fall?"

Rachel moved to the foot of the bed and adjusted the blanket, patting Annie's foot as she did.

"She's okay. Her health is good, but she sleeps a lot now."

"Does she communicate with anyone?" he asked.

"Well, once in a while she sort of wakes up…you know? We can tell because there's a flash of cognizance, then confusion, and then it usually fades pretty fast. Is there anything I can get you?"

Charlie pulled a bottle of body lotion from the sack he'd brought with him.

"I used to rub this on her feet. Is it okay if I do this, or do you think it might upset her?"

"I think that's a wonderful idea. Let's try it and see what happens. If she rejects the touch, we'll just stop, and if she doesn't, it will be a comforting thing to do for her," Rachel said. She pulled back the covers at the foot of the bed and gently removed the slippers on Annie's feet.

Charlie moved from the chair to the foot of the bed and scooted onto the mattress, patting her legs as he spoke.

"Hey, sweetheart, it's me, Charlie. I'm going to rub some lotion on your feet, okay? It's lilac…your favorite."

He took her silence as a positive sign and lifted her feet into his lap. He squeezed a dollop of the lotion into his hands and rubbed them together to warm the liquid, then began slowly rubbing it onto the top and bottom of her right foot.

When she didn't pull away, Rachel smiled.

"I think you're good to go. If you need me, just pull the cord in the bathroom. Enjoy your visit," she said and left him alone with his girl.

Charlie sat for a moment with his hands cupping Annie's foot, remembering how she used to giggle that it tickled. The fact that he was touching her now without a reaction was sobering, but being able to do this for her meant a lot to him.

He began massaging in the lotion with soft, gentle strokes,

rubbing the toes, and then along the arch of her foot and up the back of her calf with easy pressure, until it had absorbed into her skin. Then he repeated the process with her other foot, working the lotion up the back of her calf, then back down around her ankle, using just enough pressure to ease her muscles.

He was so lost in the process and the joy of touching her and being with her that a whole hour had passed and she had fallen asleep.

"Ah, baby...that felt so good, didn't it?" he whispered, then eased the slippers back on her feet and covered her up.

He thought about rubbing some lotion on her hands, but he didn't want to wake her, so he left a gentle kiss on her forehead instead and went out the door, taking the lotion with him.

The common room was nearly empty as he walked back up the hall to the door leading to the lobby. A passing aide stopped to let him out. Pinky was on the phone, so he was spared the need to speak. He stopped just long enough in the lobby to sign out.

Walking away from Morning Light into the noise and traffic of Dallas was an abrupt return to reality. He and Annie were both still living—one more than the other.

Before he went home, he stopped at a supermarket near his apartment to pick up basics. A six-pack of beer and a six-pack of pop. Cold cuts and bread. Milk and cereal. Eggs and bacon. Then he stopped by the deli bakery for sweets before heading to checkout.

By the time he got home, he was moving on autopilot. It took a couple of trips to get the Jeep unloaded. A woman who lived a few doors up from him was coming out of the apartment building as he was going in. They didn't really know each other, so there was no need to converse. A simple nod in passing served its purpose, and once he'd unloaded the Jeep fully, he locked himself in and began putting it all away.

The last thing to put up was the lilac-scented lotion, which went in his bathroom. Visiting Annie always left him with a sense of ennui and depression, but he refused to give in to it. After pulling off his shoes, changing into sweats and a T-shirt, he walked barefoot back through the house.

He hadn't eaten since breakfast, but he wasn't hungry, so he sank into his recliner, picked up the remote and turned on the TV. Charlie was too much of a conspiracy theorist to have something in his house that not only heard what he was saying and doing, but could find shows for him to watch, answered questions and initiated conversations. That was shit he didn't trust.

He finally found something he wanted to watch. He leaned his chair back and pillowed his hands beneath his head. The scent of Annie's lotion was all around him now, and in a way, a kind of comfort. He'd brought a little of her home.

Charlie wasn't the only one who had to stop for groceries. Most of the time Wyrick ordered and had them delivered to her car on the way home, but this was one of the few times she had to go inside for herself.

Too many people made her nervous, so she went only for the basics, and within twenty minutes was back in her car and on the way home. The closer she got to Merlin's estate, the more relaxed she became. The basement apartment wasn't luxury, but it was safe, and for her, that trumped elegance every time. However, she was still going with the notion of buying property, so elegance was bound to come with the level of security she would demand.

The lawn care company was mowing the grounds when she drove onto the property. They were a necessary evil, but strangers made her wary. They'd already mowed where she parked. She got out to unlock the door to her apartment, then began carrying everything inside. It took three trips before her car was empty, then she locked herself inside the apartment.

Since she didn't see Merlin when she drove onto the property, the first thing she did was text him to let him know she was back, then she began putting up groceries. Setting up the computers she'd taken with her was next, and finally, getting her things back to her bedroom.

Since she'd incinerated the prototype of her plane, there was no need to hide the remote controls, so she shoved them into the bottom of a closet before unpacking her clothes and tossing them in the laundry.

As soon as the washer was humming, she stripped down and showered, silently acknowledging her dragon as she dried off and dressed.

It was almost 3:00 p.m. and she hadn't eaten since breakfast, so she dug through the groceries she'd just bought and put a chicken potpie in the oven to bake. She poured Pepsi into a glass full of ice and headed for the computer.

She had multiple messages from her stockbroker, Randall Corne, so she checked in with him first.

"Hello, this is Randall."

"Hey, Cornie. It's me," Wyrick said.

"You know I hate it when you call me that," Randall muttered.

"You called me four times. I am returning the calls," she said.

He sighed. "Yes, well, the opportunity to buy what I was going to suggest has come and gone, so that's one phone call. The others were regarding your gaming company. You banked about six hundred million in the last six months."

"Okay," Wyrick said. "I just got home. I'll check everything out and email you in a day or two. I have a little research to do, but I'm thinking of selling all of my shares in the shipping company."

"Sure. Your call," he said, and then added. "Was it a fun trip or a work trip?"

"It was a trip to hell and back," she said. "Thanks for calling."

She took a sip of Pepsi, then went down the list of emails, deleting some, responding to others. She paid her rent via Venmo to Merlin and transferred money from four different US banks into a numbered account in Switzerland. And then, as she was logging out of her personal account, the oven timer went off.

Lunch was served.

She got her potpie from the oven, upended it onto a plate, then stuck a fork in the bottom crust to let out the steam. It rose through the cracks as she dug it apart to let it cool, and then she carried it and her Pepsi into the living room to eat.

She found a movie she wanted to watch and then blew on her first bite until it was cool enough to eat. It wasn't cordon bleu, but it was food she liked, and she settled in to eat.

Tara and Jordan were up early the next morning. Tara couldn't sleep, and Jordan kept dreaming the Master was chasing her with a gun and waking up in a panic.

When it came time to get dressed, Jordan threw away her tennis shoes and both sets of clothes she'd worn at the compound, leaving her with sandals, a red miniskirt and a red-and-white floral top to wear home. She even used a little makeup on her bruises, and after a quick glance in the mirror, saw remnants of her old self again. She packed Brownie Bear into her bag, giving him a kiss and a thank-you before zipping it up.

A brief cab ride to the airport later, they were escorted to a runway off to the side, and then they crossed the tarmac to the waiting jet. She went up the airstairs, a young, dark-haired girl in a miniskirt, with a bag over her shoulder and a weird, makeshift spear in her hand, knowing her mother was right behind her. And when they were boarded, the pilot pulled the stairs up inside the plane and helped them settle for takeoff.

Jordan's heart lifted with the plane as it took off down the runway, and the farther and faster it went, the closer she got to home.

Having the luxury of Dwight's plane at their disposal didn't end with just a flight home. The plane had been stocked with a sumptuous breakfast buffet, and as soon as the pilot radioed they could get up and move around, Jordan headed straight for the food.

"I have Dramamine if you feel airsick," Tara said.

"I'm good," Jordan said and forked a small piece of red, juicy watermelon into her mouth.

Tara smiled, but she knew Jordan's "good" was still debatable. After Tara chose some food for herself, they sat down at a table for two by a window and began breakfast, talking as they ate.

Jordan had been worrying about returning to school ever since her rescue, and now it was an inevitable fact. The girls at the compound had not been allowed that option, and she wasn't going to give up the gift of education and hide in some kind of shame for what had happened to her.

"Mama?"

"What, honey?" Tara said.

"Do you have to notify my school ahead of time that I'm back, or do I just show up?"

Tara blinked. "Uh… I hadn't thought past getting you home safe. I don't know. I'll find out."

Jordan nodded.

"Are you worried about it?" Tara asked.

Jordan shrugged. "Worried is the wrong word. But I'm not looking forward to being treated as if I've been tainted, or something."

"We can see about homeschooling for the rest of this year if—"

"No!" Jordan said, suddenly angry that this was even being discussed. "They took away my freedom once. I won't ever let that happen again."

Tara reached for Jordan's hand and then held it.

"You know I have your back."

"Yes, Mama, I do. The whole time I was there, I told the girls you would find me. I told them you'd never quit looking."

Tara blinked back tears. "And you were right. I put the best man I knew on the job, and he came through for both of us."

"Charlie Dodge saved my life," Jordan said. "And then he waited with all of us while the FBI agents arrested all the men. He told the girls he'd made up his mind to rescue all of them when he came after me."

"He did?" Tara asked.

"Yes, and I keep thinking about that, Mama."

"What do you mean?" Tara asked.

Jordan looked up. "You know how you're always telling me to look at the bigger picture…that there's always more than meets the eye."

Tara nodded.

Jordan shrugged. "So, if I'd never been taken there, then you would not have sent Charlie to find me, and the girls would still be there with no hope of ever being found."

Shock washed through Tara in waves. She hadn't seen that coming, but she couldn't deny the truth of it. The irony was that Jud Bien's betrayal had been the step needed to bring those other children home.

"I never thought of it like that, but you're right. You were the sacrifice they needed to go home," Tara said.

Jordan sighed. "I know. And it's okay, but I want to lie down. Do those seats recline?"

"Yes, and there are pillows and blankets," Tara said.

Jordan's eyes welled with tears. "I'm tired. I'm so tired, Mama. Inside, I feel a hundred years old."

After the plane ride and then a long drive through Dallas, Tara pulled up into her driveway and shook Jordan awake.

"We're home, baby."

Jordan opened her eyes just as the garage door was going up.

Tara parked inside, then lowered the garage door and disarmed the security system before getting out.

Jordan picked up her bag and followed her mother into the house. She was home. This was her world. She had such an overwhelming sense of relief she could hardly speak.

"I'll bet it feels good to be home," Tara said.

"Yes," Jordan said, following her mother up the stairs. "I'm going to unpack and change," she said, and then went into her room and closed the door.

The first thing she did was look around for her phone, and then saw it on the charger on her desk. She began going through the messages and found the one from Charlie, with the pictures he'd taken of her at the compound.

When she saw herself in the middle of the floor in that empty dormitory, her face swollen and bruised, her dark hair all wild and messy around her face and holding that spear, a wave of emotion swept over her. She *had* become her own version of Wonder Woman, and that was what saved her.

She didn't know he'd taken the other pics of her walking toward him, or the several shots of the empty compound, but in that moment, she knew she would never think of herself as a victim again. Eventually, she'd show her mother the photos, but not today.

Instead, she went to change clothes. She wore a pair of sweats, dropped her phone in the pocket and put on her oldest T-shirt because it was the softest. She went downstairs, relishing the cool feel of the hardwood beneath her bare feet.

She was home. She was safe. And she had the satisfaction of knowing that no matter what else life threw at her, she could handle it.

Tomorrow was Wednesday. She wanted the rest of the week to be home with Mama, and then on Monday, Mama would go back to work, and she would go back to school.

Wyrick made up for the days she'd been with Charlie in jeans and T-shirts and no makeup between her and the world, by showing up for work the next morning in a pale pink cat-suit, yellow ankle boots with three-inch heels and pink-and-green eye shadow. Just for kicks, she'd added two silver glitter teardrops beneath her right eye, then left her lips devoid of color to avoid being ostentatious.

On a whim, she'd stopped at a florist on her way to work, bought herself an arrangement of a dozen yellow roses and put them on her desk.

By the time Charlie arrived, she had coffee ready, mini pecan pie tarts on the pastry stand in the butler's pantry and a sheaf of messages transferred to the iPad on his desk.

It wasn't the outfit she was wearing or the makeup that stopped him in his tracks. He was used to that.

It was the flowers. He counted a dozen yellow roses and was suddenly curious who sent them.

Wyrick looked up. "What?"

"You have flowers."

"And you do not get a gold star or a smiley face for that very obvious observation," she drawled. "You have messages on your iPad that need a response."

Charlie frowned. She had secrets. She always had secrets. But he'd never known one of them might be an admirer. He reminded himself that her private life was none of his business, and stopped to get coffee on his way to his office.

The mini tarts were a nice surprise, and he snagged three to go with the coffee as he sat down and went to work.

He could hear voices in the outer office and then realized she was responding to messages left on voice mail. Everything was back to business, which was exactly the way he liked it. The presence of those roses bothered him a little, but not much.

The morning passed quickly, and it was nearing noon when Wyrick suddenly bolted into his office and turned on the TV.

"What's happening?" Charlie said.

"The girls. They're being returned to their parents and the media is having a field day with them."

Charlie recognized Katie at her home and then Randi being returned to her parents. He saw the little blonde hiding her face from the cameras and remembered how shy she'd been. Barbie...they'd called her Barbie.

They had clips of every one of the thirteen Sprites, and clips of the girls who'd gone home with babies.

"This is going to be a tough transition for them," Charlie said. "Hollywood will be after them, next."

"Jordan isn't mentioned," Wyrick said.

"Because I told Special Agent Raines to keep her name out of it. Technically, the Feds didn't go in after her, because she wasn't in the missing children database, so he didn't have a problem with that."

"Her friends know. Her school knows. And Tara's colleagues and everyone they told about it know," Wyrick said. "And when Jud Bien's name comes up as the cult member who turned on them, someone will find out why he did it."

Charlie glanced up. "What are you trying to say?"

"That she can't hide from her own truth for long. Are you going out to lunch, or do you want me to order in for you?"

"Out, I think. Want me to bring you something?"

She shook her head. "I'm on a diet," she said, then swung by the coffee station long enough to get a mini tart and took it back to her desk.

Charlie's eyes narrowed. There wasn't an ounce of fat anywhere on that freaking body of hers and she knew it. First the roses, now a diet? There was a budding relationship happening, for sure.

Tara had taken Jordan to their favorite pizza place for lunch, and they were working their way through a thin-crust supreme when Tara's phone began to signal texts, one after the other. They had a long-standing rule about no phones at their meals, but Tara sensed something was wrong.

"I'm sorry, honey. I think I need to see what all these are about."

Jordan nodded her okay as she picked a piece of green pepper from her slice before taking another bite. Then she heard her mother's swift intake of breath.

"What's wrong?" Jordan asked.

But Tara didn't answer. She was pulling up her app to CNN, and then like everyone else in the nation, she became an instant witness to the ongoing chaos in the little girls' lives.

"Oh no! Thank God, this isn't happening to you," she muttered.

"What is it, Mama?" Jordan asked.

"The girls…there's a story about them on CNN."

Jordan got up and scooted into the booth beside her to look.

"Those poor kids," Tara said, unaware Jordan was in shock.

She was watching the girls who'd become her friends being harassed outside their homes, coming out of stores, even being filmed in the family cars as they were driving down the street.

And when the piece segued to the girls with babies, and a reporter shoved a mic in front of one young mother's face and asked if she was going to miss her husband, Jordan didn't hear her answer. All she saw was the look on her face.

"Oh, Mama, why would they ask her something like that? They don't get it. They really don't get what happened there."

"I'm sorry, honey. You're right. No one can understand something like that unless they've experienced it," Tara said, immediately dropping the phone back in her purse.

Jordan moved back to where she'd been sitting, then picked a slice of pepperoni from her pizza and popped it in her mouth, trying to pretend nothing was wrong.

She knew her mama was trying hard to understand, and she knew her mama felt guilty. But having seen the other side of hell, it was hard to be in *this* world again. It took everything within her to look up and smile.

"Gosh, Mama, I'm getting full. Can we take the rest of it home?"

Tara sighed. Their lunch together was ruined and she knew it was all her fault. She could have handled this better.

"Of course," she said and signaled a waiter.

The drive home was silent, and when Jordan went up to her room to change, Tara stopped in the kitchen and sat down on one of the barstools.

The box with leftover pizza was at the end of the island. The cuckoo clock on the wall above the pantry was ticking away the time, even as she sat. The time she'd lost with Jordan was something she'd never get back, and what happened to her daughter while she was gone was something Tara couldn't change.

The rage within her was so thick and hard it was filling up her chest. She had to say what she was feeling. She had to spit it out or go mad. Even if he wasn't around to hear it.

"I hate you, Jud Bien, with every cell in my body. You destroyed our child. I don't know this girl who came home. I don't know how to reach her. I don't know how to help her. I hate you. I hate you. I hate you. I wish you were dead."

Friday morning, two days later

Charlie was on the way to work when his phone rang. He answered, then put it on speaker.

"Hello, this is Charlie."

"Charlie, Hank Raines here. I wanted to give you an update before you got to the office."

"What's up?" Charlie asked.

"We have unearthed the bodies of four young girls outside the compound, two of which had been buried with babies."

Charlie sighed. "Well, hell. Have you been able to identify them?"

"No. That will have to be done through DNA testing. But we're all well aware here that if it hadn't been for the assistance you and Wyrick gave us during this investigation, the possibility of more children dying there would have been high."

"Look, pooling our resources on this case is what made the raid successful. I'm sorry to hear this, but after the bodies have been identified, it will bring closure for four more families somewhere. I'll pass your thanks along to Wyrick, as well."

"Thank you," Hank said and disconnected.

Charlie was sick at heart, and by the time he got to the office, he was in a mood.

Walking in to Wyrick wearing funeral black slacks and a sheer black top so low that the dragon's head appeared to be emerging from below did not help it, nor did the dozen bloodred roses replacing the yellow ones that had been on her desk.

Wyrick didn't need to look twice to know he was upset.

"What?" she asked.

"Special Agent Raines called me on the way to the office.

They found the bodies of four girls just outside the compound, two of which had been buried with babies."

Wyrick flinched as if she'd been slapped. The urge to weep came swiftly, but she wouldn't do that in front of him, and she promptly stowed every emotion she was feeling. Charlie strode past her in long, angry strides, slamming the door shut between them, but she didn't take it personally. Charlie wasn't mad at her. He was just mad at life and the ugly people in it.

CHAPTER TWENTY-FOUR

It was evening before the news broke regarding the discovery of bodies outside the Fourth Dimension compound. Jordan was in the kitchen helping Tara make their dinner when the story was announced. Tara immediately stopped what she was doing and went over to the island where Jordan had been chopping vegetables and pulled her close. They stood together, watching the video footage, listening to details in disbelief.

Jordan was stunned, trying to imagine how that could happen.

"Mama, why would they kill them?"

Tara pulled Jordan even closer as she began to explain.

"I don't think they were murdered, sweetheart. The most likely explanation is that at least two of them died in childbirth, and the other two could have bled to death during miscarriages."

Jordan's eyes widened in sudden understanding.

"So they died because they didn't take them to a hospital?"

Tara sighed. "Partly, but girls that young aren't made to have babies. Their bodies haven't matured enough for a full-term baby to have room to come out. If those girls did die in childbirth, without access to a doctor, they suffered long and hard as it was happening. There isn't a punishment on earth harsh enough to make up for what those men did... what they let happen."

Jordan nodded, but the image of that suffering and death stayed with her, and that night, long after they'd gone to bed, Jordan was still awake.

The media kept calling the girls victims, but she saw them, and herself, as survivors. She kept looking at the photos Charlie took the day of the rescue, and remembering, over and over, everything she and the girls had to endure. It wouldn't go away, and she couldn't turn it off. It had become a whirlpool of dark images, and she was afraid to close her eyes for fear it would suck her under.

It was a little after midnight when she realized she had to tell their story. She couldn't go back to school on Monday without telling her truth—their truth—in the only way she knew how.

So she sent the photos to her laptop, then went to the desk where she did her homework, pulled up a blank page in a new document and started typing. One hour passed, and she was well into the second when she finally stopped editing to read her story through one last time.

Satisfied that she'd told the story the way it deserved to be told, she attached Charlie's photos and then emailed it to every newspaper and every television station in Dallas. The way she looked at it, maybe one of them would take the time to read it, and to care enough to run with it. But if not, at least she would know she'd tried.

What she didn't realize in her twelve-year-old wisdom was that she'd just set the media on fire in the city of Dallas, and that by nightfall it would be running nationwide throughout every social media outlet and every television in the country.

She didn't know she would put a knot in Cyrus Parks's belly

and the last nail in Aaron Walters's coffin. She didn't know it would be the trigger Jud Bien would pull on his own life, and if she had, it still wouldn't have changed a thing.

It was after 3:00 a.m. when she finally went to bed, and for the first time since her kidnapping, she slept without dreams.

Tara was downstairs making coffee and thinking about mixing up some pancake batter for Jordan's breakfast when she picked up the remote and turned on the TV for the morning news. The last thing she expected was to be staring at photos of Jordan that she'd never seen, or that for the first time, she'd see the actual place where Jud had taken her. The news anchor was relating full stories with details to the viewing public that Jordan had barely managed to tell her.

"Oh my God, oh my God!" Tara moaned, and grabbed her phone to call Charlie, but when the phone rang and rang without answering, she didn't know what to do.

Just as she was about to hang up, she heard his voice.

"Hello?"

"Charlie! This is Tara Bien. I'm sorry to wake you, but I thought you told me the FBI wasn't going to release Tara's name, and she's all over the morning news, and I've never seen the pictures they're airing, and did you tell—"

"Shit," Charlie said. "Hang on a sec. Let me turn on the TV."

And then Charlie was hearing what she was hearing, and seeing what she was seeing, and he realized the only person who could have done this was Jordan.

"Listen to me," Charlie said. "The Feds didn't do this. They don't have this knowledge. Jordan never talked to them at all, and told very little of this to me. I heard parts of this from the girls, but not from her. I took those pictures, but at her request. She asked me to send them to her phone at home, which I did. I asked her if she was going to show them to you, and she said you weren't ready to see them."

"Oh my God," Tara said and started to cry. "I don't know how to help her, Charlie. I don't know this girl."

"She knows who she is. The two of you need to go to counseling, but I'm sure you know that. And I don't know what triggered her to do this, but Wyrick said something to me the other day that once again proves she is always right. I'm paraphrasing here, but basically, she said Jordan couldn't hide what happened to her if she wanted to, because her school knew. Her friends knew. Your friends knew, and whoever they told knew. Jordan's presence there made her one of them, and you can't protect her from that. What I do know is that your daughter didn't want to be thought of as a freak. So maybe this is her way of stating her truth."

Tara moaned. "The other day I showed her the footage of what the girls who'd been rescued were going through, and last night we heard about the bodies they found. It must have been the last straw for her."

"Well, she certainly put the media to shame with how they're handling all this, and I'll lay odds that she'll have public opinion on her side. If she does, the media will back off. They won't want to be viewed as the vultures they are. Bottom line, what you don't do is freak out on Jordan. If she's ever going to heal from her father's betrayal, let her do it her way," Charlie said.

Tara wiped her eyes with the hem of her shirt and reached for a tissue.

"Yes, okay, I get it, and I'm sorry I accused you, and I'm sorry I woke you, and—"

"One day at a time," Charlie said and disconnected.

Tara's phone began signaling incoming calls, and when she realized they were from TV stations and local papers, she muted the ringer and put it in her pocket.

Then she washed her face and went upstairs.

★ ★ ★

The story went viral. The fact that a twelve-year-old girl had channeled Wonder Woman, a comic book heroine, to give her the courage to fight a cult, had triggered an emotional connection to her bravery for everyone.

By evening, WWWWD, What Would Wonder Woman Do, had become the acronym of the day, and Jordan Bien was the name on everybody's lips.

The media all wanted a piece of her. But after she'd called them vultures who treated victims like roadkill just to get a story, compared them to Fourth Dimension by saying they were alike, and said both the cult and the media only wanted the girls for what they could give them, the media didn't feel so good about taking her on.

Also, the fact that her mother was a lawyer was another deterrent. No one wanted to be slapped with a lawsuit. It was, however, the final paragraph in Jordan's story that touched them most.

"My mama is a lawyer. A good lawyer. She always told me that the truth will set you free. So that's our story. That's our truth. We're finally free. Now let us be."

When the girls who'd been rescued began learning what Jordan had done, and saw the pictures, it was as if they'd been given permission to live in their truth, too.

All over the country, in their homes and with their families, they began telling their own stories, of what they'd endured, and the lies they'd been told about parents giving them away and parents not wanting them anymore. And how after that, life for them personally ceased to exist—until Jordan.

They told how she'd fought the Archangels from the start, and how she'd challenged the Master. Then they began relating all the bad things that had happened to her because she wouldn't obey, and even after that happened, how she still wouldn't quit. They bragged about how she'd sabotaged the mending, and told how she'd refused to eat for fear they'd drug her. How she slept in her clothes and her shoes. How she'd made them remember playing, and how she'd made a weapon from the handle of a broom. And then on the day of the rescue, how she'd hidden them under their beds and stood between them and the Master when he came after them with a gun.

She'd given the girls back their voices. When she told her truth, they began to tell theirs. It was the beginning of their nightmare coming to an end.

Jud Bien was at breakfast with the guards and saw the same story, at the same time as the rest of the nation. The pictures. Her words. What he'd caused in his selfish search for his higher self broke what was left of him. When the story was over, he looked at the guards.

"Get your lawyers here today. If they want my testimony about Fourth Dimension, they need to video it now. I'll be dead long before your case ever goes to trial."

They didn't question what he said. That wasn't their job. But they did begin making calls. By noon, the safe house was swarming with people. They read him his rights on camera, and then he identified himself, stating his willingness to confess without having made any deals for leniency, and that he was willing to stand trial with all the rest.

After that, he started talking, answering every question they threw at him and retelling his story one more time. They had more than three hours of testimony from him when they left, and after that, Jud acted no different than he did on every other day.

They ate dinner. They watched television. And Jud went to bed just before midnight, which had been his habit.

And as was their routine, the guards did periodic bed checks on him throughout the night.

It was just before 4:00 a.m. when the guard on duty looked in on him, only to find his body swinging from the ceiling fan, hanged by a rope he'd made from the sheets off his bed.

The guard hit the lights as he ran toward him, then realized Bien was way past rescue.

"Aw, hell," the guard said and then ran to wake up his partner. "Get up. We've got a problem."

"What's wrong?" his partner asked.

"Bien hanged himself. Call the boys again, and this time tell them to send the coroner."

A glow from the street lights outside Jordan's window had found a way through the space between the curtains, highlighting the spear she and Mama had mounted over her bed.

She was curled up on her side with her back to the wall, sleeping soundly with Brownie Bear tucked beneath her chin.

The digital clock on her bed table had just clicked over to 2:00 a.m. when she suddenly woke with a gasp, struggling for breath. In a panic, she sat straight up in bed.

A faint image of her father hung within the shadows, the sadness and regret on his face unmistakable. She heard a thought. *I'm so sorry.* And then he was gone.

Jud was dead now. She knew it. And she knew he'd taken his own life. She started to go wake her mama and then stopped. There was no need to tell her now, when they'd get official notice about it later.

She peered into the shadows again, but he wasn't there. And then she got up and walked to the window, pushed the curtains aside and looked down at the street below, but it was empty.

From the window at the compound, she could see stars at night, in the thousands. From here, she couldn't see much of anything beyond the lights. Her thoughts were jumbled. Part of her felt guilty for not feeling sad, but the rational part of her knew he'd lost his right to any grief.

She let the curtains fall, then went back to bed, tucked Brownie Bear beneath her chin again, but this time turned her face to the wall, a subconscious acknowledgement that the need to watch the door for predators was gone.

The Archangels soon discovered that their special skills weren't worth shit in jail. Once they'd been arraigned and charged, they didn't need to be psychics to know they were all going to serve time. It remained to be seen how much and where they would serve it, but they were resigning themselves to their fates.

And then the story broke about the bodies found outside the compound, and murder charges were added to their crimes. And then Jordan Bien's story broke, stripping away the last vestiges of righteousness from Fourth Dimension, and their visions became painfully clear.

The State of Kentucky had the death penalty for kidnapping, *if* the kidnapping resulted in the death of the victim. And since the Feds had just dug up six bodies, two of which were babies, they didn't have a snowball's chance in hell of a lighter sentence if they went to trial.

They began requesting to talk to their lawyers, hoping to negotiate their sentences down to life versus death, and Aaron Walters was among them.

Cyrus Parks was still in cover-up mode when the Jordan Bien story broke. And while he had to admire her grit and courage she was dangerous business, and he wanted nothing more to do with her. She was part of his need to disassociate from everything and everyone connected to Fourth Dimension.

He'd already been assured that all records from Fourth Dimension were being destroyed, and Cyrus had made sure that the money trail had been scrubbed, as well.

The only person left who knew he'd been associated to the group was Aaron Walters, and Cyrus was very displeased with him.

The raid at the compound had come as a shock. He'd been assured when that compound was built that it was impenetrable from the outside. But Aaron had made a crucial mistake in ejecting one of the members and keeping the man's child, which left them vulnerable from the inside, and in Cyrus's mind, that was what precipitated the downfall. Aaron Walters had proven himself to be a Jack-of-all-trades kind of psychic, but a master of none.

Cyrus had furnished Aaron with a lawyer, with the understanding that Aaron stayed alive only if he kept his mouth shut about anyone else connected to the group, unaware that Aaron had said the same thing to Jud Bien. He was still debating what to do with him, when Aaron's lawyer called.

He wasn't happy that the lawyer was trying to reach him. There was supposed to be no traceable connection to each other, but he was curious as to what would precipitate breaking the rule.

"Hello."

"Mr. Parks, I was hoping to catch you before you left for the day. This is Frank Mallory, and I'm calling for clarification."

Cyrus frowned. "I thought I'd made myself clear."

"Yes, sir. I am perfectly clear, but it appears my client has shifted focus."

Cyrus frowned. "What do you mean?"

"I took a call today. He's asking for a meeting. Since murder charges have been added, I'm told none of the men want to go to trial, and are negotiating with their lawyers for a life sentence instead of the death penalty, which is now a possible reality. My client wishes to negotiate for a lighter sentence."

Cyrus didn't hesitate. "That's a liability. I insure myself against liabilities. I suggest you do the same." He hung up, still angry that all of this work had to be destroyed.

But then he reminded himself how many tries it always took before miracles were made, that collateral damage was part of the growth of power. Satisfied with his conclusion, he went home.

Aaron was in his cell, sitting on the edge of his bed, listening to the sounds of food trolleys rolling through the jail. Breakfast was being served.

He thought about Archangel Robert and all the wonderful mornings he'd spent in meditation, waiting for Robert to bring his breakfast. He felt like weeping. The loss of his dream was painful.

And then the trolley was next door, and he got up and moved toward the bars of his cell to wait for his tray. The trusty pushing the cart was flanked by two officers who repeatedly glared at Aaron through every meal, and this morning appeared to be no different.

"Breakfast," the trusty said, picking up a tray from the bottom shelf and sliding it through the slot in the door.

Ignoring the officers' glare, Aaron took his meal back to his bed and sat down with it in his lap. The size of Aaron's belly meant his lap was considerably shorter than most, so he held on to it with one hand and ate with the other.

He'd never cared much for oatmeal, but he didn't mind it too much if it was sprinkled with brown sugar and honey, with a little cream poured on top.

However, oatmeal in jail was minus sugar and cream, and minus flavor. There was a small pile of scrambled eggs that had originated from powder to go with it, and a couple of pieces of jelly toast, along with a cup of cold coffee.

He ate because he was hungry, downing the oatmeal first because it was filling, and because two meals a day weren't ever enough. As usual, the oatmeal was viscous and clung to the roof of his mouth like peanut butter as he worked on getting it swallowed. He ate the entire bowl in six gulps, leaving him with a slight bitter taste in his mouth, which he killed with a bite of jelly toast.

The crunchy aspect of toasted bread had long since given way, but the jelly was sweet. He downed the eggs and toast in record time, washed it all down with the cold coffee, and then slid the tray back out into the hallway to be picked up.

At this point, his day was done until the next meal. Some prisoners did pushups. Some just cursed at the world in general. Some sang. Some had conversations with the men in adjoining cells. Some jacked off. He knew because he could hear them when they came.

But Aaron still considered himself the Master and did none of the above. Not even jacking off. Not anymore. He considered himself above the masses, both intellectually and spiritually, so he went back to his bed and stretched out, trying to isolate himself from the noise by meditation.

But it didn't work.

He longed for privacy and silence, and for the sunshine on his back deck. He longed to watch birds coming to the feeder, knowing he was one with the Universe. But peace didn't come, and he couldn't concentrate. The longer he lay there, the worse he began to feel.

He tried to get up, but the room was beginning to spin, and the pain in his belly was growing exponentially with every breath. He tried to call out, but his mouth was full of spit and foam, and he couldn't do anything but grunt and cough and choke. There was a roar and an approaching blackness. His brain was on fire. Then his body began seizing and bucking, and he was kicking against the wall, in the death throes of a poison.

The irony of his life?

That he'd never seen it coming.

Special Agent Raines received the call about Jud Bien's death on the way to work. He wasn't surprised that Bien had done it, and was grateful to learn he'd thought enough about his guilt to at least video his testimony before he took the easy way out of his crimes. When he got to the office, Agent Vickers was waiting for him at his desk.

"Morning, Vickers."

"Morning, sir," Vickers said.

Hank frowned. "You being here instead of in your own office does not bode well for me, does it?"

"No, sir."

"Is it about the info on the flash drive I sent you?" Hank asked.

Vickers nodded. "Yes, sir. Considering the complicated nature of the information, it had been sent to us in a very straightforward and simple manner. We found links, and we were working on verification when they suddenly began disappearing."

Hank groaned. "She said we'd need to hurry. She must have suspected this would happen. Were you able to save enough to help us?"

"No, sir. All we have left is what's on the flash drive. But those links and money trails no longer exist."

"Damn it!" Hank said. "Our material witness hanged himself this morning, too. What else can go wrong?"

He was about to find out.

Two hours later, the phone on his desk began to ring, and he reached across the desk to answer.

"Special Agent Raines."

"Agent Raines, this is Chief Crittendon, Lexington, Kentucky PD. I'm afraid I have some bad news for you. One of the men from the Fourth Dimension raid has been found dead in his cell."

"Which one?" Hank asked.

"Aaron Joseph Walters. The one we booked in wearing the long white robe."

Shit. "Do you know what happened?" Hank asked.

"Coroner thinks arsenic poisoning, but it'll have to be verified by autopsy. We're assuming it was in his breakfast, and we're looking into who might have had access."

"Dammit," Hank said. "He was the leader, and now it's assured he won't be testifying. His death is my loss, but who did it is your headache. Thank you for letting me know."

"Yes, sir," Crittendon said and hung up.

Hank leaned back in his chair and then scrubbed his hands over his face in complete frustration. The aspects of a deeper corruption and cover-up were all over this, and whoever was at the bottom of it all had just cleaned up their own monumental mess.

"Dammit. Dammit all to hell."

Sunday morning dawned with a morning phone call to Tara from the FBI, officially notifying her of Jud's death.

A thousand images flooded Tara's thoughts, from the day they'd met, to their wedding, to the years afterward building a life together and raising Jordan, to knowing the ultimate betrayal of what he'd done to their child.

"Mrs. Bien… Ma'am, are you still there?"

"Yes, I'm here, and good riddance to his rotten soul," she said, her voice shaking with rage.

Then she turned around, saw Jordan standing in the doorway, and before she could explain the call, Jordan held up her hand.

"I am my father's child. I already know," she said and walked away.

Later that afternoon, Tara caught a story on the news about Aaron Walters, the man who called himself the Master of Fourth Dimension, having been found dead in his jail cell. Early reports stated he'd been poisoned. And that sent her into a panic about Jordan going back to school the next day. Tara was afraid to let her out of her sight.

It was Jordan, again, who finally made her understand.

"Look, Mama, I can't testify against anyone. I wasn't there long enough to witness anything but my own mistreatment, and all of the people responsible for that are either dead now, or in jail. No one wants me. No one is worried about what I know. Being psychic goes nowhere in a court of law. I'm fine. The only people interested in me are filmmakers and journalists, and they already know they have to go through you to get to me. I need you to calm down now. I have to go back to school tomorrow, and I need to know you're my backup, just like you've always been."

Tara reached for Jordan and pulled her close, feeling the warmth of her body and the brush of silky hair against her cheek.

"I love you, child, more than you will ever know. One day when you have children of your own, you will understand a mother's love and a mother's fear of losing a child. But, I hear you, and I will always be your backup. What's not going to happen is you going anywhere alone right now."

"But Mama—"

Tara took Jordan by the shoulders, looking straight into her face.

"I'm still the adult. And you're vulnerable in ways you don't even understand. Mrs. Taylor, your school counselor, has volunteered to give you a ride home for a while. I accepted, and that's going to happen. You will go straight to her office after school and she'll bring you home. Understood?"

"Yes, ma'am," Jordan said.

"And like always, you'll let me know you're here and safe, and I'll be home within the hour. Can we agree to do this together?"

Jordan threw her arms around her mother's neck and hugged her.

"Yes, Mama. We can agree."

"Okay then. So let's go pick out an outfit for you to wear for your first day back," Tara said.

They went upstairs together, hand in hand.

Monday arrived hot and muggy, with thunderheads building in the south. It would rain before the day was over.

Having already chosen what she was going to wear, Jordan kept glancing up at the spear hanging over her bed as she dressed, and then remembered Wyrick's warning. It didn't need to become her emotional crutch, and they wouldn't let her carry a weapon into school, no matter what it was made of, so she was going to have to rely on looking good—and guts.

She'd opted for her favorite pair of faded denim skinny jeans with the perfect amount of rips in the knees, and a pale yellow top in T-shirt knit, with cap sleeves and a flounce of ruffle along the loose, flowing hem.

She'd painted her toenails last night in a shade of neon yellow, and this morning they were peeping out from the open toes of her favorite sandals, and she'd washed her hair this morning. After blow-drying, it hung around her shoulders like a dark, silky veil.

A little bit of makeup was covering the last bits of faded

bruises, and she had a swipe of pink gloss on her lips. A first since she'd been beaten.

She didn't know how this day would go, but she felt good about herself, and that was half the battle, so she grabbed her purse and her book bag, and headed downstairs for breakfast.

Tara looked up just as Jordan entered the kitchen.

"Morning, baby! You look gorgeous! Waffles are ready."

Jordan smiled, setting her things aside. "Thank you, Mama. I'm starving."

She slid onto a barstool, then began fixing her waffle.

"Umm, yummy," she said as she took her first bite.

Tara poured syrup on hers and glanced up at the clock. Every morning, it was always about timing.

"We need to leave in about fifteen minutes," she said.

Jordan nodded and kept eating.

A short while later, they were driving away from the house, and Jordan was beginning to wonder if eating two waffles had been a good idea. Her stomach was beginning to knot.

God, please let this day be okay.

Tara saw the tension coming back onto Jordan's face, but she stayed quiet. Talking about what may or may not happen wouldn't make anything better.

"I have a really light day, today. So if you need me, don't hesitate to call. It won't be a problem if I need to cut the day short."

Jordan nodded. She was counting off the blocks left until they reached Bronte Middle School.

"Oh, look, there's your friend Mindy," Tara said.

Jordan had already seen her walking to school with her two brothers, but when they passed her, Jordan kept looking forward.

And then, all of a sudden, Mama was pulling to a stop by the bronze statue of a crouching lion, their school mascot.

"I'll go in with you, if you want. Just to the office to get you checked in."

"No, Mama. You called them. They know I'm coming. I'll check myself in."

Tara smiled, then leaned over and kissed her.

"Bye, sugar. I love you, and have a good day."

Jordan touched the spot on her cheek where her mother's lips had been, and then opened the door.

"I love you more," she said. She shut the door and headed up the long walk to the front door.

It took everything Tara had to drive away, but this much, she *could* do for her girl.

At first no one noticed Jordan. She was just one more kid trying to get inside. But then, one by one, they began to slow down and step aside, and all of a sudden she was walking into the building all alone.

Oh my God. Is this how it's going to be?

She lifted her chin and walked into the office.

The secretary looked up, and then a huge smile spread across her face. She came out from behind her desk and gave Jordan a quick hug.

"Oh, honey! We are so glad to have you back."

"Yes, ma'am. It's good to be back," Jordan said. "Do I need to sign in somewhere?"

"Yes, yes, right here," the secretary said and pointed to the sign-in sheet at the front of her desk.

Jordan was signing her name when the principal came out of his office, and then the counselor, Mrs. Taylor, appeared. One by one, they began welcoming her back, without mentioning a word of what had happened, or where she'd been.

"I'll see you after school," Mrs. Taylor said. "Just come in my office, and we'll leave from there."

"Yes, ma'am, thank you," Jordan said, then took a deep breath and walked out into the hall.

She had already gotten a dose of the silent treatment out-side, so she braced herself as she started walking down the long hallway to her first class. As always, it was packed with kids, but today they were lined up against the walls and no one was moving. The urge to duck her head and run was there, but she kept thinking... *I faced monsters and lived. These are my friends, and maybe they're just afraid of me.*

And then, all of a sudden, the principal's voice came boom-ing over the intercom.

"Good morning, students. It appears as if we have a bit of rain on the horizon today, but we also have something wonderful to celebrate. Our very own Jordan Bien is back. We've all been praying for her safe return, and our prayers, and hers, have obviously been answered. Let's give her a great big Bronte Lion welcome."

And just like that, the silence ended. Someone began to clap, and it spread like wildfire, with others adding cheers and shouts of "welcome back" and "we love you, Jordan." She kept walking, but this time there was a smile on her face and she was blinking back tears.

In her mind, she imagined the Sprites standing at the end of the hall, as if they were waiting for her to join them. She could see them waving and laughing, and she kept thinking, *It worked, y'all. It worked. The truth did set us free.*

EPILOGUE

Charlie was getting ready for an early lunch meeting with a prospective client when Wyrick walked into his office, gave him the once-over and frowned.

"Okay. What did I do wrong, here?" he said, holding out his arms to give her a better look at what he was wearing.

"Plaid."

He frowned. "Yes, it has a faint plaid pattern," he said, looking down at the sports jacket he was wearing.

"It's brown."

He rolled his eyes. "Crap on a stick, woman. Then go find me something better in that closet, and stop looking at me like I committed some kind of crime."

Wyrick bolted for the adjoining bedroom in his office before he changed his mind.

Charlie laid the brown sports coat across the wet bar and glanced at his watch. If she didn't hurry the hell up, she was going to make him late, and to add a little tension to the moment, his phone rang, assuring that still might be the case, anyway.

"This is Charlie."

"Charlie, Hank Raines here. One last update. Jud Bien killed himself and the info from Wyrick's flash drive no longer exists anywhere on the web."

"You're not serious," Charlie said.

"Unfortunately, I am," Hank said. "With Bien's death, and Walters dead, too, there's not going to be a trial. The men we arrested are pleading guilty and negotiating for lighter sentences. Right now there's no way to trace any further connections to the cult, and the only two people who could testify to that are dead."

"I'm sorry," Charlie said. "I know what it feels like to have everything fall to shit around you."

"It's part of the job," Hank said. "The upside is that we got a lot of lost kids back home. Someone notified Tara Bien about Jud's death yesterday."

"I hope they don't expect her to bury him," Charlie said. "She'd set him on fire, but she's damn sure not going to take on the cost of his funeral. You guys need to look deeper than an ex-wife for relatives."

"Got it," Hank said. "It's been good working with you. Have a nice life."

Charlie thought of Annie and sighed. "Thanks. You, too."

And then Wyrick came back into the room carrying the blue denim sports coat.

"Denim? Really?" he said.

"It's tailored. Your pants are black. Your boots are black. Your shirt is white. Wear this, and wear your black Stetson, not the white one," she said.

He frowned. "I thought heroes were supposed to wear white hats," he muttered as he traded brown plaid for denim.

"Heroes wear whatever the hell they please."

"No. They wear whatever the hell pleases you," he said, but he took the black Stetson with him. "Oh, that was Hank Raines who called. Bien hanged himself. All the info you gave the Feds on the flash drive has been scrubbed. And with Walters's death and the discovery of the bodies outside the compound, the men are all pleading guilty and trying to negotiate for lighter sentences."

She blinked. "What a mess. Glad that's not our problem." Then, just as he was going out the door, she called out. "When are you coming back?"

"Since I'm the hero, whenever it pleases me," he said and let the door slam shut behind him.

★ ★ ★ ★ ★